THE DOOMSDAY GIRL

A DAN RENO NOVEL

DAVE STANTON

LaSalle Davis Books

Cover art by *Steve Whan*

ISBN-13: 9780989603171
ISBN-10: 0989603172
Library of Congress Control Number: 2017948798
LaSalle Davis Books - San Jose, California

ALSO BY DAVE STANTON

Stateline

Dying for the Highlife

Speed Metal Blues

Dark Ice

Hard Prejudice

FOR MORE INFORMATION, VISIT DAVE STANTON'S
WEBSITE:

http://danrenonovels.com/

For Kris Castles and our friend,
the late Chris Andrieu

1

THE SPARRING PARTNER REX had chosen for me was about my weight, but the similarities ended there. At six-five or so, he had me by three inches, and he was still in his twenties. A large tattoo of an eagle covered his chest, and his hair was buzz-cut except for long blue strands in back. There was a wild, hostile gleam in his eyes, and I almost reminded him we were supposed to go at three-quarters speed, and no full blows to the head. But I figured he knew that and would abide by it.

It didn't take long for him to prove me wrong. He had a reach advantage, which made him difficult to box unless I moved in close. That's what I did after taking a couple of stiff jabs. I landed two good shots to his ribs, hoping to send a subtle message. I saw him wince, but I guess I just made him mad, because when I backed away he came at me with a shoulder high roundhouse kick. His heel clipped my head when I ducked, and I leapt forward with a straight kick to his thigh. It was a solid, painful shot, and his mouth turned ugly, his brow creased over his dark eyes. I danced back and held out my hands in a placating gesture and said, "Easy, now."

For a moment I glimpsed Rex standing outside the ring with his arms crossed, a smile on his face. Then the young man with the eagle tattoo came at me hard. He backed me into the ropes with three left jabs, then jumped up and threw a leaping tiger kick at my head. This type of kick has no place in training rounds; it's meant to be a knockout blow.

I dropped under the kick and lifted him by the waist and slammed him to the mat. He tried to knee me in the balls as he went down, and then he wrapped his arms around my neck. But before he could lock his grip I came down with an elbow, flush into his mouth. I felt one of his front teeth buckle beneath his mouth guard, and his eyes went dull. I almost struck him again before realizing he was out cold.

I stood and glared at Rex, who smiled and shrugged. "Nice work," he said. I took out my mouth piece and tossed it away.

"You could have at least warned me," I said.

"Naw. You reacted just fine."

I shook my head and climbed out of the ring. "Hey, someone had to teach him a lesson," he said. "See you next week?"

· · ·

I left Rex's Gym and drove my truck down old 395, heading out of Carson City and toward the Highway 50 junction. I was still annoyed with Rex, whose cavalier attitude made me wonder if he'd been hit too many times in the head. But it was my choice to spar at his gym, and I'd been doing so weekly for over a year. If I didn't dig his mojo, I could choose another way to spend my Wednesdays.

I passed a liquor store, and my foot moved to my brake pedal before I reminded myself to drive on. It was week four of my sobriety, and I'd promised myself thirty dry days. I'd make it, but I was starting to question my original rationale. Good for my health, I'd figured, good for my relationship with my live-in girlfriend, and a good test for my willpower. But I felt more tense and irritable than ever, and I doubted it was helping either my health or my relationship. As for my willpower, I'd see it through, but not happily.

I made do with bottled water as I drove down the high desert highway. The tumbleweeds dotting the flats and distant hills were coated in snow. It was a sunny afternoon, the sky a cold, cloudless blue. I passed the last casino before the junction, then turned onto 50, heading west over Spooner Pass. The road had been plowed in the morning, but there were still icy sections near the summit.

As I drove I tried to dismantle the growing sense of discord in my gut. What reason did I have to feel at odds with the world? Why let an altercation with a misguided cage fighter ruin my day? He ignored the rules and learned a painful lesson. Maybe he'd be better off for it.

By the time I reached the summit, the morning sparring session had faded from my thoughts, but my discontent hadn't. I sighed and conceded my angst was probably due to my sobriety. I recalled golfer John Daly's infamous quote, "Quitting drinking has ruined my life." I laughed dryly. Maybe a few belts of good whiskey would cure my funk. But at some level in my subconscious, I sensed something different eating at me.

When I dropped off the grade and turned south along Lake Tahoe, it was three o'clock. I drove along and contemplated what I'd do with the rest of my day. My girlfriend, Candi, would be at work until five, grading art projects at the community college. There was nothing that needed to be done around the house I could think of. I'd had plenty of time to fix things up, since I hadn't worked for six weeks. That wasn't by choice; as a licensed private investigator living in a relatively small town, my jobs tended to be sporadic. My work schedule during the four years I'd lived in South Lake Tahoe was typically punctuated by stretches of inactivity. If it lasted too long, I'd have to start visiting attorneys, business card in hand and a smile on my face.

I drove past the casinos at the state line and crossed into California. Snow was piled in four-foot walls along the roadside. A shopping development that had sat unfinished since the 2008 recession had recently been completed, and tourists were walking in and out of the new shops and restaurants. A gust of wind blew ice pellets across my hood as I passed the town's upscale resort lodge and the gondola that took skiers and snow-boarders up the mountain. My digital temp gauge read 28 degrees.

When I got home, I parked in my garage and went into the small bedroom that served as my office. I sat at my metal army surplus desk and checked my e-mail. I deleted the spam, which was all I'd received. After poking at my phone and seeing no text or voice mail messages, I wandered out to the kitchen and opened the refrigerator, but I wasn't hungry. I went and stared blankly out the large picture window overlooking the wide meadow behind my backyard. A mile out, the 10,000-foot snow-capped peaks of the Sierra Nevada were etched against the sky.

Back at my desk and idly searching the Internet, I considered driving out to Zeke's Pit, the BBQ restaurant where I had a twenty grand stake. The investment hid the cash from the IRS, and owner Zak Pappas paid me back $100 each month. I allowed him that payment plan because he was still deep in the hole for an inpatient rehab stint after nearly blowing out his circuits on top shelf booze and Colombian cocaine.

"Screw it," I said. There was no reason to go to Zeke's, other than I was bored shitless, and Zeke's had a great bar. I checked my watch, then with a sigh I opened my contact list and began calling the list of local attorneys I'd compiled. If I stuck with it I'd find a job, maybe a divorce case or two.

Ten calls later I gave up, promising myself I'd hit the road tomorrow and do it in person, drum up some business. But as soon as I set down my cell, it rang, displaying a number I didn't recognize. Hopefully one of the attorneys calling me back.

"Investigations, Dan Reno," I said in my best professional voice.

"Hello, my name's Walter McDermott."

"What can I do for you, Mr. McDermott?"

"I'm calling because of a situation we have, and, well, it's pretty serious."

The voice was subdued, uncertain, and a bit sad, and definitely didn't belong to an attorney. As for the age of the caller, I couldn't guess.

"Are you interested in hiring an investigator, Mr. McDermott?"

"I think so, yes. That is, if you think you can help us."

"That would depend. Can you describe your situation?"

"The situation?" he asked, as if the mere mention of it startled him. "I think it'd be best if we met in person. It's somewhat complicated."

"I see. Are you in the Lake Tahoe area?"

"Well, yes, we are. West side of the lake, in Tahoma. We have a place here."

"If you like I can be there in thirty minutes."

"Oh my, that's quick. Can you hold for a moment?" I heard a murmured discussion, then he came back on the line and said, "Yes, we'd like to do this right away. Here's the address."

· · ·

I threw on fresh clothes and decided to wear a sports coat under my thick winter jacket. Something in the man's voice suggested he was from a genteel class, and I've learned I have better success with people when my dress mirrors theirs. Most private eyes I know don't bother with this sort of thing, but for me it's become a habit, dating back to the days when I was desperate for a paycheck.

There was still plenty of daylight, and I drove patiently through the half dozen lights in town and turned right at the intersection known as "The Y". From there I followed 89 up a series of hairpins above Emerald Bay, until the two-lane highway straightened along Lake Tahoe's west shore. The road rose and fell through the pines, and I steered through the sweeping turns with a sense of purpose. Maybe that's what my problem was, I decided; you don't work for long enough, you lose your sense of purpose. It's like sitting and looking out a window, watching life pass you by.

Satisfied with this revelation and the prospect of a new case, I pulled into the parking lot of a lakeside residential complex. It was across the street from the single ski resort on the west side of the lake. I got out of my truck and zipped my coat. The units were single story condos, sectioned by walkways cleared of snow. My search for number 310 took me down a curved path shadowed by white fir and ponderosa pines.

I found 310 and knocked on the door. It was an end unit, right on the beach. The lake water lapped at the snow-covered sand about fifty feet from where I stood.

The door opened, and the man standing there said, "Hello, Dan Reno?" He looked at me through spectacles, and the thick lenses made his eyes look unnaturally large.

"It's *Reno,*" I said, "like Jay Leno."

"Ah, I see," he replied, nodding thoughtfully. "I'm Walter." I shook his soft hand. "Please, come in."

I followed him into the condo. He wore brown corduroy pants and a gray cardigan sweater over a plaid shirt. His shoes were suede slip-ons clearly not designed for winter duty.

Sitting on a chair in the family room was a woman about his age, around sixty. She sat rigidly and appraised me with sharp blue eyes. Her hair was gray and tied in a bun, and she had a prominent chin. After a moment she stood.

"My name is Lillian McDermott," she said. "This is my husband, Walter." Her posture was erect, and she stared straight into my eyes. "We are considering hiring a private investigator, and we'd like to interview you."

"Oh?" I said, eyebrows raised. I was usually the one doing the interviewing, and I wasn't accustomed to being on the other side of the equation. I was also surprised at her tone. She sounded stern, almost authoritarian, as if she might rap my knuckles with a ruler if I answered incorrectly. I tried to keep my expression neutral and said, "Okay, fine."

"This way," she said, pointing to the table and chairs in the adjoining kitchen. We sat across from each other. Walter stood to her side, blinking and running his hand over his wavy gray-brown hair.

"Take a seat, dear," his wife said. He lowered himself into the chair beside her.

"I'm going to describe our situation to you, Mr. Reno," Lillian McDermott said. "It's rather difficult, and frankly, I don't know if you can do anything to help. It's a ghastly, sordid state of affairs, and the police seem to have exhausted their ability."

"Were you a teacher, Mrs. McDermott?" I asked.

She looked surprised for a moment, then her eyes narrowed. "How would you know that?"

I shrugged. "Just a guess."

"We both forged our careers in academia," Walter said. "Lillian is a retired English professor. I teach biology at San Jose State University."

"That's where I went to school," I said. "Sociology major."

Walter began saying something, but his wife interrupted him. "I doubt your education is applicable here," she said. "You do come recommended, however, so please allow me to continue."

I nodded. I'd ask her about the recommendation later.

"Six weeks ago, intruders broke into our daughter's home. They severely beat her, killed her husband, and either killed or kidnapped our granddaughter. The police have been unable to find the killers, or even hypothesize a motivation. They also have no clues as to the whereabouts of my granddaughter, nor do they know if she is still alive."

I waited for her to continue. The wrinkles around her mouth deepened as she stared at her large hands, which were folded tightly on the table. After a long pause, she said, "You may ask questions now."

I paused, considering where to start. Then I said, "Was the husband involved in criminal activity?"

"No," she said.

"Not that we know of," Walter added.

"Was this a robbery? Was anything stolen?"

"The house was ransacked, but not much was taken."

"Do you know what they were looking for?"

"Yes," she said. "Gold."

"Gold? Did your daughter and her husband keep large amounts of gold at home?"

This time Walter answered. "We don't know, but possibly, yes. You see, Jeffrey was convinced the economy was bound to collapse, and soon. He believed that not only was the U.S. government wholly corrupt, but also that Keynesian economic policy is not a sustainable model, and inevitably would cause a depression so severe that anarchy would occur, and America would become a lawless wasteland."

"Sounds a little extreme," I said.

"We're not here to debate that," Lillian McDermott said. "We're here to determine if you can help us."

"Right. Where is your daughter now?"

"We can make her available, but only if we decide to hire you."

I looked at the McDermotts. Walter looked like he'd never swung a pickaxe or pounded a nail in his life, while I would have bet that Lillian, despite her erudite diction, had a hardscrabble background. Regardless, her curt tone was starting to grate on me.

"Why would they bother kidnapping your granddaughter if robbery was the motive?" I asked.

"If we knew that," Lillian said, "I doubt we'd be talking to you now."

"Why did they kill your daughter's husband, but not her?"

She shook her head, and I caught an exacerbated smirk on her face, as if my question was either inappropriate or stupid. "I have no idea," she said. "If I was the killer, I'm sure I'd know."

I looked at my watch. "I'm sorry, do you have to be somewhere?" she asked.

"Not really. I'm just wondering how much longer this interview, as you call it, will last."

"I'll let you know."

"Wrong. We're done." I stood. "Here's my card. Feel free to call if there's anything else you'd like to chat about. I charge a hundred per hour for phone consultations." I began toward the front door.

"Now, hold on," Walter sputtered.

"Mr. Reno," she said, and despite myself I stopped. "I'd like to hear how you would proceed."

"I'll make this brief, because I don't want to waste my time, or yours," I said, looking down at her. "I'd start with learning as much about your daughter and her husband as I can. Whoever intended to rob them probably knew them, or at least knew they had something specific worth stealing. I'd visit the crime scene, interview possible witnesses, see what the police will share, and go from there."

"That doesn't sound very scientific," she said.

"Go hire a scientist if that's what you want," I replied, and walked out the front door. I was halfway to my truck before I heard Walter huffing behind me. "I'm sorry, there, hold on, please, just allow me a moment."

"Yes?"

He had lost his breath during the short trot to catch up with me. "Bear with me, please." He bent at the waist and put his hands on his knees and gulped air until he straightened and said, "It's my heart, you know."

"Are you okay?"

"Yes, I think so. I'm just not a young man anymore." He smiled bravely, then said, "I want to apologize for Lillian. This situation has been incredibly hard on her. And on me, too. But she's handling it differently than I am. She's become, well, more difficult. Please understand."

"What is it you want from me, Walter?"

"Come back and finish with Lillian. She'll be cordial, I assure you."

I sighed and looked past him at the darkening skies above the lake. The temperature had dropped, and it was no more than twenty degrees outside. Walter wrapped his arms around himself and stepped in place, like a child who needed to urinate.

"All right," I said. I wanted the job, and in the back of my mind I was already chiding myself for my impatience. Sure, the woman was caustic, but I could typically handle much more than she'd doled out.

We walked quickly back to the condo and went inside. Lillian was waiting in her seat at the kitchen table. She looked at me, her jaw clenched and her lips parted, showing a chipped front tooth.

"I'm told you've killed many men," she said.

"I beg your pardon?"

"You heard me. The crimes against my family were committed by parties I wouldn't consider human. I need to hire someone who is ready, willing, and able to deal with their kind. That's why I called you."

"Do you intend to hire me, or not?"

"I have just one more question, Mr. Reno. Can you find who murdered my son-in-law, and find my granddaughter?"

I looked down and considered the different ways I might answer that. Then I met her stare and said, "No problemo."

2

AFTER A BRIEF DISCUSSION concerning my rates, which Lillian frowned at before conceding they would pay whatever it took, I asked where their daughter was.

"The doctors only released her from the hospital two weeks ago," Walter said. "She was in a coma for four weeks after the attack."

"She's recovering," Lillian said flatly. "There doesn't seem to be any permanent damage."

"When can I speak with her?" I asked.

"I'll go see if she's up to it," Walter said, and walked to a hallway leading to bedrooms.

"Wait a minute," I said. "She's here?"

"Where else do you think she'd be?" Lillian replied.

I didn't answer, and a minute later a young woman in purple sweatpants and a long-sleeved pastel blue shirt followed Walter into the kitchen. She had long brown hair parted on the side and a curvy, full-bodied figure. Her face was pretty, her nose freckled and her lips full. She could be considered either sexy or wholesome, depending on one's inclinations.

"This is our daughter, Melanie," Walter said.

"Hello," I said, standing. "I'm Dan Reno."

"Hi," she said. Her large brown eyes met mine briefly before she looked toward her mother.

"Melanie, we've decided to hire Mr. Reno, to find Mia and to find out who murdered Jeffrey," Lillian said.

"Sit here, honey," Walter said, pulling back a chair at the head of the table.

We were all silent for a moment, until Lillian said, "Please proceed."

"Your parents tell me you were in a coma," I said. "Do you remember anything of what happened?"

"Yes, I remember most of it, I think."

"Can you describe the intruders who came into your home?"

"It was two men," she said, her hands in her lap. "One was black, one white. They wore masks, so I couldn't see their faces."

"Can you tell me what they said?"

She glanced up at me, and her eyes flickered with uncertainty. "They pointed guns at us and demanded to know where the gold was. When my husband Jeff didn't answer, they tied us up. We were sitting there, tied to our dining room chairs." She closed her eyes and put her fingertips to her forehead.

I looked over at Lillian's expressionless face. "Please continue, Melanie," she said.

"They kept asking Jeff where the gold was, and Jeff kept saying he had none. The white guy did most of the talking. But then the black man had a knife and told Jeff he had one last chance." She blew out her breath.

"And then?" I said.

"Jeff was screaming and the black man was cutting him. And then I was unconscious, and that's all I remember."

I leaned forward in my chair. "Do you have any suspicions who these men were, or why they targeted you and your husband?"

She shook her head. "No. The gold thing made no sense. I mean, Jeff said eventually gold would be our safe haven, but we needed all our money to run the business. It was all in the bank."

I looked around the table. Walter's eyes were wide behind his spectacles, and he stared at me eagerly, as if hoping I'd say something reassuring. Lillian was still as a statue, her thoughts hidden for the moment. Melanie sat in her chair and moved her hair back from her forehead with a ringed finger.

"My daughter is gone too," she said, her voice breaking. "And I want to go home."

• • •

An hour later it was full dark, and the lake was as black as the moonless sky. Tree trunks and frozen boughs flashed in my headlights as I drove back to South Lake Tahoe. On the seat next to me were two pages of handwritten notes Melanie had compiled over the last two weeks, since regaining consciousness. The blow to her head had fractured her skull and ruptured an eardrum. Her four-week coma had been managed by a medical team in Las Vegas, as they worked to reduce swelling in her cranial cavity. The doctors considered it a minor miracle that she'd recovered with no detectable permanent damage. She had been airlifted by helicopter to Las Vegas after a UPS employee arrived to make a delivery, and then called police when he found their front door wide open and saw the house had been ransacked. This house, where Melanie had lived with her late husband and missing daughter, was in Cedar City, Utah. It was a small town about 170 miles northeast of Las Vegas.

When I got home, Candi was sitting on the couch, her legs tucked beneath her, our fuzz-ball gray cat on her lap.

"Hi, doll. Hi, Smokes," I said.

"Hey, you, I made a salad and put a pizza in the oven." She lifted Smoky and set him aside, then took her ceramic Sherlock Holmes pipe from the ashtray on the coffee table. "What have you been up to?" she asked, placing a small bud of marijuana in the pipe bowl.

"I just got hired for a new case."

"Really? What kind?" She lit up and walked to a partially opened window and exhaled out the screen. Her feet were bare, and she wore tight jeans molded to her hips. I walked up behind her.

"I'll probably be gone most of next week." I put my hands on her waist and kissed her neck.

She leaned into me, pushing her shapely rear into my crotch. "No, I don't think that's acceptable," she murmured.

"A man's got to make a living," I said, cupping her breasts.

"The pizza's gonna burn," she said.

I followed her into the kitchen and checked the oven. "Where are you going?" she asked.

"Cedar City, Utah. It's about an eight-hour drive, as long as it doesn't snow."

"Is that near Salt Lake?"

"No, it's in southern Utah, down toward the Nevada-Arizona border."

"What's going on out there?"

I paused. I was always hesitant to share sordid details with Candi. Even though she rarely protested the nature of my work, I saw no reason to burden her. But I didn't want to appear evasive, or worse, outright lie.

"A man was murdered by robbers, supposedly. His wife survived, but their ten-year-old daughter vanished, presumed kidnapped."

"Yikes. Why do you always get these kinds of cases?"

"I don't always. They said I was recommended."

"By whom?"

"I don't know." I began chopping a cucumber and tossing the slices into the salad bowl on the counter. When she didn't say anything, I put down the knife and turned toward her. "I don't always get to be choosy about my jobs. I don't feel right when I don't work."

She opened the oven and set the pizza on a woodblock next to the stove. Then she came close and grasped my hands.

"That's what makes you the man you are," she said. "And you never have to apologize to me for that." She began leading me to our bedroom.

"The pizza will get cold," I said.

"We'll heat it up."

· · ·

Afterward, I lay on the bed and watched Candi walk naked to the closet. She had dark brown hair, but her nipples were pink. Her stomach swelled gently before it flattened above her light pubic hair, and her ass was heart-shaped below her thin waist. Standing on her tiptoes to reach something in the closet, her thighs and calves looked sleek and perfectly proportioned. Then she bent to pick up her panties from the floor, and I said, "Too much."

"Excuse me?" she said.

"Nothing. Just talking to myself."

"Were you checking me out?"

"Maybe."

"Hmm," she said. "We'll have to see if we can cure that." She climbed back on the bed and straddled me.

"I guess I deserve this," I said.

"You sure do."

· · ·

After we finally dressed and finished dinner, I was packing my clothes and loading my truck when my cell rang.

"Dan Reno," I answered.

"Mr. Reno, it's Lillian McDermott. What time are you leaving tomorrow?"

"First thing in the morning."

"Good. I'd like you to stop by here first and pick up Melanie."

"What for?"

"She's become adamant about returning home tomorrow. We looked into flights to Las Vegas, but driving would be quicker, all things considered."

"You want me to drive her to Cedar City?"

"No, *I* don't want you to drive her. She wants you to. She's insistent upon it."

"It's an unusual request."

"You are under my employ, correct, Mr. Reno?"

"You've hired me to investigate the murder of your daughter's husband and the disappearance of your granddaughter. I wasn't aware that included taxi service."

"Are you saying you won't drive her?"

I took a moment before answering. "No, it's okay. Tell her I'll be there at eight-thirty tomorrow morning."

"Good. She'll be ready."

• • •

When I woke the next morning, the house was cold. I rekindled and stoked the stove, then made coffee. While it brewed I stepped out onto my back porch. Blowing puffs of vapor into the frigid air, I surveyed the sky. A roil of dark clouds loomed to the west, but it was still clear over the mountaintops. I suspected it would snow later in the day, but by then I'd be beyond the brunt of the storm, heading southeast across Nevada's Great Basin Desert.

I had breakfast and watched the fire dance behind the stove glass. The flames cast a shimmering pattern against the furniture in my living room. When Candi moved in a year and a half ago, she'd replaced my old couch with a leather sectional, added a modern easy chair that we rarely used, and covered the walls with various art, including her own paintings. In short order she'd transformed the interior of my three-bedroom-two-bath A-frame home from nondescript into something eclectic and inviting. In quiet moments, I still found myself marveling at the living room, as if the décor was an extension of what she meant to my life.

By the time I'd dressed and was ready to hit the road, Candi had risen and was sitting at the kitchen table drinking coffee. Smoky sat by her feet, his long gray fur impeccably groomed. Candi would not allow him outdoors because of the coyotes.

"I should know better, but how long do you think you'll be gone?" she asked.

"Around a week. Hopefully not longer."

She stood and gave me a brief hug. "Be safe and call me," she said.

"Of course, babe." I gave her a final squeeze and a quick peck on the cheek, then went to the garage and backed out my truck. I'd bungee corded my suitcase to the bed, and my gear bag was stowed in the locked steel box welded behind the cab.

As I drove out of town and around the lake, I wondered what it would be like sharing the long drive with Melanie. Would she be quiet and shy, or perhaps energized and chatty? I'd prefer the latter, because I was sure there was more she could tell me. Her two pages of notes had posed more questions than answers. But I didn't know if her injury had left her memory fully intact. I guessed I'd find out soon enough.

I pulled into the lakeside condo parking lot right on time and knocked on the McDermotts' door. Melanie opened the door as if she'd been waiting there. To her side were two large suitcases. She looked at me expectedly. Lillian McDermott appeared behind her, followed by Walter.

"Good morning," I said. "Ready to go?"

"I'd like to have a word with you first, Mr. Reno," Lillian said. "In private."

"All right." I went into the house and followed Lillian to a room where a sliding glass door faced the lake. The waters were gray and the tiny white caps looked fringed with ice.

"Melanie has been through a lot, as you know," Lillian said. "Walter and I originally planned to accompany her back to Cedar City. Unfortunately, we have pressing business that will keep us here at least another forty-eight hours. We pleaded with Melanie to wait for us, and allow herself more time to heal. But she insists she's fine, and is unwilling to delay her return."

We stood side by side, looking out at the beach. After a moment, Lillian turned toward me. "My daughter's life has been invaded by unspeakable evil, and we don't know if any danger still exists. But she is ready to reclaim her life, as she must."

I started to respond, but Lillian stopped me with her piercing, steely blue eyes. "These men who killed her husband, and maybe her daughter—they must be found. If my granddaughter is still alive, she must be found, and returned to Melanie. The police force in Cedar City, if they can truly be called a police force, has proven woefully inadequate. I don't know exactly what they've done, but I can tell you it's not much."

"I understand."

"As for Melanie, know this: she is my only child, and she must be protected, above all else. Again, I don't know what threat may lurk in Cedar City, but I'm not at all comfortable with her returning so soon."

"It is her home," I said.

"Yes, and she needs to live there, or try to sell that… property." Lillian shook her head and her lips turned downward.

"Is there anything else?" I asked.

"I suppose not." She turned toward the door.

"Mrs. McDermott, you said I came recommended. By whom?"

"An investigator we spoke to in San Jose. A massive bear of a man. Cody Gibbons, if I remember his name correctly. He said he was too busy, but this case would be right up your alley. Those were his exact words."

I stared at her silently for a moment. "You know him, I take it?" she said.

"Yes," I replied. "I know him."

We walked out to the main room. Melanie wore blue jeans, pink trail shoes, and she'd put on a thick jacket with a fur collar. She opened the front door and pulled one of her suitcases down the step. I grabbed her second bag, but Walter stopped me.

"Please," he said. "We're counting on you."

I shook his hand and squeezed a little harder than I meant. Then I patted him on the shoulder and walked out the door.

3

SITTING QUIETLY IN MY passenger seat, Melanie didn't seem eager to chat. In fact, within a minute of taking off, I saw her eyes were closed, and I heard her deep, rhythmic breathing. I let her doze as we wound around the lake, then into South Lake Tahoe. It was only after we'd crested Kingsbury Grade and dropped out of the mountains that she stirred.

"I'm sorry, I guess I'm really tired. I didn't sleep much last night," she said. She wore a white ski beanie over her auburn hair.

"You've been asleep for an hour."

"The doctors said I might take more naps than usual. Where are we?"

"West of Gardnerville." We were on a long, straight section of road traversing pastures that stretched as far as I could see. To either side, cattle grazed on the sparse vegetation that rose through the snow. Behind us a series of granite peaks loomed, the ridges jagged and streaked with white.

She removed her shoes and tucked one leg beneath her. "So much empty land," she said.

"There's a lot more of that to come."

"It's kind of pretty, I guess."

"I figure we'll stop for lunch in Tonopah. It's about the halfway point."

"What's in Tonopah?"

"Not much. It's an old mining town in the middle of Nevada."

"Oh," she said.

We drove in silence for a while before she spoke again. "Did you read my notes?" she asked.

"Yes."

"Don't you have any questions?"

"Yeah," I said, but her two pages seemed little more than a smattering of disjointed thoughts, and I wasn't sure where to start.

"Maybe it'd be easier if you just tell me about your life with your husband and daughter."

"Well, okay," she said, and for the first time I saw a modest smile on her face. She had white, even teeth, and her brown eyes had a certain sparkle. She was quite pretty, I decided.

"I met Jeff in high school, in San Jose. I was a freshman, and he was a senior. I have to admit, at first I really thought he was a big dork. But he had charm in his own way. I mean, he was confident and cool, and he always said it was love at first sight for him. We got married when I was twenty, after Jeff's career started going."

"What did he do for a living?"

"At first he worked for a construction company, managing projects. Then he formed his own company, as a contractor. He specialized in upgrading apartment complexes. I kept all the books for him."

"You managed his money?"

"The company's money. He did business as Jordan Contracting."

"Your last name?"

"Yes," she said. "I'm Melanie Jordan. I suppose I can still keep that name, even though Jeff is… gone." I looked over and her eyes were downcast.

"Of course you can," I said.

"It's hard, you know," she said through a sniffle. "He was my life, my family. I mean, I really haven't come to terms with it, I mean, any of this."

"It'll take time," I said. I didn't know what else to say, but the comment sounded empty as soon as it left my mouth.

"I suppose," she replied. "But I have no idea what I'm going to do without him, and without…" Her voice cracked, and I saw her lips tremble. "And without Mia, my daughter."

"You have to go one day at a time," I said. She didn't respond and stared with red-rimmed eyes out the windshield. I always hated this part of the job. Dealing with distraught women never failed to jangle my nerves, even though I'd done it plenty of times, endured their sadness and grief and anger and hysterics. I'd utter things straight from the counselor's playbook, but none of it ever seemed to ease their pain or solve anything. A lady once told me that women just want to be listened to, while men, fools that we are, we don't want to listen, we just want to fix the problem. Her advice to me was simple: shut up and listen, and quit trying to fix what can't be fixed.

We turned south onto 395, driving down the California-Nevada border. To our right, the early sun lit the east flank of the Sierra Nevada, and to our left the high desert plains stretched eastward.

A few minutes passed before Melanie spoke again. "Let's do this chronologically," she said. "I think that's the most logical way." Her tone was now flat and even, and as she talked I kept glancing at her quizzically. There was no longer any grief or sadness in her voice, as if she had become vacated of emotion. It was as if she'd shifted from a helpless, damaged victim to a woman who was utterly stoic. I was struck that I was witnessing a hidden side of her, maybe her mother's genes at play. But as she described her life leading up to the attack, I became increasingly perplexed at how detached she sounded. It was a bit eerie, as if a switch had been clicked inside her head. In this almost robotic manner, Melanie recounted her existence since meeting Jeff Jordan.

He was a big man, broad-shouldered and thick in the chest. His eyesight was poor, which prevented him from playing sports in high school. Doctors told him a minor surgery would make his vision perfect, but his divorced parents considered it unnecessary, or perhaps were unwilling to spend the money. Jeff paid for the procedure himself once he could afford it.

More than anything, Jeff's personality was defined by an intense desire to rise above the standards set by his family. His mother suffered from depression and spent weeks at a time alone in her dark house. She refused all pleas by her family to seek treatment. Jeff realized she was mentally ill, but he could not forgive her for lacking the will to better herself.

Jeff's father, Bur Jordan, was largely absent. He worked for the government and spent long months overseas. The nature of his work was something he did not share with his family. Over time, Jeff came to suspect he was involved in covert operations, and was probably a spy. Bur Jordan, during the short times he was at home, would never respond when asked about his career. What exactly he did for the government remained a mystery to Jeff.

When Jeff was fifteen years old, his parents divorced. This was, for the most part, a non-event in Jeff's life. His father sent monthly support checks until Jeff turned eighteen. After that, Jeff never heard from Bur Jordan again. The meager relationship Jeff had with his father became nonexistent from that point.

As for Jeff's siblings, he had an older brother and sister. His sister married a man in Connecticut and rarely stayed in touch. Jeff's older brother went to college and played football. After graduating, he bounced from job to job, had alcohol problems, became involved in several failed business schemes, and was divorced twice.

Melanie's parents viewed Jeff dimly and hoped the relationship would be temporary. But Melanie saw in Jeff not only strength and determination, but also confidence and the ability to work tirelessly. She didn't care that he never went to college. She knew he'd be successful in whatever he set his mind to. And besides, she loved him.

After marrying, they moved from San Jose to Salt Lake City, where Jeff worked in construction. He quickly became a manager and within three years decided to branch off on his own. Headstrong and viewing his previous bosses as lazy and incompetent, Jeff founded Jordan Contracting. He was twenty-six years old. Shortly afterwards, Melanie became pregnant, but miscarried.

A year later, Jeff had three full-time employees. He and Melanie bought a home in a suburban neighborhood at the base of the Wasatch Range. Melanie became pregnant again, and this time gave birth to a daughter, Mia. For the next five years, Melanie's primary role was that of a mother, but she also had an instinctive knack for accounting, which was not among Jeff's strengths. She began managing the books for Jordan Contracting.

At age twenty-eight, Melanie's life could be considered idyllic. She loved her husband and her daughter, and she was quite content living in their large home, especially after Jeff remodeled the kitchen and bathrooms. He'd also offered to put in a swimming pool, but Melanie insisted he wait until Mia was older and could swim. Melanie also thought the money could be put to better use, and she'd opened tax-deferred retirement accounts for both of them.

Melanie began to think of her existence in terms of an article she had once read on the Great American Dream. She had her husband, the house, plenty of money, and a daughter. The next logical step was a second child. But when she spoke to Jeff about getting pregnant again, he was strangely evasive. It was only after she confronted him that she first learned of certain opinions he held.

"I was completely blindsided by this," Melanie said, some emotion creeping back into her tone. "He had been reading things on the Internet about conspiracy theories, about government corruption and secrecy, about the impending collapse of the world economy. I never had any idea he was into this stuff."

Over the next year, it became clear to Melanie that this was not a passing phase, as she originally hoped. Jeff Jordan became increasingly obsessed with the notion that the global economy was a house of cards, and the point of critical mass was looming. The ensuing implosion would be catastrophic, he believed; the United States, along with the rest of the world, would descend into a state of apocalyptic chaos once a worldwide depression replaced the current bubble economies. All governments would fail, as violent protests erupted. Bankrupt, the U.S. government would no longer make basic services available. Without funding, utility services, police and fire departments, and the military would cease to operate. Food would become scarce and the streets would fill with starving mobs. Desperate to survive, the law-abiding citizenry would resort to crime. Gun stores would be quickly cleaned out. Anarchy would reign.

"Did you believe any of this?" I asked.

"At first, no. I thought it was ridiculous. But Jeff made me read things on the Internet. 'Thank god for the Internet,' he'd say. So I read different articles, and there is a basic argument that Keynesian economic policies are not sustainable. From an accounting point of view, I understand the logic."

"But do you believe we're headed for anarchy?"

"No," she said sharply. "I never believed that."

"Did that create any problems for you with Jeff?"

When she didn't respond I looked over and saw her palms pressed to her forehead. "I'm sorry," she said, her voice faltering. "All this talking is making me tired. I'm going to close my eyes for a few minutes. Why don't you turn on some music?"

I found a light rock satellite station and turned the volume low. We were now heading east, away from the Sierras and into the desert. The two-lane highway split vast fields of sagebrush and was straight until the road merged with the sky. We were driving into an expanse where only a few tiny towns existed, relics of the silver or copper mining industries.

I drove on for thirty minutes and didn't see another vehicle. A spider-webbed pattern of white clouds stretched across the brilliant sky. In my rear view mirror, I could still see the Sierras, which were now under a dense shroud of storm clouds. Next to me, I didn't know if Melanie was sleeping, but I saw no need to bother her. We still had six hours of drive time in front of us.

When she spoke again, we had just passed the exit for Luning, a town with less than a hundred residents. "Three years ago, Jeff told me we needed to move," she said, turning the radio off. "He said we'd have a ranch with cows and chickens and a water well and windmills. He said we needed to become self-sufficient, and that meant being able to survive on our own. 'Imagine if there are no stores,' is how he put it."

"So you moved to Cedar City?"

"About ten miles north of the city. Jeff bought a twenty acre parcel and built our house."

She paused and seemed deep in thought. Then she said, "The goal was to be off the grid. Are you familiar with that?"

"It usually means hiding from the law," I said.

"No, that's not what I'm talking about. For us, it meant not relying on any public utility or institution. We had our own water supply, our own power, our own food source, our own health care. We also home-schooled Mia. That is how we lived."

"So, if the world went to hell, you'd be ready to survive."

"Prepared is the word. Prepared to survive. Jeff was determined to be prepared and protect his family. He felt that ninety-nine percent of the population was hopelessly oblivious and gullible. He referred to them as 'sheeple.' He said that when the day came, the sheeple would run around like fools, while we were prepared."

"Bizarre," I said.

"Is it? Do you believe everything the establishment tells you?"

"You mean newspapers and television?"

"Yes. The establishment, the mainstream mass media. Your local news channel or CNN, or the New York Times or USA Today. They're all government and corporate mouth pieces, brainwashing the lemmings to make them feel that all is secure and stable."

"Is this your opinion? Or Jeff's?"

"He tried to convince me, and I went along with it. He thought he was doing what's best."

"But you didn't buy into the whole doomsday scenario."

"There are worse ways to live. And Jeff was always a good provider."

"He was still running his business while all this was going on?"

"Oh, yes. Money was always important. It's not cheap being prepared. Jeff worked constantly. He traveled all over for different jobs."

"And you spent most of your time at home?"

"I almost never left. There was a lot of work to be done, way more than I could handle. We had over a hundred chickens and we were farming an acre, growing potatoes, tomatoes, cucumbers, watermelons, and more."

"Did you hire people to help?"

"A couple times a week I'd bring in teenagers from town for various things."

"Do you think any of these kids might have been somehow involved in the attack at your home?"

"Oh, no. I doubt it. I mean, that never occurred to me."

I noticed I was going over ninety and eased up on the gas. "Did Jeff have any disputes with his customers, or employees, or people he did business with?" I asked.

"Well, sure," Melanie said. "That's unavoidable in business."

"Anything that stands out? Like someone seriously pissed off?"

"Not really. There was one guy who worked for us who was kind of trashy. Jeff fired him and he got bent. That's how Jeff put it."

"I should talk to him. Anybody else you can think of that Jeff might have had issues with?"

"No, not really. Despite his views on the world, Jeff was a pretty normal guy. He didn't have enemies or anything like that."

"Let's talk about the gold. The perpetrators invaded your home specifically to rob you of gold. Is that correct?"

"That's what they said."

"I asked you before if there was gold at your house."

"And I told you, if there was, I didn't know about it."

"But you said Jeff talked about gold, and didn't believe in banks, right? So it seems plausible he had gold hidden on your property. Would it surprise you if that was the case?"

"No, but even if Jeff had bought some, it couldn't have been much," she said.

"But he never confided in you, huh?"

"Nope."

"Melanie, how about helping me out here? You say you loved your husband, and you stuck by his side even though he uprooted your life. You also say you managed his books, so you know where your money was. But you're just drawing a big blank on the gold question. We need to get to the bottom of that."

I could almost feel the air change in the space in which we sat. I believe the human body emanates certain wavelengths, invisible but real. The frequency and height of those waves is something we can intuit on a subconscious level. A happy person emits a certain profile range, while someone upset, discontent, angry, or nervous would project a very different range. As for Melanie, I could feel her vibe change, and it felt as if the air had grown denser.

"You're making me feel like I'm either stupid or a liar," she said.

"Are you lying?"

"No, I'm not. And if you don't trust me that's your problem."

I clamped my jaw shut and stared out the windshield. I could feel her glare on my face. We were cutting through a plain so featureless it looked almost cosmic. The only sound was the hum of my tires on the pavement. I turned on the radio.

Melanie reached out and switched it off with an angry flick of her wrist.

"We were both busy, all right? I had a lot to manage at the house, and he worked his butt off. I trusted him and didn't micro-manage his life. So yes, he could have had gold hidden away, but if it was more than a couple thousand dollars' worth, he didn't buy it with company money."

"Did he have any other income source?"

"He sometimes did small side jobs, but it was only a thousand here or there."

"If he made a lot on a side job, would he hide it from you?"

"Why would he?" she snapped.

I saw a tiny speck on the horizon, and after a minute I could tell it was a car coming in the opposite lane. I looked over at Melanie.

"You said Jeff was paranoid. Maybe he thought the gold would be safer if you didn't know about it."

"What gold?" she screamed, thrusting her arms outward and jerking in her seat. "I don't know that he had any!"

I kept my eyes on the road and watched the approaching vehicle grow larger until it became a red sports car. Then it passed by in a flash, the high-pitched growl of its motor loud for an instant before the sound faded behind us.

Melanie sighed and sunk back in her seat. "Listen, Jeff sometimes said things were best kept on a 'need to know' basis. But it always seemed he was kidding—I never thought he was serious about it."

"I see," I said. I was tempted to ask if she ever suspected her husband was unfaithful. But when I looked over, she sniffled and wiped at a tear.

"I'll tell you everything I possibly can. I just…I just want to hold my daughter again." The grieving, vulnerable Melanie was back. She put her hands between her legs and seemed to shrink into herself as if the burden she faced was more than she could bear.

We drove in silence for a few minutes, until I said, "The men who invaded your house. A white man and a black man. Is there anything about them that hinted why they targeted you? Anything they said?"

She shook her head. "No."

"Are there many black men who live in Cedar City?"

"Not that I know of."

I grunted and turned the radio back on. I didn't yet know what to make of Melanie Jordan. My initial impression of her, that she was wholesome, sweet, and a defenseless victim, was fraying around the edges. I was having a hard time reconciling her two personas; the grieving, widowed parent, versus the dispassionate wife of a successful businessman who had turned into a paranoid nutcase.

"Their voices," Melanie said.

"What about them?"

"They were foreign, not American. They had accents."

"What kind?"

"I don't know. Nothing I recognized."

"Spanish? Indian? An Asian accent?"

"I don't think so."

"British? French?"

"No. For the white guy, maybe Eastern European is the only thing I can guess. The black man only said a sentence or two, and his accent was different, not like anything I've heard."

"Interesting," I said, just as my phone beeped with a text message. I took a quick glance and saw it was from Cody Gibbons. We were now climbing a slight grade and there were a few bends in the road. As soon as the road straightened, I read the text: *Referred you a job. As usual, you owe me.*

I shook my head. Cody had been my best friend since high school. After he was fired from San Jose PD, he got an investigator's license, and we'd worked a number of cases together. I'd once told Candi that Cody's approach to crime solving sometimes skirted legal convention. That was as politely as I could put it. If I were in a more forthright mood, I might have said his methods were often illegal and invited violent confrontation. In almost every instance, working with him made me question my career choice.

For the next hour I drove south through the Great Basin Desert. The name implies low altitude and hot temperatures, but most of the elevation is over four thousand feet, and it was twelve degrees Fahrenheit in Coaldale, where the highway turned east. From there it was a straight line into the heart of the high desert. We climbed a thousand feet to where black sagebrush clung to rocky slopes topped by bitterbrush and Pinyon pine. Then we came off the grade onto a massive plain scabbed with patches of shadscale. As we descended, I could see the road led due east, the strip of pavement becoming thinner and then disappearing into the horizon. I laid into the gas and drove at a hundred miles an hour for the next thirty minutes, until speed limit signs marked the outskirts of Tonopah.

The highway gave way to the main drag, and we slowed, looking for a restaurant. Beyond the small collection of hotels and shops, three distinct pyramid-shaped buttes preceded a ridgeline scarred by strip mining. We passed the old Mizpah Hotel and the Clubhouse Saloon, then doubled back and parked at the town brewery. It was a large, single story building, but there were only two cars in the parking lot, and I wasn't sure if it was open.

"How many people live in a place like this?" Melanie asked.

"Couple thousand, maybe," I said. "It's part of Nevada's silver mining history. Mostly caters to tourists now."

"Makes me think of cowboy movies."

We got out of my truck. The outside air was dry and bitter cold. I suspected the joint's entrance might be locked, but the door swung open. We went into a cavernous, dimly lit room, where a man wearing a white chef's hat and a waitress sat at a long bar.

"Kitchen open?" I asked. The chef nodded as we took a table. The waitress brought us menus, we ordered quickly, and then Melanie stood.

"Excuse me, I'm going to use the ladies room," she said, walking toward the back of the place.

I sat and gazed wistfully at the beer taps behind the bar, then I dialed Cody Gibbons, but he didn't answer. I hadn't spoken to Cody much since our vacation in Mexico last October. He had made the arrangements after we'd finished a difficult case, professing that we deserved "rest and relaxation." That was a hard point to argue, so Candi and I had traveled with him and his sometimes girlfriend, Heidi Ho, down to the southern tip of the Baja Peninsula. The resort was nicer than I expected, the weather perfect, and I found the Mexican food and tequila to my liking. Cody was charming and ebullient, and our dinners were festive events that went late into the evening. After three days I felt my head decompress. I took to strolling on the beach in the mornings, the Sea of Cortez lapping at my feet, the sun warming my skin. My mind would go blank, and I would just walk and enjoy the natural elements.

Then, on the fourth day, we pulled our rental car into a gas station outside of San Jose Del Cabo. We were immediately surrounded by a dozen attendants, some wearing white shirts with petrol company logos, and some dressed only in T-shirts. They spoke loudly and one made a pretense of washing the windshield and another insisted on pumping the gas. But as soon as the gas began flowing, I saw the pump meter wasn't on.

Cody and I stood outside the car while Candi and Heidi Ho waited in the rear seat. Once the tank was full, the man who pumped the gas said, "one thousand pesos, *señor.*"

I looked at the sign advertising the cost per gallon and did a quick calculation. "You're charging us double," I said in Spanish.

"It's for the service. The service is not included in the price," he replied, waving at the sign.

"I'll give you six hundred pesos. And that's being generous," I said.

Another man stepped forward at that moment. At around 5'10" and 175 pounds, he was the largest in the group. When he spoke his lips curled and his eyes were flat.

"It's one thousand pesos, *señor*. It's not negotiable."

"Really?" I said.

"What'd he say?" Cody asked.

"They're trying to charge us double for the gas. It's a scam."

"No shit?" Cody said. Cody went to the man and peered down at him. "Tell you what, *muchacho*. Take your punk-ass gaffle and hit the bricks. *Comprende?*"

The man looked up at Cody, and if he was concerned about giving away seven inches and 125 pounds, he didn't show it. I also doubted he understood exactly what Cody said, but I guessed he understood enough of it.

"One thousand pesos, or you're breaking the law," he said to me. The other attendants, some who obviously did not work at the gas station, were watching silently. A few of the bolder moved closer to us.

Cody glanced at me and I said, "He wants us to pay up." My inclination was to hand over five hundred pesos, then simply get in the car and drive away. But that would be to ignore everything that made Cody who he was.

Cody stepped forward, fitted his huge paws around the man's neck, and lifted him off the ground. The man gasped and punched ineffectually at Cody's arms. A younger guy rushed forward, but I stopped him with a stiff arm to the chest.

"Okay, there, *pendejo*, here's the deal," Cody said. "Under normal circumstances, I'd slap the shit out of you. But you get a free pass since I'm on vacation and teaching religion to scum like you is something I get paid to do. So consider this your lucky day."

The man couldn't breathe and his face turned tomato red as he clutched at Cody's arms. Cody held him there for a long moment, then threw him into two of the nearest attendants. They all went down in a heap.

I gave a folded stack of pesos to an attendant. "Five hundred, *amigo*," I said. *"Adios."*

As we drove back to our resort, I hoped this minor occurrence wouldn't disrupt the tranquility of our trip. If Cody and I had been alone, it certainly wouldn't have. But to assume our women would let it go was probably wishful thinking. Candi had never seen Cody in action before, and I suspected she would view his behavior as irresponsible and dangerous.

But after a few pointed questions in the privacy of our room, Candi seemed quite willing to discount the event. She even seemed a bit titillated by Cody's antics. In the eighteen months Candi and I had lived together, she'd become more accepting of certain things related to my profession. It helped that her father was a lawman in Houston.

Heidi Ho, on the other hand, apparently was not amused. She was sullen at dinner that evening, and would barely look at Cody. I did my best to humor her, but it grew increasingly awkward. I finally gave up after Candi pinched my leg. When the waiter came around, I ordered a double shot of tequila.

At eleven that night, after Candi nodded off, I met Cody at the outdoor bar overlooking the ocean. It was warm and the long beach was deserted and moonlight glinted off the breakers. The sound of waves washing over the shoreline was steady and almost hypnotic. We sat looking at the sea and drank and laughed and reminisced until the bar closed. The

We returned to the table, and she crossed her legs and poked at her salad. I took a few bites off my sandwich and watched her eat. She took small bites and used her silverware in a dainty manner. She caught me staring at her and put down her fork. "God, I didn't even have time to do my nails," she said, holding up her hand. "You're not much for conversation, are you?"

"Depends who I'm talking to," I said.

"Nothing wrong with the strong, silent type, I guess."

"Would you excuse me for a minute?"

"Don't leave me alone too long. I might stray if you're not careful."

"Be right back," I replied. I walked to the far corner of the room and stood near the door to the kitchen. Watching her from behind, I called the number for the McDermotts. The phone rang and rang and finally went to voice mail. "Shit," I muttered. I ran my hand through my hair and wondered who else I could call.

Melanie turned to look at me, and I started back to the table.

"I was hoping you'd bring me a drink," she said as I sat.

"I don't think that's a good idea. You've had a serious head injury."

"My head's just fine. So is the rest of me, don't you think?" She turned and struck a pose, shoulders back, her chest forward. She ran her finger along the exposed portion of one breast.

"We should eat up and hit the road," I said.

"What's the hurry? There's a hotel right down the street." She pursed her lips and winked.

"We've got a long drive. Finish your salad."

"Do you mind if I pay you a compliment?" she said. "I love those big arms you have, the way the vein runs up your biceps. It's very sexy."

I pinched the bridge of my nose and looked at Melanie. She raised her eyebrows and touched her upper lip with her tongue.

"Do you happen to have the phone number for your doctor in Las Vegas?" I asked.

"You are such a stick in the mud."

"Sorry about that. How about the phone number?"

"I don't know what you're talking about, but Vegas sounds great. Let's go there."

I concentrated on my food, then caught the waitress's eye and waved my credit card at her. She brought the bill, and I waited for Melanie to finish eating. When we stood to leave, she put her arm around my waist. I peeled her fingers from my belt loop and held her hand and led her like a rambunctious child to my truck.

"Put your seat belt on, please," I said, pulling out of the lot. She had reached over with her left hand and I could feel her fingernails on my jeans. I squinted into the sunlight and hit the gas. We were more than four hours from Cedar City. There were only a few ghost towns along the 230 remaining miles to the Utah border. In a minute Tonopah was a spec in the rearview mirror and I was accelerating into the stark desert.

Thankfully, within five minutes Melanie was asleep again. I stole a glance at her, and her face looked sad beneath her exaggerated makeup. I wondered what she might be dreaming of, if anything. I also wondered about the extent of her brain injury, and if it was causing some sort of delayed psychosis. My only knowledge of multiple personality disorder was from a college psychology class over ten years ago. I had a vague recollection that multiple personalities were a coping mechanism to deal with something too painful to accept. But could multiple personalities be brought on by a blow to the head?

Either way, something was seriously haywire in Melanie. I considered rerouting and driving straight to Las Vegas to get her to a hospital. We were about ninety minutes from Junction 93 south, which would take us there. It would be shorter than driving to Cedar City.

Melanie stayed asleep as we passed through the ghost town of Warm Springs. A few minutes later I saw the green sign declaring Nevada 375 as the Extraterrestrial Highway. Ahead was the tiny hamlet of Rachel, which is at the center of what's commonly known as Area 51. I drove past an OPEN RANGE sign warning drivers to beware of cattle on the road. On the sign was a drawing of a flying saucer over a cow.

My phone rang and Melanie stirred. I saw it was a return call from the McDermotts. I answered and said, "Hold on a minute." Then I hit the brakes and pulled onto a thin coating of snow on the shoulder. To either side of me, the frost-covered plains stretched for miles.

I grabbed my coat and stepped outside. It had gotten colder, even though we were now many miles south of Tonopah.

"Walter?" I said.

"Yes. Is this Dan?"

"Yeah. Listen, about your daughter."

"Is everything okay? Where are you?"

"Out in the middle of Nevada. I have a few questions about Melanie."

"Of course. Go ahead."

"Since she regained consciousness, has her personality seemed normal to you?"

"Her personality? Why, yes, I suppose it's been normal, all things considered. She's been through something horrible, you understand."

"I know that. Have you noticed anything different about her, like multiple personalities?"

"She's had her ups and downs," he said. "She's been depressed at times, which I consider normal. She's grieving for her husband, and is very worried over her daughter, but multiple personalities? I think not."

"You're sure?"

"Yes. Why are you asking this? Is Melanie acting oddly?"

I looked in my truck and saw Melanie had folded down the passenger-side visor so she could look at herself in the inset mirror.

"Yeah, she seems sad, then very matter of fact, and then…"

"Yes?"

"We stopped to eat, and she went in the bathroom and came out with a ton of makeup on. She told me her name was Sasha and started coming on to me and suggested we go to a hotel room."

"What?" His voice had gone up a notch.

"It really threw me, Walter. I don't think I've ever seen anything like it."

Walter sputtered a bit, then finally said, "Can I speak with her?"

"Hold on." Melanie was removing the makeup around her eyes with cotton balls. I got back in the cab and handed her my phone. "It's your dad, Melanie," I said.

"Oh. Okay." She took one more swipe at her eyes before jamming the blackened cotton balls in a small plastic bag.

I started my truck and pulled back onto the highway. Melanie's conversation with her father consisted mostly of her repeating that she was fine and lasted only a minute before she handed me the phone.

"She sounds okay," Walter said. "But Lillian and I will contact her neurologist and ask about what you said."

"Please do. I wasn't exaggerating. Also, can you text me the contact info for her doctors?"

"Sure, but hopefully you'll not need to contact them," he said.

"Hopefully not," I replied.

4

I DROVE WITH A heavy foot, reeling in the miles, but the afternoon felt like it had no end. The road was occasionally interrupted by a sweeping turn or two, for no reason I could fathom other than to avoid some unseen variance in the terrain. Nameless brown ridges rose and fell in the distance, and the shadow of my truck appeared before us as the sun finally dropped. Melanie asked that we stop in the ghost town of Crystal Springs, but I stayed hard on the gas for another half hour until we reached a dot on the map called Caliente. It was four p.m. and I looked for a likely restroom, passed a few closed restaurants, then stopped at a tiny bar named the Hide Away Club.

Melanie had been quiet since lunch. Her face was free of makeup and the freckles on her cheekbones made her look younger than she was. When she walked into the cold sunlight, her expression suggested nothing but vulnerability and innocence. She'd removed her heels and was again wearing her pink trail shoes.

We went into the dusky bar, where the only patrons were two old ranch-hands with leathery forearms and scarred knuckles. They sat silently, sipping from Coors bottles and smoking Camels. Melanie headed to the ladies room, and I asked her to be quick. I wanted to get the drive over with before full dark, and I didn't want to give her a chance to become Sasha again.

In my career I've dealt with all sorts of miscreants, and a fair amount of the criminally insane. For the most part, they are a predictable bunch. Criminals usually behave based on habit, just like law-abiding people. That's why recidivism rates are so high; bad habits are hard to break. But I'd never experienced a multiple personality. I didn't know what to expect from Melanie from one minute to the next. It was unsettling, especially since I was trapped in my truck with her.

I sighed and studied the slot machines against one wall, then I turned and looked at the bottles on the tiered shelves behind the bartender. He caught my eye and said, "You like a pop, mister?"

I shook my head, but at that moment I felt a great surge of weakness. This was the type of bar where I might have holed up for a weekend in bleaker days. An old, ramshackle joint where a smoky darkness filled the spaces between the neon lights. A bartender with a knowing glance, and a quick bottle at the ready. A place far from reality, where time is meaningless, and the blurred conversations are forgiven or forgotten.

But those days were in my past, I reminded myself. I didn't drink like that anymore. Not unless I had a damn good reason to, and that wasn't often. I'd survived my binges, pointless or otherwise, and had outgrown my self-destructive tendencies. With age I'd developed an appreciation for moderation. I watched the bartender pour whiskey for the two ranch hands, and my mouth suddenly went dry, and I felt myself pulled as if my bones were metal and the bar was a giant magnet. The barkeep looked over and gestured with the bottle of Jim Beam he held.

"A coke, please," I rasped.

He hurriedly poured me the soft drink, as if he suddenly understood my predicament and wanted no role in it. I stepped back and sat at a table, and when Melanie came from the ladies room, I rushed her out of the place.

"What's the matter?" she asked.

"Nothing. We need to get back on the road."

And so we did, fleeing the late afternoon for wherever the pavement would take us, which in twenty minutes was the Nevada-Utah border. Melanie began chatting aimlessly as we crossed the state line, telling me a story about a high school friend of hers, then about a movie she'd seen, and then about her technique for growing tomatoes. She asked me questions and answered them herself, hardly pausing long enough to catch her breath. It occurred to me she was nervous to be nearing her home, to the site of the crime that turned her life upside down. But at least her chatter seemed normal, just a release of tension, a typical reaction to the anxiety I imagined was building in her. I was pleased to hear her continue on. Her soft voice had a comfortable rhythm to it, the words almost like a quiet song. I sensed this was the real Melanie speaking, or at least the one who existed before the attack.

Melanie's patter ceased when we reached the outskirts of Cedar City. It was twilight and a low cloud bank looked on fire in the purple sky. A long red rock escarpment rose east of the town, and beyond it, taller ridges were coated with snow.

"North, right?" I said, as we approached Interstate 15, which ran west of the city.

"Yes," she whispered.

Once we'd driven a couple miles, Interstate 15 was nearly as desolate as the highways in Nevada. Only power poles, a few billboards, and random fence lines indicated much in the way of population. A series of mesas and low hills stretched for miles across the desert grasslands before disappearing in the distance.

"While I was in the hospital, my parents came and sold the chickens," Melanie said. "So at least that's done. I mean, I'd hate to see them all starved and dead."

"What else did they do?" I asked.

"My mother said that once the police finished their inspection, or whatever you call it, she cleaned the place and locked it up."

We drove for a few more minutes until Melanie said, "Turn here." It wasn't a marked exit; the dirt shoulder off the interstate simply broadened, and then I saw a narrow road leading off into some low hills. I slowed and began down the gravel track.

"It's two miles in. We'll come to a gate soon."

The road turned behind a rise, and a metal cattle gate appeared. My tires crunched to a stop. The gate was secured by a stout chain, but when I got out, I saw the chain was missing a lock. I pushed and the gate swung open, the chain dropping to the ground.

I climbed back into my truck, and Melanie said, "The gate was always locked."

I looked at the terrain to either side of the track. The ground was uneven, but the scrub was low and any decent four-wheel-drive vehicle could have driven around the gate. I got back out and spent a minute kicking through clumps of sagebrush, searching in the fading light for a discarded padlock.

"What are you looking for?" Melanie asked when I returned. I started my motor and drove through the gate.

"Somebody must have cut the lock. But it could have been the police."

"I don't know," she said.

"Did you see the vehicle that your attackers drove?"

"No, I never saw it."

"Did you hear the vehicle? Did you hear anything before you saw them?"

"No. I was in the kitchen making dinner, and Jeff was in the other room watching TV. I didn't hear a thing until one of them came up behind me."

"And the other one went to where your husband was."

"That's right."

"Was it light outside?"

"It was around six-thirty, just getting dark. About like now."

"This was early December, right?"

The road dipped and turned to the right, and I saw a reddish building. "Yes, it happened on December first," Melanie said.

As I drove around the bend, a house came into view, and then a third building.

The house, the largest of the three buildings, was single story, and not only struck me as terribly out of place in this rugged landscape, but it was also an unfortunate mishmash of styles. The facing was a pinkish stucco, which I supposed was an attempt at a Mediterranean look, but the front door was set in a circular, gray stone section that rose above the shingled roof in a medieval castle motif. The porch was shaded by a tile-roofed portico supported by squared colonnades, as if the designer couldn't decide whether to use a hacienda or colonial style, and resolved the matter by choosing both. Regardless of the architectural incongruities, the home looked well-constructed, with considerable attention to detail. It was also big, at least three thousand square feet I estimated, and no doubt expensive to build.

The structures to either side of the house were painted barnyard red. The one on the right, about twenty yards from the house, was a barn, and beyond it, toward the base of a gentle hillside, was a corral where two horses grazed. The building left of the house was narrow and rectangular, and looked like a chicken coop. In front of it was a forty-foot tall windmill, its blades spinning soundlessly in the evening breeze.

I parked my truck in the paved driveway, stopping a few feet before the garage door. There was no lawn or shrubbery in front of the home. A faint dirt trail led to the porch. I shut off the motor.

"Who's been taking care of the horses?" I asked.

"My mother has the number for the high school kids I hired. She said they've been here every other day."

I nodded and sat looking out my window, then I climbed out into the cold dusk and turned in a slow 360. If a car were to approach from the single available road, there was no hidden place to park. If intruders wanted to reach the house unseen, they'd have to leave their vehicle back behind the rise, about a quarter-mile away. Then they could come around from the side of the home, which would be a more stealthy tack.

I opened my truck door and looked in at Melanie. Her eyes were wide with uncertainty.

"Is it safe?"

"Yeah. No problem. I'd like to take a walk before full dark. Why don't you grab your coat?"

She got out as I unlocked the steel box welded behind my cab. I grabbed my industrial strength flashlight and re-locked the box. "What do you want to look for?" she asked.

"I don't know yet."

"We own twenty acres." She pointed up the hillside behind the house, and then out across a broad field of jade sagebrush and short juniper trees.

"You can see the fence line out there," she said. "That's where the water well is. They had to drill down four hundred feet."

"Sounds like a big job." I looked out at the land, unable to make out much detail in the twilight.

"Let's start over here," I said, walking back the way we'd driven in. "I want to try to recreate the path of the intruders." She followed me until we reached a spot I felt could be a likely pathway from the road to the house. The sagebrush wasn't over two feet high, and not dense enough to prevent passage. It would have been easy enough to follow a serpentine trail through the brush, ducking low, and arrive unseen in the twilight. Especially if no one was expecting them.

I turned on the flashlight and started hiking into the scrub. A thin coating of snow covered much of the bare spots between the sagebrush. We walked for a minute, making our way toward the road. Given the snow, finding footprints was unlikely. I trained the flashlight on the ground, looking for anything to suggest someone had been here.

"Would you or anybody ever be along this trail?" I asked.

"No," Melanie said. "There's no reason to."

We continued for another minute. It was growing dark quickly, and we were at the crest of the small rise that overlooked the house. I stopped at the base of a juniper tree about my height and studied the ground, then I knelt.

"Did your husband smoke?" I asked.

"Only occasionally."

"What brand?"

"Marlboro Lights."

I plucked aside a broken tangle of twigs and carefully removed a crushed cigarette butt. It was weathered and water-damaged and there wasn't much color left in the paper. Finding it had been pure luck; I might have missed it even in broad daylight. Holding it between my fingernails, I put it under the light and tried to read the lettering on the filter.

"What is it?" Melanie asked.

"You know anybody who smokes Pacific cigarettes?"

"Pacific? I've never heard of that brand."

I dropped the butt into a plastic baggy, folded it neatly, and placed it in my shirt pocket.

"Me neither," I said. "Let's go inside, it's getting too dark."

We made our way to the front door. She took a set of keys from her purse and unlocked the doorknob and a deadbolt. She pushed the door open, and we peered into the entrance.

"Was the door locked when the intruders came?"

"No," she replied. "We never locked the house when we were here."

We walked in and Melanie flipped a light switch. The foyer was circular and tiled in gray stone. To the left, the front room was carpeted but unfurnished. Curtains were drawn over a large window that faced the front yard. We went to the right, into a spacious kitchen and dining area. The countertops were plywood, but everything else looked finished; polished wood plank flooring, white cabinets, and stainless steel appliances. In the dining room, a walnut table surrounded by six chairs was lit from above by a modest chandelier.

Melanie stood in the kitchen, looking around as if stupefied. Then she took a step toward the dining room. I noticed some dark spots in the carpet beneath one of the chairs.

"There," she said, pointing. "That's where Jeff sat. That's where I last saw him."

I walked to the chair, then around the table and into an adjoining room. The walls were wood-paneled and a sectional leather couch faced a television mounted on the wall. To one side of the TV was an entertainment center, and on the other side rested a long, glass-doored credenza.

A brick fireplace dominated the furthest wall. I walked to it and stood looking through an archway that led back to the unfurnished room in the front of the house. From this vantage, it was easy to imagine the assailants quietly entering through the unlocked front door, walking through the front room into the family room, where Jeff Jordan watched TV. From there, they could enter the dining room and kitchen, where Melanie was preparing dinner.

"How about the bedrooms?" I said.

We went down a hallway. The doors were all closed. Melanie stood outside the second door and put her hand on the knob. She stood there for a long moment, and then I saw her shudder. "This is Mia's room," she said. Her voice was high-pitched and almost childlike. She twisted the knob, and the door opened.

The bed was made and a small white desk was in one corner. Hand drawn pictures of ponies were taped above the desk and a pink stuffed bear lay on the frilly lavender bedspread. The room was orderly and had probably been looked through by the police and then cleaned by Melanie's mother, just like the rest of the house.

Melanie stood in the center of the room. She crossed her arms over her chest, her fingers touching her shoulders. "Mia?" she whispered. She turned in a circle, her eyes glassy and red, her body trembling. "Mia?" she said again. "Where are you, baby girl? Your mom is here and I love you."

She turned in a circle again, tears streaming down her cheeks. She reached her hands upward as if beckoning to the heavens. Then she tilted her head back and let out a low moan that started deep in her chest. The moan rose in intensity until it became an anguished, ear-piercing wail. As soon as she ran out of breath she collapsed onto the floor, sobbing.

I stood over her until she sat up. "I'm sorry, I'm so sorry," she said. "But I feel her here, in my heart. I'm having a hard time dealing…"

I reached out and helped her to her feet. "Take your time, try to relax," I said.

"My head is spinning."

"Do you need to sit down?"

"No, I'll be okay."

She stood staring at the floor, until she mumbled, "Let's go." We left Mia's room and I closed the door behind us.

"Is that your room?" I asked, pointing to the end of the hallway.

"Yes," she said, but before I could take a step she grabbed my arm, her fingernails digging into my skin. "She's alive. Dan, my daughter is alive. I know it."

I looked down at her tear-streaked face, and her round eyes stared at me. "I believe you," I said.

"You have to find her. Please find her. I don't care about anything else."

"I'll do everything I can."

"When?"

"As soon as I have some idea what happened to her."

She took a deep breath, seemed to steel herself, then she led me down the hall and opened the door to her bedroom.

"This is where I slept with my husband," she said.

It was large for a bedroom. A king-sized bed was in the center, and there were a dozen empty feet to either side. On the opposite wall was a long closet with mirrored sliding doors. I put my hand on the slider, then looked at Melanie.

"Go ahead," she said. She sounded tough and resolute, as if committed to harnessing her emotions.

In the closet were clothes on hangers and folded shirts on shelves. In the center there was an open space where the closet was deeper. I saw a cord, partially hidden behind a hanging coat. I pulled, and a light came on.

"What's back here?" I asked.

"Some of Jeff's stuff. Just storage."

I slid through the narrow opening, and behind the hanging garments, cardboard boxes were stacked against the wall. "Anything valuable I should know about?"

When she didn't respond I turned and, not seeing her, I sidestepped out of the closet. She was at the opposite side of the room, next to a nightstand. In her hands was an opened jewelry box.

"Melanie?"

She looked up, a deep frown on her face. "My wedding ring is gone. All my jewelry is gone," she said.

"Are you sure your mother didn't take it for safe keeping?"

"She would have told me."

I walked over and stared down at the empty box.

"Those men must have taken it," she said.

"That would be the most likely conclusion. But I'll double-check with your mom."

She didn't say anything for a long moment, then she snapped the box shut and tossed it down onto the nightstand. It clattered off the surface and fell to the floor. She shook her head and muttered, "Just great." She put her hands on her hips, then turned and walked out of the room.

We went into the kitchen and she opened a cupboard and grabbed a bottle of red wine. "Would you mind opening this for me?" She handed me a corkscrew.

"Are you sure you should be drinking?" I said.

"I'm not sure of anything, except that I need a damn glass of wine."

I sighed and uncorked the bottle. She set two stemmed glasses on the kitchen bar and sat on a padded stool. She poured herself a glass, but I moved the second glass away from her. "I'm on the wagon," I said.

"That's too bad. You look like you could use one."

I sat at the counter next to her and rubbed my eyes. "You didn't have much for lunch. You should eat something," I said.

"We have plenty of food downstairs. Assuming they didn't steal that too."

"You have a basement?"

"Just one big room, where we store our food reserves."

"Like what?"

"Freeze-dried meals, canned meats, vegetables, and starch. All with long shelf lives."

I watched her sip from her wine glass. Her straight hair was shiny and fell over her shoulders and onto her chest. She took a longer drink, and the freckles under her eyes glowed. Looking at her, I realized I had no idea who she was. She could be a distraught victim one moment, a stoic accountant the next, then a seductress, and then return to the role of a grieving wife and mother. I wondered if behind it all, she may not have been all that unhappy to lose her husband. I couldn't discount the possibility she'd hatched a scheme to get rid of Jeff. If so, the end result was obviously not what she had in mind. Hell, she'd been lucky to survive.

The McDermotts said the doctors claimed Melanie had recovered, but the fractures in her personality suggested otherwise. If she simply had rapid emotional swings, from sadness to dispassionate to bitter, that might be explainable given the dramatic upheaval of her life. But I kept on remembering her walking out of the Nevada restaurant ladies room, strutting on high heels, swinging her hips, her makeup overdone, touching her bare breast with her fingertip. She claimed her name was Sasha, and that obviously indicated some of her screws were loose.

But Melanie's mental stability, or lack thereof, was not my concern, I reminded myself. I'd been hired to find her daughter, if she was in fact still alive, and also to bring Jeff Jordan's killers to justice. To those ends, I was just getting started.

I assumed I'd be spending the night here, rather than driving into town for a hotel. I'd have been surprised if Melanie asked me to leave; I didn't sense she was ready to be alone in her big house. I'd need some private time to map out a strategy. This was my typical approach to any investigation. The early stage always felt like a confused jumble of indefinites. To get past this, I'd first outline primary lines of inquiry, then drill down to secondary questions. In this case, I was beginning to think it might result in a fairly lengthy document. Almost everything Melanie had told me so far raised more questions, more possibilities. Hopefully the variables would quickly condense once I had some answers.

I knew I had to thoroughly interrogate Melanie, but I wanted to wait until I felt she was in a stable mood, or at least well rested. I also needed to talk with the Cedar City police. They'd be able to fill in some blanks. As long as they were cooperative.

"Come on downstairs with me, let's pick something for dinner," Melanie said.

"All right." I followed her down the hallway toward the bedrooms. We went through a door opposite Mia's room, into a small office. She opened a desk drawer and reached deep inside. There was a metallic click, then she went to a large oak bookshelf against the far wall and pulled on a screw head protruding from the wood. The entire unit swung into the room, revealing a lit staircase heading downward. A rush of cool air came from below.

"Jeff built this himself," she said. "He said it'd be pointless if anyone except us knew about it."

I shrugged. "I promise to never tell."

"As if it matters anymore."

We went down the wooden stairs and into a concrete room lined with shelving. Florescent tube lights hung from the ceiling and illuminated rows of cans with handwritten labels. Cases of soft drinks and water bottles were stacked on the floor beneath the shelves. Tucked in a corner was what I immediately recognized as a gun safe. It was about five feet tall and two feet deep. Fireproof, and probably weighed well over five hundred pounds.

"Jeff owned rifles?" I asked.

"Yes, plenty. Assault rifles, pistols, ammo."

"For what? He expecting a war?"

"He kept them to protect us."

"You mean from the economic collapse, the anarchy?"

"That's right," she said. "Ironic, isn't it?"

"I guess so. Do you have the combination for the safe?"

"I'll have to look for it. How about chicken with sundried tomatoes and asparagus?"

"Sounds good."

She handed me the can and we went back up the stairs and into the kitchen. After opening the container she prepared two plates and put one in the microwave. Then she poured herself a second glass of wine.

"Tell me more about this doomsday stuff," I said.

"I bet you think it's totally crazy, right?"

We went into the dining room and sat at the table. "I don't know enough to say," I said.

"When most people first hear about it, they think it's just a bunch of silly conspiracy theories."

"Is it?"

"I'll try to explain it to you," she said. "Then you can decide."

"Okay."

"It starts with the Illuminati. They were a group of intellectuals that formed a secret society back in the seventeen hundreds. Their main goal was to create a new world order, which they were in charge of. This would mean the elimination of countries and their governments, and the establishment of a global ruling elite."

"But that never happened."

"No, but that doesn't mean they're not still trying, and making progress. From the Illuminati came more secret societies. You've heard of the Freemasons, right? Their aim is the same thing, to create a world where they rule everyone. They would eliminate today's religions and make everyone practice their version, which is more like Satanism than anything else. To do this, they have to brainwash the masses, to get us to behave and cooperate."

"How would they do that?"

"You have to understand who they are. We're talking about the most powerful politicians, businesspeople, intellectuals. You'd be surprised who belongs to the Freemasons. These people truly believe they are genetically superior to the rest of us, and that we only exist to serve their ultimate vision."

"Okay, but how can they succeed?"

"Let me give you the most obvious example: nine-eleven. There is overwhelming evidence that the mainstream media version is a total lie. There is no way a group of Arab terrorists could have pulled it off, for one. But then you look at all the other disconnects. For instance, Building Seven. This was a smaller building, forty-three stories, about two football fields away from the main towers. Hours after the main towers were hit, Building Seven mysteriously collapses. But it's not really much of a mystery; the collapse was caused by preset bombs, which were also what caused the main towers to collapse. All sorts of well-known structural engineers have testified to this fact, that there's no way the planes could have caused the buildings to fall like they did."

"And how do the Freemasons play into this? What do they have to gain?"

"Here's how they work: they use their powerful positions to secretly arrange events that lead the unsuspecting population to false conclusions that in turn justify certain government reactions. In the case of nine-eleven, the government reaction was to invade Iraq. But if you look at the result of the Iraq war, what do you see?"

"The rise of ISIS. The world is now more dangerous than before."

She looked at me with a sly smile. "So, you do pay attention to world politics."

"I read the newspaper."

"So," she said, "that's exactly what the Illuminati and Freemasons want; to make the world a more dangerous place. Because in order for them to get control, to establish their one world order, they need to tear down much of our current civilization. That means they work behind the scenes to create wars, and also environmental disasters and health plagues like AIDS and Ebola. And of course, one more critical thing they'll orchestrate—the failure of the world economy."

"And then what happens?"

"Once they unleash enough disasters, the oblivious citizens will lose faith in their governments and demand change. This is when we'll see new political figures emerge, claiming a globalist approach is the only way to save the planet. They plan to take control and make the world population slaves in their new social order."

"A massive dictatorship," I said.

"Yes, but that's just the beginning. To maintain power, they'll need to dramatically reduce the earth's population. That means killing off literally billions of people. Their goal is to go from six billion down to less than one billion. After they achieve that, they'll then implement a mandatory eugenics program. You've heard of it?"

I nodded. "Selective breeding."

"That's right. They'll pick who gets to reproduce. Inferior offspring will be killed, inferior parents killed, only those who fit the purpose of the elite will be allowed to live."

The microwave pinged, and I went into the kitchen, replaced the first plate with the second, and hit the start button. I found silverware in a drawer and brought Melanie her dinner.

"Go ahead and eat," I said.

"I'm really starving all of the sudden. Would you mind bringing the wine?"

"You shouldn't drink on an empty stomach. Eat something."

She shot me a disparaging glance, but began eating. The food looked and smelled better than I expected. She ate voraciously, and half her plate was gone before she looked up and said, "I won't be offended if you don't buy into any of what I just said."

"I try not to draw conclusions too quickly," I said.

"But you're skeptical."

"I'm skeptical about most things. I also like to know what I'm talking about before spouting off an opinion."

"You're a deep thinker, are you?"

"Not really. But I think a lot of people go through life pretending they know things they don't. They talk without thinking and usually sound pretty stupid."

"Do you think I know what I'm talking about?"

I heard the microwave and went to get my plate. She asked that I bring the wine and this time I complied. I sat across from her and said, "You seem informed on your subject."

"I should be. Jeff spoke on and on about it. He called it his 'awakening' and he believed every word of it."

"And you? How much of it do you believe?"

She filled her glass and stared at me frankly. "Less than I used to. Without Jeff here…" she shrugged, palms up.

"Do you think Jeff was off-base?"

"He had me convinced, somewhat. But when I was in the hospital, I talked to a psychiatrist who said something that helped me figure it out."

"What was that?"

"He said that people who feel powerless or alone, or who have low self-esteem, often embrace conspiracy theories. It makes them feel more knowledgeable, more powerful, more important and worthy. He also said the Internet has given these people easy access to all sorts of extreme and wild information that's presented as if it's factual and scientific. Previous to the Internet, this kind of information was only found in publications like the National Enquirer, which everyone knows is a crock. But now, anyone interested in conspiracies can read endlessly about them online."

"Did Jeff have low self-esteem? I thought he was doing pretty well."

"He was, but he grew up basically fatherless and his mother suffered from depression. I don't think he got much in the way of positive reinforcement when he was a kid."

"You don't think he overcame that as an adult?"

"Some things you never fully overcome."

· · ·

After we finished eating Melanie showed me to the guest room, which was next to Mia's bedroom. The interior was Spartan; a twin bed in one corner, and a small desk against the opposite wall. There were no drapes over the single window, and the sky outside was black and starless.

I set up my computer and placed Melanie's two pages of notes to the left. Then I began typing thoughts, first in a random mode, and then with increasing structure. Soon I had the beginnings of an outline. More ideas and questions resulted, and I rearranged the elements until they were somewhat organized.

While working, I kept looking back to Melanie's handwritten jottings. Most of it we'd already covered in conversation. A white man and a black man looking for gold that Melanie had no knowledge of. Jeff resisting, Jeff being cut. The remainder chronicled the hours previous to the invasion. Jeff had run errands earlier in the day, a trip to the Cedar City Home Depot, and a possible stop at a local bar for a single beer.

An hour later I'd completed a plan for a detailed interrogation of Melanie. I hoped to sit with her the next morning at the dining room table, and ask questions until I was confident she'd revealed every scrap of information, every idea, and every conjecture she could offer. At this stage of the investigation, Melanie was my sole resource, available and willing, and I needed to extract as much from her as possible.

I stood and looked out into the dark night. There was no moon, and I could barely make out the curve of a distant hill. If you wanted to live away from people, with plenty of space and privacy, this location fit the bill. But being isolated comes with risk; in any emergency, help is not nearby. That's why criminals view remote residences as good potential targets. No close neighbors to see or hear, the nearest police miles away.

It was 9:30. I spent the next hour and a half on the Internet, reading various perspectives on conspiracy theories. I didn't know how or if Jeff's belief system might be involved in his murder, but I thought it'd be a good idea to get more familiar with the subject.

As Melanie said, there seemed to be an endless number of sites warning the unsuspecting masses that secret, nefarious groups were plotting to take over the planet. To facilitate their evil schemes, they needed to make the population docile and submissive. Their means included fluoridating water supplies to reduce intelligence, preventing pharmaceutical companies from providing cures for major illnesses, and rigging airplane engines to leave poisonous contrails (referred to as *chemtrails*) in the sky.

Other popular theories involved JFK's assassination (arranged by CIA leaders controlled by the Illuminati), AIDS (a CIA-Illuminati plot to kill off the black race), Pearl Harbor (Illuminati members with high ranking positions in the U.S. military knew in advance of the attack, but kept it quiet), and of course 9-11, which the Illuminati hoped might prompt a nuclear holocaust in the Mideast.

I also found a number of sites dedicated to debunking these theories. The tone of these sites was often derisive, and the "facts" they offered seemed no more credible than the claims by the conspiracy theorists.

By eleven p.m. I'd read enough. My conclusion? Whoever said "Don't believe most of what you read on the Internet," was right. With that thought, I shut down my computer.

When I went to the guest bathroom to brush my teeth, I heard a faint patter from the television. I walked to the kitchen and through the archway leading to the family room. The television was tuned to what looked like a local news station. From my angle I could see the back of Melanie's head. I walked around to where she could see me.

"I'm gonna go to sleep," I said. "Just wanted to say goodnight."

She didn't respond, and I stepped directly in her line of sight.

"Hey," I said, thinking she could have been dozing. But she wasn't. Her eyes were open and staring straight ahead as if she was captivated by the screen.

"Melanie?" I bent low, so she was looking right at my face. But she didn't react.

I took the clicker from the coffee table and turned the television off. Then I waved my hand in front of her. She continued staring, trancelike. I paused for a second, then knelt and put my hand on her shoulder. I shook her gently. "Can you hear me?" When she didn't respond I jostled her, first with one hand, and then with my hands on both of her shoulders.

"What the hell?" I muttered. Then I clapped loudly.

She blinked hard and a small cry escaped her lips. She looked around the room and then at me, panic in her eyes. "Hey, it's just me," I said. "Are you all right?"

Her face looked terror-stricken for a moment, then her features slowly relaxed.

"I'm… I'm fine. I must have fallen asleep."

"Were you dreaming?"

She leaned back as if exhausted. "I don't know. I don't think so."

"Maybe you should go to bed. You look pale."

"I'm very thirsty. It must have been the wine."

"Maybe so. I'll get you some water."

"I'm not used to the alcohol."

I went to the kitchen and returned with a glass of water. She drank half of it and her color returned.

"I think I will go to bed. I'm a little dizzy."

"Take my arm," I said as she stood. She stumbled for a second and grasped my forearm tightly. "You're still recovering from a head trauma. You need to take it easy."

"No more wine," she murmured.

I walked her to her room, and she let go of me and said, "See you in the morning."

"Good night."

Back in the guestroom, I lay on the bed and decided I definitely needed to call Melanie's doctor in Vegas. Her condition was clearly not right. The stress of returning home might be too much for her. In a worst case scenario, could she slip into a coma again?

"Wonderful," I muttered. I undressed, got under the sheets, and tried to sleep.

•   •   •

It was three a.m. when I woke. My door was open and light from the hall shined in my eyes. A figure stood in the doorway.

"Melanie?" I croaked.

She turned on the light, and I sat up in alarm. She was naked. Not only that, she stood tall on high heels, and her makeup was fully done, heavy around the eyes, her lips bright red. She stepped toward me.

"Hi, there," she said. Her heavy breasts swayed when she moved, the light brown nipples flat and large. She took another step, her hips full and curvaceous, and the patch of hair between her legs was trimmed and at my eye level. I held my hand out to stop her. But she turned her back to me and posed. "You like?" she said.

Her behind was round, each cheek like a ball. I winced as I felt an electric charge in my groin. When she turned to face me I clapped my hands and yelled "Melanie!" as loud as I could.

"No, Sasha, ding-a-ling," she said. She was now within arm's reach.

"Stay back," I said, but she leaned down on me, and I pushed her away by her shoulders. She retreated, her face pouty, then she pounced, her knees on the mattress. One of her breasts bumped against my cheek, and I jumped off the end of the bed and stood facing her. She was kneeling on the sheets, her right hand at her crotch, the middle finger caressing a spot above her vagina. I wore only my undershorts and was half-erect.

"Melanie!" I shouted again.

Her eyes jumped, and she looked perplexed for a moment, then she crossed her arms over her breasts and ran out of the room. I quickly closed the door. For a minute I stood there, holding the door shut, not fully convinced she wouldn't be back. I saw the light go off in the hall, and I waited another minute before returning to bed.

"Oh, boy," I said.

5

I WOKE ABRUPTLY THE next morning, at the tail end of a Kafkaesque dream. The conversations lingering in my mind centered on a problem involving Candi and some undefined threat. I couldn't remember much detail, but the dream seemed to have gone on for a long time.

It was 7:30, and when I dressed and went into kitchen, I was surprised to see Melanie up and preparing breakfast.

"Good morning," she said. "Would you like coffee?"

"Yeah, thanks." I found the pot, poured a cup, and sat at the counter. Melanie was wearing jeans and an apron over a pink shirt. I didn't see a hint of the makeup she wore a few hours ago. She stood over the stove, scrambling eggs, and said, "I found bacon in the freezer. Would you like some?"

"Sure," I said. She seemed energetic and chipper, moving about and cooking breakfast.

"Sleep well?" I asked.

"I did. Like a log. Didn't even wake up once."

"Oh. That's good."

"How about you?" She glanced over her shoulder at me.

"I woke up about three. Heard a noise."

"Really? It's usually very quiet here."

"I'm sure it is."

Melanie hummed as she tended to the stove. She looked quite content, and I imagined that preparing breakfast for her husband and daughter might have once been a comfortable routine for her.

"I'll be right back," I said. I walked back to the guestroom and grabbed my notepad. Melanie apparently had no recollection of her nocturnal excursion into my room. It would be as good a time as any to interview her.

I returned to the counter and drank from my coffee cup. "Melanie, I'd like to ask you some specific questions."

"Fire away," she said, over the sizzle of bacon.

"You said the intruders demanded gold. And you said Jeff talked about gold, but you don't know if he owned any, or if he did, where he got the money to buy it."

"That's right. But, just so you know, Jeff bought some silver coins about a year ago. It was only a thousand dollars' worth. He kept it in a safe deposit box at the bank in town."

"You're sure he didn't keep any hidden here?"

"Not that I ever knew. He kept it at the bank."

"I thought he didn't trust banks."

She turned from the stove and set her eyes on me. "He didn't. But it was in a safe deposit box, not an account." She removed strips of bacon from the griddle and prepared two plates.

"I don't know if Jeff was keeping anything from me," she said, sitting across from me at the table. "But in the few weeks before he died, he was acting a little strange."

"How so?" I asked, both pleased and a little puzzled at how open and cooperative she seemed. It was in marked contrast to our conversation about gold during the drive across the desert. But I shouldn't have been surprised, for I'd already learned to expect the unexpected from her.

"Well, he'd make phone calls, or get phone calls, and go outside to have conversations. That wasn't typical for him. Plus, he'd driven to Las Vegas a couple times. He has no business in Vegas. He drove to California all the time, but not Vegas. It was out of his way. All his jobs were in California."

"How'd you know he was in Vegas? Did he tell you?"

"No. But there's an app on his phone that allowed me to see where he was."

"Did he know about that?"

"Yes, but he never used it, and I think he forgot about it."

"Did you check on him often?"

"Every now and then. He spent half his time driving from here to Southern Cal or Northern Cal. So I'd sometimes check to estimate when he'd be home."

I jotted some notes. "What do you think he was doing in Vegas?"

She finished chewing and sipped from her coffee cup. "I thought he may have been talking to gold or silver brokers. Jeff wanted to convert our savings into precious metals. But we had to keep all our cash in the bank, to run the business."

"Did he ever withdraw large amounts, maybe buy gold behind your back?"

"Not a chance. I managed the books and knew where the money was."

"Did you argue with him about it?"

She patted her mouth with a napkin. "Jeff knew I didn't fully buy into his theories on the economic collapse. I told him we needed to keep our portfolio diversified, and it would be foolish to put all our eggs in one basket."

"How did he react to that?"

"After a while, we stopped talking about it."

I tapped my chin with my knuckle. "Why would he talk with gold brokers if he had no money?"

"He sometimes got money from side jobs, but it wasn't a lot."

"Would you have cared if he spent that money on gold?"

"Not really. It's better than wasting it on toys or…"

"What?"

"You know, drugs, hookers, booze. Jeff may have been a little kooky, but he was a good man. He wasn't into that stuff."

"There's a lot of that stuff in Vegas."

She shook her head. "That wasn't his thing."

I ate a forkful of eggs and scribbled a few more notes. "You said Jeff sometimes went outside to make phone calls. Any idea who he was talking to?"

"Elias Pullman, for one. He's a die-hard survivalist, lives about ten miles up the highway."

"Anyone else?"

She shook her head. "Jeff was too busy to have many friends."

"Were you ever suspicious he might have been cheating on you?"

She raised her eyebrows. "Jeff? No, he wasn't like that. He was a loyal husband."

"Are you sure?"

"A wife knows."

"Okay." I gulped the dregs of my coffee and got up for a refill. "Do you know where Jeff's cellphone is?"

"Oh," she said. "No, I don't. I mean, maybe the intruders took it. Or, maybe the police did."

"Did he usually leave it in a specific place?"

"On the table near our bed. But it's not there."

"How about computers? You and Jeff had PCs, right?"

"Yes, but they were both stolen, my mom said. I'll need to buy a new one."

I looked out the small bay window above the kitchen sink. The morning was overcast and gray. "Do you have the login and password for Jeff's e-mail account?" I asked.

"Maybe. I'd have to guess at it."

"Okay." I studied my outline. "Back to the gold. Do you think Jeff kept any in his gun safe?"

"I doubt it," she replied. "It would take up too much room, and the safe was pretty full with his arsenal, as he called it."

"Can you find the combination? I'd like to take a look."

She tilted her head. "It should be in one of a few places. Come on." She got up and I followed her to the master bedroom. Inside, it smelled faintly of perfume, and I recognized it from Melanie's visit to my room. The scent prompted a vivid recollection of her nude body, and I quickly pushed the thought aside.

Melanie opened her nightstand drawer and poked around, moving things, then she went to the closet. She stepped into the recess behind the hanging clothes and knelt. I heard the thump of boxes and papers shuffled.

"Need any help?" I asked.

"Nope," she said a moment later. "I got it." She emerged with a sheet of paper.

We went to the small office and Melanie reached in the drawer and released the mechanism that allowed the bookshelf to swing outward. I went behind her down the stairs, into the cool cellar.

"It's been a long time since I've done this," she said. She punched buttons on the safe's keypad, and then had to start over. "I hope he didn't change the combination," she said, but I heard a loud click. She turned the handle, and the heavy door opened.

The lighting in the room was not great, and the safe was in a shadowy area. Melanie stepped back and said, "Check it out."

The interior was crowded and Melanie was right, there was no room for gold. I counted eight rifles on one side. Four AR-15 assault weapons, an Uzi submachine gun, a large bore hunting rifle, and two shotguns, one sawed off. The center shelves were stacked with ammo. But my attention immediately went to the left, where a handheld rocket launcher, disman-tled into two pieces, rested in the space. The warhead looked like two gray metal funnels attached at the mouths.

I shook my head. It would be a perfect weapon to destroy a car, assum-ing one knew how to aim it. But it didn't do Jeff Jordan a bit of good, locked away while murderers entered his home. Neither did his other arms, for that matter. And his arms were plentiful, for on the inside of the safe door were eight holsters, each holding a handgun. One was a Beretta .40 cal, the same piece I owned. The others were an assortment of Glocks and revolvers.

Below the holsters were five zippered compartments. I unzipped the largest and found boxes of various ammunition. I zipped it shut and opened the next two. One was stuffed with manuals, and the other two held more bullets. I closed them and unzipped the smallest compartment at the bottom. It was not as full as the others.

Inside were two items. One was a small address book. I glanced at the pages, and noted what looked like a carefully drawn diagram. I dropped it in my shirt pocket, then picked up the second item, a black pouch. It was made of a silky material and felt like it contained a handful of sharp pebbles. "What's that?" Melanie said, looking over my shoulder.

I moved into better light. "Hold out your hand," I said. I pulled on the tie string and shook the contents into her palm.

"Oh, my," she said, staring at about twenty glittery stones. They were multi-colored, the shapes varied and irregular.

"Were you aware of these?" I asked.

"I had no idea," Melanie replied. "Jeff never said anything about this." The stones, despite their rough edges, were dazzling in the light. There were a mix of clears, yellows, blues, and pinks.

"Do you think they're real diamonds?" she asked.

"I don't know," I said. "But fake diamonds wouldn't be in raw form like this. I think we should talk to a jeweler. Is there one in town?"

"Yes, a couple."

I held open the pouch, and she dropped the rocks back inside. "Best leave them in the safe," I said. "Let's head outside, I want to take a walk."

.   .   .

It was about ten degrees above freezing outside, but the dry air felt colder. We stood outside the front door, looking over the terrain. The sky was white and there was no wind. I could see the glint off a metal fencepost a few hundred yards away.

"The bulk of your acres are this way?" I said, pointing to the right.

"Yeah. Our home is built near the backside of the property line."

"Show me around."

We began down a faint trail. A pair of thousand-gallon propane tanks sat to the side of the rectangular building next to the house.

"For chickens?" I asked, walking to the building.

"Yes, and storage."

We went inside. The air was foul and spider webs hung from the rafters. A long row of empty chicken coops lined both sides, and I walked past them to where bags of feed, rolls of chicken wire, and shovels, rakes, and other yard tools were leaning against the walls. Nothing struck me as out of place or unusual.

Back outside, we continued down the path. We headed across a field of purple sage, stepping over icy patches. A row of stakes in the ground led out toward the fence.

"This marks our water line," Melanie said. "The well is out there." She continued down the trail, and I fell in behind her. As I walked, I took the address book from my pocket and flipped to the page with the diagram. It was hard to decipher, but I thought it might have been a map of the property. But if it was, it was drawn to be less than obvious, or maybe even to obscure its purpose.

We hiked along, nearing the well site, until we reached a large, cultivated plot, perhaps fifty yards square.

"This is where we grew our crops." She shook her head. "Most of it looks dead now." We followed the trail at the head of the plot to a small structure near a four-foot wire fence at the property line.

"The well's beneath us." Melanie rapped on the wood facing of the structure. "There's a pump inside." I opened the unlocked door. A thick, cast iron apparatus was bolted to the concrete floor. There wasn't much room for anything else.

I closed the door and squinted into the domelike, colorless clouds. "Do you know where Jeff was killed?" I asked.

"No, no I don't," she stammered. "I mean, I assumed it was here… somewhere."

"You spoke with the police, right?"

She nodded. "I talked to them on the phone, right before I left the hospital. Two cops asked me a bunch of questions."

"Did you get their names?"

"I don't remember them."

"Cedar City cops, right?"

"Yes, I think so, why?"

"Sometimes state police get involved in crimes like this. Especially in small towns. Do you remember what they asked you?"

"For descriptions of the intruders, mostly."

"Huh," I grunted. "What's this way?" I stood looking out over flat terrain that rose into a series of knolls.

"Not much. Riding trails mostly. For ATVs, or horses."

I took the lead this time. When we reached a trail with parallel tracks, Melanie said, "This runs right down the middle of the property. Jeff would sometimes go exploring, out in those hills." I looked down and saw both tire tread and horseshoe tracks leading down the trail.

"Come on," I said, heading away from the house.

"There's nothing out there."

"You can go back if you want."

"I think I will. It's freezing out here." Melanie turned and began hiking away.

"I'll see you in twenty minutes or so," I said.

I went the opposite direction, out toward the far reaches of the acreage. After a minute I stopped and again studied the diagram in the address book. There were two parallel lines drawn, and from them were five off-shoots, like branches on a tree. Each branch was marked with a small X on either the right or left side.

I looked back toward the house, and saw Melanie hiking along, hugging herself against the cold. Then I turned and continued down the trail. It took a couple minutes to reach a smaller path to the right. I checked the diagram and followed the path for another minute until I saw broken strands of yellow crime scene tape nailed to a pair of twenty-foot junipers. Between the trees was a small clearing, and near the base of one tree a hole had been dug. It was about two feet deep and a foot in diameter.

Studying the diagram again, I concluded that this was the location of one of the five X marks. It was also evidently where Jeff Jordan was murdered, or at least where his body was found. I peered into the hole, took a picture, then stepped back and took more pictures.

It would have been easy to draw a few conclusions at this point. The intruders forced Jeff to lead them here, where gold, or something, was buried. Once the criminals had what they'd come for, they killed Jeff and either killed or kidnapped his daughter. Whether she was dead or alive, I wasn't sure, despite Melanie's intuitions. But if they'd killed her, I couldn't imagine why the body hadn't been found.

That left me to consider that they'd most likely kidnapped her. Since no ransom had been demanded, there must have been some other motivation. The possibilities for a ten-year-old girl were grim.

As for the bag of uncut gemstones, maybe they were junk and of no significance. But if they turned out to be worth more than a thousand bucks or so, it would definitely indicate Jeff was involved in something he had not shared with his wife.

I went back to the main trail and followed it for a hundred yards until a single track veered to the left. I checked the diagram and took the path, which became so faint that I wasn't sure I was actually on it. But I kept going, pacing toward a single juniper near the property boundary that coincided, more or less, with an X in the diagram.

When I reached the tree, I searched for any sign a hole had been dug. The sage was thick and tightly bunched and I found only a few spots where a square foot of ground was free of brush. Sweeping aside loose dirt with my boot, I saw an area where the ground looked slightly indented. With my heel I scraped an X on the spot.

It was midmorning, and the day showed no sign of warming. If anything, it had gotten colder. I blew into my hands and took off at a fast jog toward the chicken coop. I got there without breaking a sweat, went inside, grabbed a shovel and a pickaxe, then jogged back to where I'd marked the ground. I was sweating now, and by the time I'd dug down a foot I was wiping my brow to keep the salt out of my eyes.

Because of the angle, digging the final twelve inches took twice as much effort as the initial foot. I worked without pause, swinging the pick and shoveling the hole clean. It took ten minutes before the pick crunched into something pliant. I worked with the shovel until I saw the top of a plastic container. Jamming the shovel aside it, I was able pry the container free after a minute.

The pick had cut a crease in the lid, but not deep enough to reveal the contents. The container was about eight inches square and weighed ten pounds or so. I peeled the lid up, then untied the cord binding the canvas sack inside. It was full of coins, gold coins. I removed a couple and held them in the daylight. Although I'd never held a gold coin, I was pretty damn sure these were the real McCoy.

I left the shovel and pick and jogged back to the house, holding the container in my arm like a football. I went through the front door without knocking and yelled for Melanie. When she didn't respond I checked the main rooms, then peeked hesitantly into her bedroom. The last thing I wanted to do was catch her undressed, maybe coming out of the shower, and prompt Sasha to reemerge.

But Melanie wasn't in her room. With growing concern I searched the house, until I went through a door into the garage. I saw her at the far end, above a blue Jeep. She was halfway up a ladder, her hands in a cardboard box. Plywood flooring had been installed in the rafters, and boxes and various items, including a tricycle and an old bed frame, competed for the available space.

She was holding a tiny dress by the shoulders. "Hey," I said, but she ignored me for a long moment before folding the dress and returning it to the box.

"I found something you need to see," I said. She climbed down and came around the Jeep to where I stood at the front of a late model Chevy pickup. Her eyes looked vacant, her face without expression. I set the plastic container on the hood and pulled open the canvas bag inside.

"Gold coins, about ten pounds worth. Buried out there."

"Out where?"

"About a third of a mile out, on your property."

Whether she was surprised or perplexed, I couldn't tell. She seemed in a daze.

"Here," I said, and handed her a coin. She held it in her fingers and it gleamed with a dull luster under the fluorescent lights. Then she blinked and said, "Wow. What's it worth?"

I poked at my phone, and found a website listing the market price for gold bullion, by the kilo. I did a quick calculation and said, "About two hundred grand."

We went inside to the kitchen. I put the dirt stained box on the counter and we sat with it between us. "You told me you had no knowledge of Jeff owning this much gold," I said.

"That's right," she said.

"Well, now you do." When she didn't respond, I said, "Are you surprised?"

"I'm—I'm surprised it's so much. I mean, I don't know how he could have two hundred thousand dollars without me knowing."

"I got news for you," I replied. "I think there's three more boxes stashed out there. I think Jeff's killers got one box, but there's five total."

"How would you know that?"

I took the address book from my pocket and opened it to the page with the diagram. "This is a map of your property. Each X marks where a box is buried."

"Where'd you get this?"

"It was in the gun safe."

"And just by looking at it, you could find the spot?"

"I also found the hole where the first box was, and where I assume the police found his body."

Her eyes widened and she looked startled. "All that, this morning?"

"Your parents are paying me for my time. I'm on the clock."

"I'm impressed," she said.

"So now, Melanie, I need to ask you again: Do you have any idea where Jeff got the coins, or the money to buy them?"

"No," she said without hesitation. "It doesn't make sense. Our business was going good, and I managed all the cash flow. There's no way I wouldn't know about that kind of money. It didn't come from our business, I can tell you that." She shook her head defiantly.

"It came from somewhere," I said.

.   .   .

By 1:30 I'd found the three remaining boxes. My hands were blistered despite the canvas gloves I'd worn, and the muscles in my upper back were tight against my shirt. There was grit in my hair and when I wiped at the sweat that ran down my face, the back of my hand came away streaked with dirt. I'd worked nonstop and my body had that empty, satisfied feeling that comes after hard exercise. I hiked back to the house, the pick and shovel over my left shoulder, thirty pounds of gold coins cradled in my right arm.

Melanie was standing on the porch waiting. When I set down the yard tools, she said, "What did you find?"

"Your buried treasure."

Her mouth fell open. "Three more ten pound boxes," I said.

She stared at me and sputtered a few unintelligible words. Then she said, "You must be starving. Come in, I made you lunch."

I followed her in and washed my hands and face. My clothes were dirty, the knees of my jeans dark with mud, my T-shirt sweat-stained. But I was hungry, and I sat at Melanie's dining room table and ate from the plate of heated leftovers she'd prepared for me.

"Why would Jeff bury the gold in five separate places?" I asked. I could see Melanie in the kitchen, hovering over the four plastic boxes on the counter.

"Part of the reason," she said, coming to the table and sitting across from me, "comes from basic survivalist tactics. You're never supposed to keep your important things in a single place. Food, weapons, medicine, should all have alternative stores, in case of emergency."

"Like what?"

"Well, a fire, for instance. If our main supply was destroyed, we would have a secondary supply."

"I see."

"But also as a backup in case desperate people tried to take our supplies."

"If the anarchy occurred, right?"

"Yeah. Jeff said that we needed to be ready for the worst case scenario. If we were overwhelmed by numbers and our main caches were raided, we'd still have hidden supplies."

I set my silverware down and wiped my mouth. "I guess that ultimately ended up being a good strategy," I said. I nodded toward the kitchen, where roughly eight hundred thousand dollars in gold sat, the sacks of coins heavy and cold in their dirty plastic boxes.

"I mean, if it had all been buried in a single place, the intruders would have got it all," I said.

"I guess so," she said after a moment.

I finished my plate. "I'm gonna shower then head into town."

"Can I go with you?" she said, standing.

"Why?"

"I want to put this gold in a safe deposit box. I'll have to rent a bigger one."

"Good idea."

"I also want to get those stones looked at," she said. "I can't imagine where they came from."

I showered in the guest bathroom, then loaded the gold into my truck while Melanie retrieved the bag of gemstones from the safe. When we drove away from the house, tiny pellets of snow were rattling against my windshield. The white sky had turned a shade darker.

Once we reached the highway it was snowing steadily, but it wasn't quite cold enough to stick. I pulled out behind a semi towing two large trailers, and as soon as I caught up to it I buried the gas pedal and passed in the opposite lane.

"Are we in a hurry?" Melanie asked.

"You need to get to the bank before it closes."

"It's only two-thirty. We'll be there in ten minutes."

I eased off the gas. "How are you feeling?" I asked.

"Just fine. Why?"

Because I can't take that for granted, I thought, glancing at her. It wasn't my job to watch her every moment, but her mother had asked that I protect her. Given Melanie's mental instability, that might include protecting her from herself.

A few minutes later I took the exit for Main Street. The boulevard was lined with shops and stores. Like most small towns, the majority of Cedar City's retail businesses existed side by side on a single street. Restaurants, furniture outlets, hardware stores, clothing shops, banks, tire companies, a post office, and at the end of the main drag, a Walmart and a Home Depot. A few miles out, a series of red rock ridges marked the eastern boundary of the valley.

I passed the police station in the center of town and drove another mile before pulling to the curb in front of a Wells Fargo bank. I got out of my truck and looked up and down the street. Cars pulled in and out of parking lots and drove slowly down the street, leaving wet tread marks on the pavement. The pedestrian traffic along the sidewalks was minimal.

I'd put the four ten-pound containers in a single cardboard box. I lugged it from my back seat and Melanie and I went into the bank. I stood holding the box until she was seated at a desk and speaking with a manager. Then I set it at her feet and told her I'd be back in a minute.

I went out to the sidewalk and stood in front of the bank, watching the street. Eight hundred thousand in gold coins was enough to attract plenty of troublesome attention. I didn't know if anyone might have been anticipating Melanie's return, watching and waiting for an opportunity to rob her. I saw no sign of it, but I still didn't know what I was dealing with. Those who murdered Jeff Jordan could be long gone, or scheming to complete an unfinished job.

I went back inside, where Melanie was filling out a form. I tapped her shoulder.

"How long will this take?"

A bank employee, a man with hair parted and sprayed in place, approached with a dolly and slid the ledge under the box. Melanie stood and said, "Shouldn't be more than a few minutes. They have free coffee. Have a cup."

I sighed and sat in a chair against the wall. When she didn't reappear after a minute I Googled "Cedar City PD" on my smartphone and found their website. I tapped a link to a message from the Chief of Police. After a paragraph noting that Cedar City was settled in 1851 by thirty-six men sent by the Mormon Church, he said how proud he was of the forty-five member police staff he managed. I tapped another link and saw they had both a patrol and operations division. It mentioned an investigative sergeant and detectives.

Five minutes later Melanie came out from a door behind the tellers. "It's all locked away now," she said.

"Good. Let's go talk to the cops."

"You want me to go?" she asked, blinking.

"I think it'd be a good idea."

Her face creased with concern. "Well, I—I guess I wasn't expecting to. I mean, isn't that your job?"

"They might be more cooperative if you're there."

"Oh," she said, then paused. "I suppose you're right."

"You don't have to if you're uncomfortable."

"I'm not. I'll be okay," she said, but doubt was etched across her down-turned mouth. Maybe she was worried the police might reveal painful details of her husband's murder, things she wasn't ready to hear. Maybe my request of her was not only insensitive, but worse, could bring on another breakdown. Her behavior had been better today; no personality deviations, no trances, and no appearance of the specious Sasha. But I didn't know what a pressure situation might do to her.

Regardless, I felt it was worth the risk. Alone, I was a stranger from out of town. With Melanie, the police would likely be far more cooperative.

We got in my truck and drove back up the street to the police station, a brick building that also housed the mayor's office. I parked, and we hurried out of the cold and into the lobby. A young deputy sat behind the counter.

"Afternoon," I said. "This is Melanie Jordan. We'd like to speak with the detectives investigating Jeff Jordan's murder."

He looked startled for a moment, then stood abruptly. "And who are you?"

"Dan Reno, private investigations." I handed him my card.

He took his time studying it. "Please wait here," he said, and disappeared through a doorway behind his desk.

"I guess we're going to learn some things," Melanie said, her words catching in her throat.

"I hope so," I replied.

The deputy returned a minute later with a man wearing pleated khaki pants and a red rugby shirt. His curly hair was so blond it was almost yellow, and he looked at us with light blue eyes. He was of average height and I guessed a couple years younger than me.

"Hello," he said. "I'm Detective Taylor Humphries. Would you like to come on back?" He pointed to an opening at the end of the counter. We came around and followed him through a doorway and into the squad room. He led us past a dozen desks to a room twelve feet square with a desk in the center.

"Please take a seat," he said. He went behind the desk and we sat across from him. "How may I help you?" he asked.

"I've been hired by Melanie's family to investigate her husband's murder and the disappearance of her daughter."

"It was a terrible thing. I'm sorry for your loss," he said to Melanie. He rested his chin on his fists and his eyes looked almost watery.

"Detective, can you share the status of your investigation?"

"The status? Well, the state police have taken over."

"Why's that?"

He leaned back and rested his hands in his lap. "Mainly because we don't think the crime was committed by a local resident. We think the criminals were from out of town."

"Based on what?"

"For one, there are only two black families in Cedar City. There's only one black man who fit the profile, and his alibi was ironclad."

"How about anybody with an Eastern European accent?"

"We asked around and it went nowhere. It's a pretty vague thing to investigate."

"I see. What kind of other leads did you develop?"

He licked his lips and his face reddened. "There was really very little to go on. There was no DNA, no fingerprints, no witnesses, except of course for you, Melanie."

"How about motive?"

"Robbery, obviously."

"By someone who specifically was after gold?" I asked.

He shook his head. "We never found evidence of that. We interviewed Jeff's friends and business contacts in Cedar City. He didn't keep his, uh, fondness for gold a secret. But nobody thought he had enough worth killing him for."

I rubbed at the stubble on my chin. "What about Mia Jordan, detective? Any leads on her disappearance?"

He cleared his throat. "Nothing solid. It's not likely she's still in Cedar City, if she's… you know." He gestured with his hands and when he looked at me his eyes darted.

"Melanie, tell you what," I said. "Why don't you wait outside while Detective Humphries and I finish talking?"

She hesitated, and for a moment I thought she might insist on staying. But the defiant glimmer in her eye quickly faded, and she said, "I'm fine with that." She left the room and closed the door behind her.

"I spoke with her a couple weeks ago, when she regained consciousness," Humphries said. "She didn't provide much help, but then again, she'd been in a coma for four weeks." He rubbed at his ear. "Is she okay now?"

"I don't know, to tell you the truth."

"It must be very hard for her."

"What do you think happened to Mia, detective?"

"They either killed her and disposed of the body, or took her out of town."

"That's it?" I asked, unable to hide the reproach in my voice.

"Look," he said, a vein twitching below his eye. "We put a full court press on the case for the first two weeks. Every one of our detectives made it their first priority. Our Chief of Police supervised the investigation himself. We interviewed over a hundred people, and put up signs all over town. I called the state police and brought them into it. I sent out an AMBER alert, and that's nationwide. But we never found a decent lead. She just vanished."

I didn't reply for a long moment, until he said, "Stop looking at me like that."

"If they killed her, why would they let Melanie live?"

"I suspect they thought Melanie was dead. I don't think they intended to leave any witnesses."

"Any thoughts on where Mia might be if she's alive?"

"Yes, unfortunately. Kiddie porn rings operate out of Vegas."

"Did you contact LVPD?"

"They were contacted, but understand, we have nothing more than conjecture."

The room became quiet. The redness faded from his face, and was replaced with a pale gray. His lips were a thin, colorless line.

"I understand a delivery driver called nine-one-one when he arrived at the house," I said. "Were you first on the scene?"

"No, a patrolman drove out there. He called me afterward. That's when I..." He stopped for a moment and took a breath. "That's when I found Jeff Jordan's body."

"By the hole out there."

"Yes."

"Shot?"

"Yes, and..."

"And what?"

"I'll be right back," he said, and left the room. Before thirty seconds passed he returned. He dropped a file on the desk. "See for yourself," he said.

I opened the manila folder and thumbed through the police report until I came to a series of crime scene photographs. The first was startlingly vivid. A large, white male lay face-down in the snow, near the same hole I'd seen a few hours ago. The snow was stained red around his face, and a gunshot wound was clearly visible in the back of his head. Blood was splattered beyond the body as well, patterned against the snow as if it had been sprayed. I drew a breath through my teeth. There was nothing remarkable about the cause of death; it was execution style; get on your knees and say goodbye. What was surprising was that the victim's arm had been hacked off above the wrist, and the forearm and hand lay about a foot away.

I looked up at Detective Humphries. His blue eyes met mine briefly before he looked down.

"Was he mutilated postmortem?" I asked.

"We don't know for sure. Our medical examiner said he may have lost his arm right before they shot him, or right after." Humphries put his hand to his chest. "Pretty sickening," he said.

"Any idea what it means?"

"It's the work of a psychopath, a sadist, a lunatic, or maybe all of the above. Take your choice."

"But it was a robbery. There was gold buried in that hole."

"You're sure?"

"Yes," I said.

"So then you have a violent robber."

"Yeah, but why cut off his arm? Wasn't killing him enough?"

"Apparently not," Humphries said.

I turned back to the photograph, and noted some cuts on Jordan's other forearm, which I assumed were inflicted inside the house. Then I looked at the following pictures. They were graphic and looked almost as if the photographer had made a special effort to find angles that would highlight the gruesome nature of the scene. Like all murder photos, they exposed the stark finality of death, the wounds gaping open, the death stare of the sightless eyes, the lifeless body's agony frozen in place.

I closed the folder. "Can you give me the names of the state police working the case?"

"Sure," he said. He wrote on a sheet of paper and handed it to me.

"Thanks. How about Jeff's cellphone? Did you find it at the house?"

"No, and he wasn't carrying it either. The place had been ransacked, and my assumption is the perpetrators stole it, along with whatever else they found small enough to carry."

I rubbed my jaw with my knuckle. "Seems odd they'd bother. They were there for a bigger score."

"True, but thieves have sticky fingers. They take whatever they can get their hands on. It's in their nature. They can't resist."

"Maybe you're right," I said.

"We did contact the phone company, though, and got a couple months of call records. You can see them at the back of the folder."

I opened the file again and found the copies of Jeff's cellular bills, which included a lengthy list of phone numbers. The numbers were highlighted in a variety of colors and all were assigned handwritten letters.

"There were twenty-six numbers he called over the sixty days before his death. I verified each one and listed them A through Z."

The last page in the folder was typed and showed the letters and corresponding company and individual names. One number was highlighted in yellow. It began with a zero and had fewer digits than the others.

"Anything suspicious?" I asked.

"That one was the only number we couldn't reach. It was to a prepaid cellphone, with no owner of record. Other than that, nothing looked unusual."

"Could I get a copy of this?"

"I'm sorry, no. But you can make some notes if you like."

I scanned the page and jotted down a few of the most frequently called numbers, including the one beginning with zero.

"Look, I'll help any way I can," Humphries said, his tone apologetic. "I still have nightmares about this. This is a peaceful, churchgoing town. Nothing like this has ever happened here."

I stood to leave. "Thanks for your help, Detective."

•   •   •

"What did you talk about?" Melanie asked as we climbed into my truck.

"The detective doesn't think any locals were involved. The Utah state police have taken over the investigation. I'll call them."

"What about Mia? Did he tell you anything useful?"

I turned onto the boulevard. The snow was now coming down in tiny flurries, and a thin coat was building on the rooftops. "Not really," I said.

We drove down the main drag in silence. The skies were white and the colorful storefronts were obscured by the descending weather. It felt as if we were shrouded in a dome of mist. I hit my brakes to avoid a sedan fishtailing out of a parking lot.

"Shit," I muttered. The weight of the crime scene photos sat in my gut like a flat beer. I had no notion why those who invaded Melanie's house not only shot her husband to death, but also hacked his arm off, possibly before he died. It didn't follow any logical line of reasoning, other than the killer was a sadistic son of a bitch. If so, that would be a clue, but not much of one.

As far as the implications for Mia, I didn't want to contemplate that, but that's what I was being paid to do. If I was alone, at that moment I'm sure I would have found the nearest bar. I'd start with a shot of Jim Beam and a cold draught. I'd sit at the bar staring into the rows of bottles and drink until my mind went numb. Then maybe, once my thoughts slowed and my emotions became muted, my intuition would kick in.

Or maybe I was just making excuses, because I'd always drank my way through my most sordid cases, and it seemed damned unfair and unreasonable to be riding the wagon now. But I'd committed to thirty days, and I hated breaking promises to myself as much as to others. It was a matter of principle. Besides, I only had two more days to go.

"Are you okay?" Melanie asked.

"Yeah, why?"

"You have a look on your face like you want to punch somebody."

I tried to smile. "I'm fine," I said. "Is that the jeweler?"

"Yes. Turn in here."

I steered into the parking lot beside a long building with a gray brick façade divided by massive wooden pillars. It was a pawn shop. We went through the glass doors and walked past a section where hundreds of rifles and pistols were displayed, then past guitars, sporting goods, and electronic devices. At the end was the jewelry section. Beneath the glass counter top were rows of rings, bracelets, watches, and necklaces. A white-haired man with spectacles low on his pug nose sat at a small table in the corner. He held a disassembled watch and poked at it with a tiny screwdriver.

"Excuse me," Melanie said. "I have some stones for you to look at."

"I'll be right with you," he said, his eyes fixed on the watch. He gave the screwdriver a final twist, then set it down.

"What have you got there?" he asked, as Melanie set the black pouch on counter. She pulled the strings and shook two of the stones onto the glass. One was colorless and about a half-inch in diameter. The other was larger and had a purplish hue.

The man removed his spectacles and fit a loupe against his eye. "May I?" he asked, holding out his fleshy hand. Melanie put the clear stone in his palm. He pinched it between his thick fingers and peered at it. Then he set it on a black mat and examined it some more.

"It's an uncut diamond," he said, looking at us with raised eyebrows. "Are you looking to sell it?"

"It depends," I said. "For now, we're just looking for an appraisal."

"I'll bring up my microscope. Wait here, please."

He disappeared into a back room and returned with a twelve inch microscope. Melanie handed him the stone again, and he put it on the tray and switched on a light. After adjusting a few dials on the scope, he repositioned it with a pair of tweezers. A minute later he looked up at us.

"It's about four carats. I can't say for sure since it's rough, but I would predict VS1 clarity, D color." His face was impassive, but he couldn't hide the interest in his voice.

"What's it worth?" I asked.

"I can offer you forty thousand."

"What?" Melanie said.

"Take a look at the purple one," I said.

Melanie placed the large jagged stone on the tray. The jeweler lowered his head to the eye piece and after turning the rock a few times, he switched off the light.

"I'd have to call New York to get you an appraisal on this one. I almost never deal in uncut rocks. But I can tell you, the clarity and color are extraordinary. It's also quite large, but I can't predict how many carats. I'd have to see it cut."

"What's your best guess on its worth?" I said.

He returned his spectacles to his face. "Definitely over a hundred thousand."

Melanie returned the stones to the bag and cinched it shut.

"Just out of professional curiosity, do you mind if I ask where you got these diamonds?"

"An old inheritance," I said.

"I have virtually unlimited access to funding," he said. "I'd be happy to make you cash offers."

"We'll keep that in mind. Thanks for your time."

"Well, thank you," he said, following us to the exit. "Please take my card. Eugene Baxter is the name. Always happy to be at your service."

We got in my truck and I started the engine. Melanie sat clutching the black pouch in her small hand. When I looked at her she seemed lost in thought.

"There's probably over a million dollars' worth of diamonds in that bag," I said. "Your bank should still be open. You need to get them locked away."

"I can't figure this out," she said. "First the gold, and now this? I was the money manager. I can't believe Jeff hid this from me."

"The good news is, you're rich."

She didn't reply, and when I glanced at her there were deep furrows around her mouth. It wasn't until we reached the stop light across from her bank that she mumbled, "Rich and alone."

I went into the bank with her and waited while she followed a teller into the back. When she reappeared a minute later, the frown was still on her face, and her gloom was palpable. Clearly, she didn't view her new-found riches as reason to celebrate. I tried to conjure some words to cheer her. I thought she might burst into tears.

We stepped onto the sidewalk and stood under the archway. "Hey," I said. I faced her and squeezed her shoulder with one hand. "I'll find Mia and get to the bottom of all this. It's gonna be okay."

She looked up at me, her eyes big and childlike, and I saw tears form-ing. "I don't know what to believe anymore," she said.

"Believe this: you're young and have most of your life ahead of you. There's no reason you can't have a great life. You'll get past this."

"Thank you," she murmured, then she came forward and gave me a brief hug, but it felt obligatory and shallow.

We started back to my truck. "What now?" she asked.

"Let's head back to your place. I want to see if I can talk to Jeff's friend, the one ten miles up the highway."

"Elias Pullman," she said.

"Right," I said, spinning my tires on the grainy snow as I steered my truck into the white haze.

6

FIFTEEN MINUTES AFTER DROPPING off Melanie at her house, I spotted the solitary mailbox she told me to look for. I eased onto the highway shoulder and turned down a rutted track leading to the right. It was not unlike the dirt road leading to Melanie's place, except it had not been graded and had to be driven more slowly. After two patient miles, I reached a gate in front of a short wooden bridge. I got out of my rig and stood at the gate and looked down at the icy stream running a few feet below.

The gate was locked, but not by chain and padlock. Instead, a metal box attached to a post housed an electronic keypad and two large buttons, one green and one red. I rattled the gate and peered at the keypad, and then, shrugging, I pressed the green button. An ear piercing siren split the air, loud enough to cause deafness. I cursed and jumped back, covering my ears and running for my truck. Even with my windows closed, I jammed the gearbox into reverse and backed up to get away from the noise.

From a hundred yards, it was tolerable. I waited there for five minutes, until I saw a Toyota pickup with oversize tires come around the bend, approaching from the opposite side of the gate. The siren ceased as it neared the bridge, and when the truck stopped a man standing in the pickup bed hopped down.

He wore an orange hunting jacket and held a shotgun in his gloved hands. He stood staring in my direction. I got out of my cab and waved at him with both hands over my head, in what I hoped he'd view as a friendly gesture. After briefly conferring with the driver, the man with the shotgun waved for me to drive forward.

When I was within ten yards, he held out his hand to stop me. I killed my engine and waited for him to come to my lowered window.

"Who are you and what do you want?" he said. He was young and unshaven, maybe still a teenager. The blue baseball cap he wore advertised a brand of generator motors. The end of the shotgun rested across his shoulder. If I wanted to, I could have snatched it out of his hands.

"My name's Dan Reno," I said. "I'm investigating Jeff Jordan's murder, and would like to talk to Elias Pullman."

"No shit, huh? Wait here." He went across the bridge and spoke to the driver, who then spent a minute talking into a cell phone. Then the young man came back to my window.

"I need to check your ID. Are you carrying weapons?"

I handed him my California driver's license. "No weapons," I said. He looked at my license and handed it back to me. "Step out," he said. I paused and watched the driver exit the Toyota and walk across the bridge. He wore a Western holster carrying a large revolver. I stepped onto the dirt and allowed the man with the shotgun to perform a one-handed pat down. After exchanging nods with the driver, the young man said, "You can come back now, if that's what you want. We'll drive. You sit in the passenger seat."

The driver spit a brown streak of chew into the snow. "You got a problem with that?" he asked. He was thick-bodied, had a bushy goatee, and wore cowboy boots.

"Nope," I said.

I walked across the bridge and got into their pickup. The teen climbed into the bed and knelt, his left hand holding the rusted roll cage, his right grasping the shotgun by the stock. We drove the bumpy trail for three minutes. During that time, our conversation consisted of five words:

"Cold out," I said.

"For you, maybe," the driver responded.

The truck came around a low rise and rolled to a stop. I sat staring, my hands on my knees. In front of us was a collection of buildings unlike anything I'd ever seen. The compound comprised three main structures, if that's what they could be called. The structures were forty-foot shipping containers, stacked two high. The unit in the center was orange, topped by a blue container. To either side, set at forty-five degree angles, were similarly stacked containers. One had a silver bottom and a green top, while the other was gray and red.

A twenty-foot overhang had been built in front of the center containers. Beneath it were a table and chairs, and a fire pit surrounded by blackened rocks. At the table sat a man in cargo shorts and army boots laced high on his white shins.

I followed the driver and the younger man to the overhang. The man at the table appraised me as I approached, one eye squinted and the other wide and bulbous. He wore a heavy camouflage print jacket and was smoking what I first thought was a marijuana cigarette, but when I got closer I smelled burning tobacco.

"Private eye, is it?" he said. His round face was white and clean shaven, and his thin brown hair was cut unevenly. About fifty years old, five-eleven, two hundred pounds. His calves were big, but his fingers were thin.

"That's right. Dan Reno." I handed him a business card. He looked at it, then said, "Boys, why don't you go inside and help Mattie while I talk to Mr. Reno here." The two fellows grunted and walked by us to a metal door in the center of the orange shipping container. After they went inside, the man opened a cooler next to him and pulled out a wet can of discount beer.

"You're Elias Pullman?" I asked.

He drank from the can and belched softly. "That's right. Go on, sit."

I sat across from him. The chair rocked unsteadily on the dirt. Snowflakes were drifting down and the afternoon was growing darker.

"Who hired you?" Pullman said.

"The parents of Jeff Jordan's wife."

"What, they don't trust the local authorities?" he said, his eyes askance.

"Guess not."

"Well," he said, his home-rolled cigarette burned down almost to his knuckles. "Jeff Jordan was a friend. He was good people, and he didn't have his head up his ass like most do. You got questions, shoot."

"Okay," I said. "The men who killed him came to his house looking for gold, and they found it. Any idea who would know Jeff had gold on the property?"

Pullman flicked away the scant remains of his cigarette and grimaced. "Now, that was a problem Jeff had. Diarrhea of the mouth. You talk too much, the wrong people are bound to listen."

"Wrong people like who?"

"You never know, do you? Take a look around, this country's on the verge of a collapse unlike anything you could imagine. People are getting desperate, even though they don't know why. But they can sense it's coming."

"You mean the apocalypse."

"That's right, son. Maybe you're not as blind as most."

"Was Jeff involved with any other women? Anything going on the side?"

"You mean, was he a poon hound? No, that wasn't his thing."

"You're sure he didn't have a girlfriend or two stashed away?"

"Let me fill you in on some basic human nature, maybe this will help you down the road. When a man has gash on the brain, and he's having some success, he's gonna talk about it. He'll brag to his buddies, whenever they'll listen, about his sluts and blow jobs and what not. But I never heard Jeff say anything about getting his pole waxed. You hear me?"

"Yeah," I said, as he raised his can and guzzled it down in long, noisy swallows. Then he crushed the can, wiped his mouth, and grabbed another.

"Is there anybody in particular you think may have targeted Jeff?" I asked.

"You see my property here?" he replied, waving his hand at the stacked containers. "You probably think I'm suffering from a mental disease. But those steel walls are reinforced and bulletproof. When the day comes, when I'm sitting on ten years of food supply and the masses are starving, guess who wins? You tell me."

I took a deep breath.

"Wrap your head around this," he said. "The oblivious out there are getting brainwashed on a massive scale. Those of us who woke up and smelled the coffee are digging in for the long haul. But we pose a threat to the evil motherfuckers who want to control us, to take away our freedom and run our lives. Jeff didn't quite understand that, he didn't quite get how dangerous it's becoming. Because even without money, the awakened are a threat. But with money, that's a combination asking for trouble."

"Trouble from who?"

Pullman took a plastic bag from his coat pocket and began rolling a smoke. It took him less than ten seconds to finish, and the result looked almost as perfect as a store bought cigarette. He lit up and dragged deeply, then spit a stray piece of tobacco into the air.

"The globalists, my friend. Who are they, you want to know? Top politicians and businesspeople, intellectuals, the richest people in the world. A secret society of them, going back hundreds of years, plotting to fuck over the common man, and I mean *fuck* us over, as in eliminate us until they shrink the world population small enough to where they can rule it." He drank off his beer, but his eyes never left mine.

"I see that look on your face," he said. "I've seen it a lot. You know what it's called? Cognitive dissonance. It happens when people are presented with cold, hard facts that are too upsetting to accept. So they create rationales to negate the truth."

"I see," I said.

"Hey, don't feel bad about it. It doesn't mean you're a dumbass. It just means you're uneducated."

"Thanks for the insight. Back to Jeff—"

"Let me give you a perfect example: World Trade Center Seven. It was a smaller building a hundred yards away from the Twin Towers. No planes ran into WTC Seven. But it collapsed just the same, in the exact way it would if it was professionally demolished. Our government claimed debris from the Twin Towers caused a fire in WTC Seven, which caused its frame to weaken and collapse. But leading engineering and architecture experts say there's no way a fire could have caused the building to fall that way. So what happened? Here's a clue: The CIA had an undercover office in WTC Seven, where they stored all sorts of secret and classified documents. They were all destroyed."

"And?"

"Within two years, we invade Iraq, under the false premise that they possessed weapons of mass destruction. Thousands die, Vice President Dick-head Cheney makes millions off Halliburton stock, and with the rise of ISIS, the world is now a far more dangerous place. Think it's coincidence?"

I looked at my watch. "You said Jeff had money. Do you know where he got it?"

"Hell, boy, he earned it. He ran a business."

"Did he have any other income source?"

"Not that I ever knew."

"Okay. Did the police interview you after Jeff died, Mr. Pullman?"

For a moment he stared at me, face ablaze, then the fervor left his eyes. He made a scoffing sound and shook his head. "Yeah," he said. "But I don't think I was much use to them."

"Where were you the night Jeff Jordan was murdered?"

"Right here, all night with my family. Just like I told the Cedar City cops."

We sat in silence for a long moment. Then he chugged his beer and said, "I'll get Randy to drive you back to your car."

"No need," I said. "I'll walk."

· · ·

I made it back to my truck quickly and began down the dirt road toward the highway. What conclusions had I drawn from my conversation with Elias Pullman? First, I saw no indication he knew more about Jeff Jordan's murder than he'd confided. But I also wondered about the potential of a man whose extremist views dictated a lifestyle I could only describe as freakish. While Jeff Jordan subscribed to much of what Pullman prophesized, Jordan seemed to be seeking a balance of sorts. Just because Jordan lived in a remote location, didn't trust our financial system, and sought to reduce his dependence on public utilities, I didn't view him as crazy. Elias Pullman, on the other hand, seemed completely unhinged. I was certain he could explain away even the most obvious realities to justify his beliefs. Could a person like him justify murder?

I steered around a deep rut and saw the paved road up ahead. Elias Pullman was no doubt well-armed, and his cigarette-rolling prowess was something that could have been learned in prison. Could he be a murderer? I couldn't eliminate him as a suspect, but the fact that he'd not run, but remained nearby, made it extremely unlikely. He may have been crazy and paranoid, but I didn't think he was stupid.

Right before I reached the highway, my cell rang. I looked at the screen and recognized Cody Gibbons' number.

"What's happening, Cody?"

"Dirty double-crossin' Dan," he said. It was the nickname he'd assigned me for life. Something about a woman in a bar during a long night of drinking many years ago.

"I'm southbound, old buddy. Heading to Vegas. Remember my daughter I told you about?"

"Your daughter?" I asked, eyebrows raised. "You mean the one you haven't met?"

"Yeah, but that's old news. We had a long talk recently, and I'm going to visit her."

"How did this happen?"

"I called Betty Lou from high school and got her number. Abbey is a criminal justice major at UNLV. Can you believe that?"

"From you, sure."

"What's that supposed to mean?"

"Criminal justice runs in your veins. She must have inherited it."

"Oh. Goddammit, you're probably right. Anyway, I'd like to introduce you to her, being that you're in the trade and all. Aren't you nearby?"

"I'm in Cedar City, working on that case you sent my way. It's in southern Utah."

"So, what, you're two or three hours away? Take care of business, then get your ass to Vegas. I'm gonna be there for about a week."

"I'll see what I can do."

"Hey, Dirt, it's my daughter. It means a lot to me."

"Okay, buddy."

"Call me and let me know," he said.

We hung up, and I shook my head as I drove through the murky twilight. The idea of Cody as a parent would take some getting used to. Cody had never mentioned wanting kids, and I wondered what was going on in his brain when he contacted the daughter he'd never met. Maybe guilt, or maybe it was just an impulsive thing. Whatever the case, it came out of left field, but that's how Cody was. I smiled as I recalled some of his past exploits, but I also felt an undercurrent of concern for my friend. I hoped this development would be a positive one for him, but given his inclinations, anything could happen.

The sky was dark when I rolled to a stop in Melanie's driveway. The solitary light above the front door flickered weakly through the cold mist, as if it were a candle flame that might die at any moment. I parked and turned the doorknob, but it was locked. I rang the doorbell and waited, then knocked loudly. I jabbed the doorbell again, listening to it through the small glass windows next to the door.

I kept ringing the bell for five minutes, wondering if she was taking a shower, or perhaps listening to music through headphones. An inch of snow had built on the ground. I stood with my hands in my coat pockets. "You got to be kidding," I said, and pushed the doorbell once more. Another couple minutes went by until I heard a noise inside and the door opened. Melanie had a blanket wrapped around her shoulders.

"I'm sorry, I fell asleep. I'm not feeling that great."

"Are you just tired?" I said, closing the door behind us.

"Maybe. Were you out there long?"

"No."

"I'm a little dizzy. I think I'll lie down again."

I followed her into the family room. She sat on the couch, then lay on her back with her knees bent. She rested one hand on her forehead.

"Have you had enough water? You might be dehydrated."

"I drank a bottle when you dropped me off."

"How about food?" I asked. "Have you had anything to eat?"

"I'm not hungry. Could you turn the light off, please?"

"Sure." I took a long look at her, then hit the switch and left the room.

For the next hour I methodically searched the house, looking for Jeff Jordan's cellphone, or anything else that might help me. I started in Melanie's bedroom and spent some time poking through the boxes in the closet, hoping to spot paperwork related to how Jeff came to possess a million in gold and probably more than that in gemstones. Finding nothing, I moved from room to room, looking under couches and in drawers and cupboards and behind furniture. The longer I searched, the more I felt that the intruders must have taken the phone. They would have been foolish not to, because it likely contained text messages and phone numbers, if not actual e-mails, that would reveal where and how Jeff got his mysterious treasure. And this information, I was reasonably certain, would lead to who robbed and killed him.

Or maybe I was assigning the killers too much credit; maybe they didn't bother with his phone. Only the most professional criminals do a decent job covering their tracks. Most crooks make an effort, but in a hurry and under stress, they leave key evidence. I tended to think Jeff Jordan's murderers fell in the latter category; the mutilation seemed an act of rage, or psychosis. These weren't the kind of men that were disciplined.

I finished searching and found nothing. The only room I hadn't covered was the family room, and when I went in, Melanie was still asleep on the couch.

Sighing, I went into the den and pulled the lever hidden in the desk drawer. When the bookcase swung open, I went into the cement-walled basement and grabbed a can. Then I proceeded to prepare dinner for myself, the pasta in red sauce splattering in the microwave.

I was hoping Melanie would wake and join me, because I wanted to search the family room, and also ask if she could provide Jeff's email login and password. If so, I could access his email on my PC.

I'd just finished eating when I heard moans from the family room.

"Melanie?" I switched on the light.

She sat with her head in her hands. "I have a migraine. I think I'm going to throw up."

"I'll get you some aspirin."

"I took some earlier. It's not doing anything." She stood abruptly. Her face was colorless and dotted with perspiration. She rushed past me to the hall bathroom and I heard her retching. I followed her and stood in the doorway. After a minute she collapsed next to the commode and curled into the fetal position.

"I'm taking you to the emergency room," I said.

• • •

The road to the highway was coated in white, but my truck didn't falter, and I drove aggressively until I power slid onto the pavement. Then I kicked it up a notch, flooring it and bringing it up to eighty on the long straight. It was an unsafe speed on a dark, snowy road, but Melanie was weeping in pain, her body hunched over in my passenger seat.

I made it to the medical facility on Main Street in fifteen minutes, and they took her into a room promptly. I stood outside the room, speaking to the emergency room physician, a middle-aged woman in green scrubs.

"Six weeks ago she was hit on the head, and spent four weeks in a coma in a Las Vegas hospital," I said. "They said she'd recovered, but she's been having some issues, and now this."

"We'll give her an intravenous pain killer and keep an eye on her. That's our standard treatment for a severe migraine."

"How long will you keep her here?"

"At least ninety minutes. The pain killer might make her drowsy. You'll need to contact her primary care doctor tomorrow."

"I'm taking her to the hospital in Vegas first thing in the morning."

I left the building and stood under the awning in the stark light. It was no longer snowing and the night had become colder. A few cars drove by, their tires crunching and slipping on slush that had turned to ice. I blew into my hands then poked at my phone until I found the number for Melanie's parents.

"Hello?" Walter McDermott said.

"Mr. McDermott, Dan Reno. Is your wife there?"

"Well, yes."

"Put me on the speaker, please. I'd like to speak to you both."

"Hold on," he said, followed by muted voices and scuffling sounds. Then Lillian McDermott spoke.

"Yes, Mr. Reno, what is it?"

"I'm at the emergency clinic in Cedar City. Melanie had a migraine and she's being treated now."

"A migraine? Is that the doctor's diagnosis?"

"For the time being. But I can tell you, Melanie is not ready to be on her own. Her behavior is erratic and she needs someone watching over her. She should also be near doctors who understand what she's been through. I'm taking her to the hospital in Vegas in the morning."

"You really feel this is necessary?" Lillian said.

"I'm not a neurologist, but I goddamn know when someone's not right."

"You don't need to swear in front of me."

"Listen, I can't work this case and be Melanie's caretaker at the same time."

"What are you suggesting?"

"Catch a morning flight to Vegas. I want you to stay with Melanie until my work is done."

"You mean, until you find Mia?" Walter said.

"That, and deal with Jeff's killers."

"Deal with?"

"We need to think about this," Lillian said. "In the meantime, I'm paying you for your time, so please make sure Melanie is safe."

"Call me back tonight," I said.

We hung up, and I went back into the clinic waiting room, then spun on my heels and walked out to my truck. I drove past the storefronts, which were now mostly closed and dark, and gunned it onto the highway and back toward Melanie's house.

Peering through my windshield at the deserted two-lane, my eyes felt red and tired. It was nine o'clock, and my day had started early. This was typically the time I'd be sitting in my house having a drink with Candi, while she toked off her Sherlock Holmes pipe. Pleasantly buzzed, we'd relax and enjoy our time together, like a normal couple. Often we'd have sex in the evening, sometimes not even making it to the bedroom. It was during this time that I never allowed myself to think about work. I locked the sordid ugliness away behind a wall, temporarily rendering it not part of my life. Over time, this had become easier to do.

But tonight I was still on the clock, and I reminded myself to not complain, because I hadn't worked for weeks. If I couldn't tolerate occasional long hours and late nights, I could always seek a regular forty-hour job, maybe even as a detective at South Lake Tahoe or Douglas County PD. Those opportunities had been there for me, but I'd never seriously considered being a cop. The structure, the rules, the politics, those were headaches for others. As for the challenges of my job, at least they were varied, and allowed me some "freedom of expression," as Cody called it.

When I arrived at Melanie's house, I saw we'd left the lights on. No surprise there, I'd been in a hurry to get her to the clinic. It bothered me to see her in such pain, and I wondered if this was just my natural response to a woman in distress, or if it was heightened because she was starting to grow on me. She was pretty and definitely smart, despite her mental issues.

She was also vulnerable, but I sensed she possessed an underlying toughness. As for her nude body, I couldn't deny my physical reaction, but Candi was everything to me, a once in a lifetime find. I would never risk that.

I went through the front door and into the family room. Sitting on the couch, I imagined Jeff Jordan watching television while Melanie prepared dinner. Did he have his phone with him, maybe texting or checking e-mails or playing video games? If so, the intruders could have grabbed it as soon as they entered the room.

I looked around for the remote control, thinking to turn on the television, maybe recreate the scene. But it wasn't on the coffee table, nor did I see it on the entertainment center. My hand reached between the leather cushions, then I stood, staring at the couch. I removed the center cushion and sure enough, found the remote. Then I removed the cushions to either side and ran my fingers in the spaces between the frame and the upholstery. The cracks were narrow, but my fingertip hit something solid. I jammed my fingers in deeper, and something was definitely there, but I couldn't see it. Pushing hard with both hands, I heard a muted thump as an object fell to the carpet. I dead-lifted the couch, tilting it back until I saw it laying there. A Samsung smartphone.

"Bingo," I said, grabbing the phone and lowering the couch. It was a lucky break. The battery was dead, but it used the same power cord as mine. I went into the kitchen and plugged it in. Two minutes later it came to life.

The device was encrypted and required a password. Most people view this as a hindrance and choose passwords that are easy to enter. I tapped four zeros, then four ones, four twos, and after I reached four sixes it locked me out. I rebooted and started again with four sevens. Lucky sevens unlocked the device.

I sat at Melanie's dining table and looked over the icons on the home screen. Then I tapped the Gmail tab and began reading through Jeff

Jordan's email history. It didn't take long to conclude that he used email solely for his contracting business. He only sent five or six messages per day, and they were a mixture of job quotations, instructions to sub-contractors, and purchase orders sent to construction material wholesalers. In twenty minutes I scanned almost two months of activity and saw nothing that made me pause.

Next I opened the text message application. There were more than twenty conversation strings. Except for one, they were all identified by a first and last name, which meant the individuals were in Jeff's address book. The sole exception was a string titled by a number sequence beginning with a zero. I opened it and saw a total of three incoming messages and Jeff's response to each.

November 13, 8:45 p.m. Zero #: *eta 11-16 pola*

November 13, 8:48 p.m. Jeff's response: *let me know exactly when and where*

November 14, 2:12 p.m. Zero #: *scheduled dock is 5:15am*

November 14, 2:14 p.m. Jeff's response: *exactly where?*

November 14, 3:30 p.m. Zero #: *berth 207. park on street 6am. I'll call you*

November 14, 3:32 p.m. Jeff's response: *got it. will wait for you*

I spent another ten minutes looking over the other conversation threads on Jeff's phone, and saw nothing suspicious. I stood, then sat again and reread the zero number thread. Mid-November, roughly two weeks before Jeff was shot. An early morning meeting with an unknown person. A dock, a berth: boating terms, but berth suggested larger vessels. And *pola*—what was that?

Shrugging, I tapped the redial function for the number beginning with zero. It immediately went to a recorded message saying the call could not be completed as dialed.

I checked my watch and swore under my breath. I'd spent more time here than I meant to, and would be late getting back to the clinic.

Hurrying, I locked the house and hit it down the dirt road. But after a minute I slowed, my mind preoccupied with the text messages. A dock and a berth obviously indicated a body of water. It could have meant any number of lakes in the western U.S. There were two, both fed by the Colorado River, that came to mind. Lake Mead was in Nevada and a short drive from Las Vegas, less than an hour. It would no doubt offer plenty of docks and boat slips, as it was popular with recreational boaters. The same could be said for Lake Powell, which was a couple hours east of Cedar City, in southern Utah. Hell, it could even mean the Great Salt Lake up north, but the water was far saltier than the ocean and I doubted it was desirable for boating.

"*Pola*," I muttered. It was an acronym or an abbreviation. It could mean Lake Powell, although *Lapo* would have made more sense.

Confident and pleased I was making progress, I looked down at my speedometer and saw I was poking along at 35 MPH. At that moment an air horn blared and lights flashed in my rearview mirror. An eighteen-wheeler barreled by me, its tires crushing the snow and spraying blasts of icy crust against my quarter panels. It was towing a white forty-foot container that said "China" on the side in bright red letters.

The truck swerved in front of me and I slowed to give it some distance. The driver seemed intent on making time, even if it meant driving at an inadvisable speed through the wintery darkness. If he jackknifed, I wanted to be well behind him.

The taillights on the trailer dimmed quickly, and I accelerated. It was no longer snowing and had turned colder, as it often does following a storm. My digital temp gauge read 24 degrees. I let off the gas and cruised at forty. The road was slicker than it had been two hours ago. These were black ice conditions and required caution, even on the straights.

If the doctor said Melanie was okay, my plan was to pick her up and return to her place, where hopefully she could get a good night's rest before we left for Vegas. As for her parents, I anticipated they'd meet us there sometime tomorrow. They needed to care for their daughter, but I was still waiting for their return call.

About two miles from the city limits, the road swerved gently to the right. I eased off the pedal and steered along the two black tire paths cut into the thin coating of snow on the highway. I could feel my tires slide and then regain traction on the thicker snow along the edges. I slowed to thirty, and in the distance I saw what looked like headlight beams perpendicular to the road. As I drew closer, there was a series of diagonal skid marks on the ice, followed by dark furrows in the snow field aside the road. It was the big rig that had passed me. It had slid off the highway, and the cab was in a shallow ditch. Behind it, the trailer was upright in the brush.

I pulled over and stopped near the cab. I could see the driver in my headlights. He wore a cap and was pounding his palms on the steering wheel. I got out and walked up to him. He glanced at me with jittery eyes. His unshaven cheeks were hollow and his jaw was knotted as if his molars had been clenched for hours. He rolled down his window.

"I don't see any damage. Think you can drive out?" I asked.

"I intend to," he said. "I've got to be in Port of Los Angeles by morning or my ass is grass."

"Best take it easy. It'll be dicey until you get farther west."

He shook his head at me. "I've made the drive before, pal." I saw a dusting of white around one of his nostrils.

I looked toward where his headlights illuminated the white flatlands. Then I turned and started back to my pickup.

"Hey," he said loudly. "You don't need to make a phone call on this. Right? We clear on that?"

I looked back at him and smiled. "Cedar City's a small town, full of god fearing folk. So you best check your attitude, and hide the coke."

"What? What kind of wiseass crack is that? You some kind of poet?"

"Sure, why not?" I said, then I left him to his issues and drove away.

•   •   •

The emergency room nurse told me Melanie was sleeping, and they'd wake her shortly. I sat in a chair in the deserted waiting room. It would be close to midnight before I got her home. I worked on my smartphone while I waited, searching for information on Lake Powell boat slips or berths. I couldn't find any reference to a berth 207.

I leaned my head forward and shut my eyes, declaring I was done for the day. Every thought that entered my mind, I tried to shove aside. I should have called Candi, just to check in, but that could wait until tomorrow. She was good that way; for the most part, she didn't worry or pester me while I was working. I think she acquired this from her mother, who was married to a career sheriff in Texas.

After a few minutes of concentrated effort at keeping my thoughts at bay, I began to drift off. Images of the eighteen-wheeler deep in the sagebrush danced on my eyelids, and I saw the jagged angles of the man's face and the white rim around his nostril. Then I heard him speak, and I jerked awake, stunned for a moment.

"Port of Los Angeles, *pola*," I said out loud. "I'll be goddamned."

The receptionist looked up. "Sir?"

"Just talking to myself, it's an old habit," I said, but she'd already turned her eyes back to her computer screen. I did the same, working my phone again. It didn't take long this time. The site for the Port of Los Angeles included various maps, including one of the port cargo terminals. Berth 207 was near the far end of the complex. It took some searching, but I finally found a map showing the waterway that hosted berth 207. There were probably massive cranes there, positioned to hoist containers from the ships and lower them onto railroad cars.

At that moment the door opened and Melanie came into the waiting room. She looked sleepy and a little disheveled. The same lady physician I'd spoken to earlier was by her side.

"She should be okay now," she said. "Acute migraines can happen for any number of reasons. I can't say if it's related to her injury and coma. You should have her looked at by a specialist."

"That's the plan," I said.

"Here's some pain pills. If she feels the slightest onset of more pain, have her take two. With migraines, you have to catch the pain early."

I stuck the bottle in my pocket. "Thanks, doctor."

She left us, and I turned to Melanie, who stood holding her hands and looking at the floor.

"Better put your jacket on," I said. "It's cold out."

I led her out to my truck and we drove down Main Street. "You're feeling okay?" I asked.

"My head feels empty. It's like the pain was replaced by this big emptiness."

"It's probably the drugs. You look a little pale."

"I feel very relaxed, actually. It's like everything's in slow motion."

We reached the end of town and I turned onto the highway. There was no moon and I drove carefully, expecting black ice, sometimes driving on the white rather than risking dark portions of the road that might be treacherous. We forged ahead without speaking, my tires popping and spitting, the engine a steady drone.

I glanced at her and saw her eyes were wide open. "Do you remember Jeff being in Los Angeles recently?' I asked.

"Maybe," she said. "He had jobs there."

"Right."

I passed the section of road where the eighteen-wheeler had slid off the pavement. The truck was no longer there. "Do you remember him saying anything about meeting someone at the Port of Los Angeles?"

"No. I don't remember anything like that."

My cell chimed, and I saw I'd received a text message. It was from Walter McDermott, and read: *Landing in LV tomorrow 11am. Please meet us then. Will call you.*

"If you're up to it, you should pack your bags tonight," I said.

"Why?"

"We're driving to Vegas in the morning, to meet your parents."

"Huh? What for?"

"The doctors who cared for you need to do a checkup."

"Oh. What will you do, then?"

"I'll be working," I said.

. . .

When I woke the next morning I opened the front door and saw that much of the cloud cover had dispersed, and a portion of the sky to the southwest was a pale blue. The sun was mostly hidden behind a bank of low clouds, but I guessed it would break through shortly. The weather had passed; it would be a good day to drive.

I made coffee and sat in the kitchen and worked on my PC while I waited for Melanie to wake. I found some more detailed maps of the Port of Los Angeles, which were easier to view on my larger screen. Berth 207 handled containerized cargo that could come from anywhere and contain anything. The number of freight and logistics companies that frequented this berth and those near it seemed virtually limitless.

I spent half an hour searching, looking for any detail that might provide some clue as to why Jeff Jordan had a clandestine meeting with an unknown person near this particular berth. I closed my screen just as I heard Melanie's footfalls.

"Good morning," she said. She was dressed and looked ready to go.

"Morning," I said. "Coffee's hot."

"Did you eat?"

"No."

"I'll make breakfast then. I'm all packed."

"Great. How's the melon?"

"Excuse me?"

"Your head. Any pain?"

"No, not a bit. I feel really good, to be honest. I slept straight through, eight hours, didn't wake once."

"Glad to hear it," I said, then I pulled her ex-husband's cell from my pocket. "By the way, I found Jeff's phone last night, crammed in the couch frame."

"You did?"

"Yeah. I went through it and found a curious text conversation. I'd like you to take a look."

She came to the table and stared down at the screen. Then she picked up the phone and spent a minute reading before she said, "I have no idea what any of that means."

"Do you recognize the number?"

"No."

I took the phone from her. "Best I hold onto it for now. Your folks will be landing in Vegas at eleven. If we leave soon we can get there by noon."

Twenty minutes later we got into my truck, and if Melanie was hesitant to leave the place where she'd lived with her daughter and late husband, I saw no sign of it. The sun had risen above the clouds and bathed the house in light. Water was trickling beneath a band of snow that lay in the sun's path, and it was warming quickly. It was the type of day that may have held promise for many, but it offered no cheer to me, for at that moment I felt the weight of a widow with a missing child. I also had the beginnings of a plan in place, but Melanie's presence would only impede my efforts, and I was anxious to leave her in the care of her parents.

The highway was still icy, but easier to drive in the daylight. Once we were south of Cedar City, the road turned wet in the sunlight. I made good time on the straights, until Melanie asked me to stop in Saint George. While she used the ladies room at a fast food joint, I stood near my front fender, breathed the brisk air, and stared at the surrounding red rock formations. Then I took a folded sheet of paper from my pocket and dialed the number I had for the Utah State Police.

"Detective Batterman," a voice said.

"Hello, detective. My name's Dan Reno, I've been hired by the family of Melanie Jordan to look into her husband's murder, and the disappearance of her daughter. I'd like to compare notes with you on the case."

"Down in Cedar City, right?"

"Yes."

"It's an ongoing investigation. That's all I can tell you."

"I understand. Have you interviewed Melanie Jordan yet?"

"She was in a coma."

"She was released from the hospital two weeks ago. I'm with her now."

"Is that right?"

"Yes. You work out of Salt Lake, correct?"

He paused, and when he replied his voice sounded constricted. "What's your point?"

"Have you been to Cedar City recently?"

I heard him take a breath. "Their local force is handling it."

"They said Utah State Police has taken charge of the case."

He paused again. "What did you say your name was?"

"Reno."

"Okay, Mr. Reno. I'm going to conclude this conversation now. But first I'll leave you with two things. One, Salt Lake is dealing with a huge gang problem. If you were unaware of that, feel free to pick up a newspaper."

When he didn't continue, I asked, "What's the second thing?"

"Don't call me again," he said, and the line went dead.

I put the phone in my pocket, leaned against my fender, and watched Melanie come out of the restaurant. "Prick," I mumbled.

"What's that?" she said.

"Nothing. Just talked to a Salt Lake cop about your case."

"What'd he say?" she asked, climbing into my cab.

"Not much." I pulled out of the parking lot. "It doesn't sound like the state police have done much of anything."

"That's exactly what my mother said."

I steered back onto the highway, and ten minutes later we crossed into the northwestern corner of Arizona, a few miles north of the Grand Canyon National Monument. The winding road followed the Virgin River Gorge, a deep canyon carved from limestone. In places, the iron oxide content was so dense that the serrated cliffs looked almost a fluorescent orange.

"This scenery is awesome," Melanie said.

"Jeff would have driven this way," I said. "It's the quickest route into California."

We came out of the canyon and the cliffs became small hills, and then flattened entirely as we entered Nevada. It was sunny and the road was dry and we were now in the Mojave Desert. The flatlands stretched for miles to distant ridgelines that barely dented the horizon. As we drove, Melanie seemed alone with her thoughts.

I left her to her contemplations, and fell into my own. The tone of the conversation with the Utah State detective hadn't surprised me. In general, cops view private investigators dimly. We have the potential to interfere with their work, or worse, make them look bad by solving cases they've neglected. In many instances, I'd seen police forces lack the desire, tenacity, or resources to effectively address their caseloads. But that certainly didn't motivate them to welcome private eyes into their domain.

Of course, not all cops are created equal. I've run into detectives and patrolmen who are overzealous, sometimes fiendishly so. I've also dealt with those who are lazy, corrupt, or just putting in their hours and waiting for their pensions to kick in. While not all fall into the latter categories, a fair amount do. It was hard to completely blame them, I suppose. The common citizenry rarely consider that cops spend the bulk of their hours dealing with pissed off, resentful, drunk, or desperate people. And that's on good days.

On the bright side, I was fortunate to enjoy a positive working relationship with the top cop in South Lake Tahoe, Sheriff Marcus Grier. I'd saved his ass a few times, and in return he treated me fairly, and sometimes as an ally. Although Grier was a strict nine-to-fiver, he worked hard during those hours, and did his best to serve the community. And I couldn't blame him for wanting to get home on time; he had a loving wife and two teenage daughters who worshipped him.

And then there were cops like Cody Gibbons had been. I shook my head, rejecting the thought. No, there were no cops I'd ever met who behaved at all like Cody did during his seven-year stint as a San Jose officer. Cody didn't just scoff at the rule book; he lit fire to it.

An hour later we reached the northern outskirts of Vegas. The densely clustered mega-resorts on Las Vegas Boulevard rose from the desert floor like a cosmic oasis. If the gods had dreamt up this place, they definitely had a warped sense of humor. I always thought of Las Vegas as a place where people went not to find anything, but rather to lose themselves. And if Sin City failed to claim their souls, they could always wander off and surrender to the unforgiving vastness of the desert.

Las Vegas had grown immensely since 1960, when less than 200,000 people lived in the greater Las Vegas area. Today the population is over two million. The bulk of the tenfold increase occurred after 1989, when the Mirage, the first mega hotel-casino in Vegas, was built. Many more casinos followed, and the number of hotel rooms in the city grew to over 150,000.

Of course, where growth and prosperity occur, crime always follows closely behind. Criminals are no different than honest citizens; they go where the money is.

We passed the old downtown district and a mile ahead the thin parabolic structure of the Stratosphere casino rose 1100 feet, overlooking the section of South Las Vegas Boulevard known as The Strip. Home to Vegas' most famous and extravagant hotel-casinos, The Strip does its best to paint the hard core business of gambling as glamourous and thrilling. Talk to the poor chump staggering out of a casino in the wee hours of the morning, drunk and wondering how he'll pay his mortgage, and you might get a different perspective.

My phone beeped with a text message. It was from Walter McDermott: *Just checked in at the Hampton near the airport.*

I continued south for a few miles. To our left, the hotels on The Strip glittered in the cold sunlight, their glass walls rising into the sky and sparkling with gold and silver reflection. I took the exit for the airport and drove past it to the Hampton Inn, then parked and lifted Melanie's suitcases from my truck bed.

"What now?" she asked, standing at the tailgate.

"Your mom and dad are going to take care of you for the time being. You should go see your doctors here."

"What are you gonna do?"

I looked over to the hotel lobby entrance, and saw Lillian McDermott open the door.

"Follow up on some leads. Look for Mia."

We walked to the entrance, where the McDermotts were waiting. Walter stood holding the door, as if he was unsure whether our conversation would take place on the steps, or inside the lobby.

"It's cold," Lillian said. She grabbed one of Melanie's roller bags and wheeled it inside. Melanie and I followed, with Walter trailing. "How are you, little girl?" he said.

"I'm okay, Dad."

"I'd like to hear from you daily, Mr. Reno," Lillian said. "We'll stay here with Melanie for as long as required."

"Good," I said.

"May I know when I can expect some results?"

"I've made some decent progress."

"That sounds less than encouraging. It also sounds evasive."

I looked down at her, right into her steely gray eyes. "If you like, we can sit down for a couple hours, and talk about a whole bunch of maybes and what ifs. I consider that a waste of time, but it's your dime."

"You don't need to take that tone with me."

I looked away and briefly considered a retort about *her* tone, but after a long moment decided against it. "I'll contact you with daily updates, if that's what you'd like," I said.

"Have you identified any suspects?"

"Not yet."

"I'm going to be very forthright now," Lillian said. "Since hiring you, I've done some further research into your background. I've been told that you are both a drunkard and a man given to violence without cause."

"Mother!" Melanie exclaimed. She was standing next to Walter, who shifted his weight from foot to foot, his eyes darting behind his spectacles.

"Who told you that?" I asked.

"Other private eyes. Also policemen."

"That figures, I guess."

"I hope I haven't made a grave mistake in hiring you."

"Mrs. McDermott, I certainly do enjoy a few drinks on occasion, but I'm not a drunk. So you've been misinformed."

"And what about the violence?"

"Wait a minute. I thought you hired me after learning I've killed men. I thought that was one of the reasons you contacted me."

"True enough. But I've now heard that your killings have not always been warranted, and you've been lucky to avoid prosecution."

"Every man I've killed was an act of self-defense. They all had it coming, ma'am."

"Others put it differently."

"Some cops don't like me, especially when I get done what they can't. And as far as other private eyes, let me ask you this: Were they trying to get hired when they offered their opinions of me?"

Lillian McDermott paused before answering. "I suppose so," she said.

"Is there anything else?"

"Yes," Lillian said. "You've promised to deliver results, Mr. Reno. So please see to it without delay."

"My point exactly," I said, spinning on my heel and heading for the door. But before I got there Melanie said, "Dan?"

"Yeah?"

She came forward and hugged me, her breasts pushing against my torso, her head touching my shoulder. "Thank you for everything," she said. I looked up at Lillian, and she shook her head in denial. Walter just stood there looking perplexed.

7

AS SOON AS I left the parking lot, I called Cody Gibbons. He
answered on the first ring.

"Dirty Double Crossin', what's drinkin'?"

"Water."

"Christ, are you still on the wagon?"

"Yep."

"Why punish yourself?"

"A little clean living is good for the soul."

"That's an interesting bit of philosophy," Cody said. "Where are you?"

"Just rolled into Vegas. I'm over near the airport."

"Really? Why don't you meet me over at the Hard Rock? Have lunch
with Abbey and me."

"You sure?"

"Why wouldn't I be? Step on it, I'm starving."

• • •

When I walked into the restaurant adjoining the Hard Rock Casino,
I spotted Cody and his daughter right away. They were sitting across
from each other at a four-seat table near the bar, and Cody's huge frame
looked crammed into his chair. His beard was neatly trimmed and his

unruly blond hair was shiny with gel, as if he'd made a concerted effort to tame it.

"Hey, Cody," I said.

He reached up, grabbed my hand, and drew me to him in a clumsy hug. His chair creaked in protest. "Dan, great to see you. Abbey, this is my partner, Dan Reno."

"Hello," she said. I offered my hand, and she grasped it and squeezed so firmly I was almost temped to squeeze back, as if it were a contest. When she finally let go I took a seat, Cody to my left, Abbey to my right.

"Dan, like I told you, Abbey's a criminal justice major at UNLV. She's doing an internship with Las Vegas PD."

"No kidding?" I said. I looked at her, and she stared back frankly, an amused glint in her green eyes. She had reddish hair, wide shoulders for a woman, and when she smiled her mouth seemed to test the confines of her jawline. Her face struck me as large, but necessarily so to accommodate her smile and wide-set eyes. In the center of her face, in contrast to her other features, her small, freckled nose looked very girlish.

"Do I not look like a cop to you?" she asked.

I smiled back at her. "Well, cops come in all shapes and sizes, I suppose."

"Do you deal with policewomen very often?"

"Every now and then."

A waitress walked up and asked for our drink orders. "Let's see," Cody said. "How about a root beer? What do you say, Dan? Root beer?"

"Diet Coke."

"And for you, miss?"

"Vodka tonic."

"Hey," Cody protested.

"What?" Abbey said.

"It's a little early, don't you think?"

"You're one to talk."

"Just because I drink doesn't mean it's a good idea."

"Sounds like a double standard to me, pops."

"Pops?" Cody's expression had turned incredulous, and his ears were turning red, the way they did when he was either angry or embarrassed.

"Just because you're twenty-one doesn't mean you should abuse the privilege," Cody said. I stared at him curiously.

"You finally meet me after twenty-one years, and now it's parental lecture time?"

Cody looked down and the table became quiet. After a moment his eyebrows rose and he said, "I'm sorry."

"Don't sweat it, big dude," Abbey said.

"It's just because I care."

"Wow, you need to lighten up. You sure you don't want a beer or something?"

Cody looked down again and put his fingers to his forehead. But then he leaned back and laughed briefly. "Ain't you a piece of work, Abbey? Just like your old man."

"You never know," Abbey said, and at that moment I saw in her face something that went much deeper than a family resemblance; I saw in her Cody's persona, his carefree irreverence and fearlessness. It was in her genes. I could only hope she possessed a watered-down version.

"So, tell me about the case you're working," Abbey said.

I didn't respond for a moment, until Cody said, "Come on, Dan. Give us a little shop talk."

"All right. A family was attacked in Utah, a couple hours northeast of here. The husband was murdered, the ten-year-old daughter kidnapped or possibly killed, and the wife was struck on the head, spent four weeks in a coma, but survived. The wife's parents hired me to find their granddaughter and bring the killers to justice."

The waitresses brought the drinks, and Cody eyed his without interest and moved it aside. "Motives?" he asked.

"The husband had gold buried on his property. The perps apparently made him dig up one lot of it, about two hundred grand worth."

"What about the little girl?" Abbey asked. "Her body wasn't found?"

"There's no sign she was killed. But there's been no call for ransom, either."

"If she's not dead…" Cody said, his voice trailing off.

"Then there's two possibilities," Abbey said. "Either she's in the hands of a pedophile, or a victim of human trafficking." The skin on her face seemed to shrink and pull tight, and her eyes retreated deeper into their sockets.

"I have a few leads on the husband and maybe the gold," I said. "Nothing on the girl yet."

"I work on a child pornography task force," Abbey said.

"What? As an intern?" Cody jutted his head forward.

"That's right. I volunteered for it."

"They have no right to assign an intern to that."

"Yeah, I got some push back, but I can be pretty insistent."

Cody straightened in his seat and widened his eyes, then his brow furrowed. He picked up his spoon, examined it, and carefully returned it to the table.

"Abbey, I think it's great you're doing an internship with the police. But I'm confused why you'd want to be involved in something as grim as child porn. I mean, there's plenty of other options."

"Like what, traffic detail? Maybe bust commuters for going ten miles over the speed limit or rolling through stop signs?"

Cody seemed stunned for a second. He started to say something, then stopped, frozen in mid-syllable.

"I'm not worried about it. Why should you be?" Abbey said. She tasted her drink, then took a long sip. "And please, no concerned parent lecture. That would really be ridiculous. You get that, right?"

Cody glanced at me, his eyebrows peaked high. His mouth was still open, as if a gear was jammed in his brain.

"Cat got your tongue, pops?"

"Excuse me," Cody said. "I got to go to the men's room." He stood, his chair falling until he caught it at the last moment.

"So you two go way back, huh?" Abbey said, once Cody was out of earshot.

"I met him in high school. His parents had kicked him out of the house."

"Yeah, I heard all that."

"From your mother?"

"Yeah. She said she would never have considered marrying him. She also said he got married once, and it lasted maybe a year."

"What else did she tell you?"

"That he's a booze hound and a pot head and runs around with strippers and sluts, and that he's done things that would land most people in prison, but he's somehow avoided it."

"I see."

"She said it's no surprise it took him more than twenty years to get in touch. She said to not be surprised if it's a temporary thing."

Her eyes were burning into mine, and I looked down and found myself staring at the drink in her hand.

"You got nothing to say?" she said.

"Your father saved my life twice. He's the most unselfish and loyal friend a man could have. He's got the biggest heart of anyone I know."

Abbey tilted her glass and drank until I heard the ice cubes rattling against her teeth. When she wiped her mouth, her eyes looked red-rimmed and glassy. "Then where was he all these years?"

I watched the bartender pour pints of beer from the taps, the foam spilling over the glass rims. "Trying to deal with his past. Maybe trying to find himself."

For a brief moment I saw a pall of sadness cloud her face, like a passing shadow. But then she burst out laughing. "God, that's corny. Is that the best you can come up with?"

I shrugged and tried to smile. "Your dad's not perfect, but who is?"

"What does he want from me?" she asked.

"To have a relationship. To be there for you."

Abbey squinted and her face again looked pained. When she didn't respond, I said, "Is he too late?"

"We'll see," she said quietly, as Cody approached.

• • •

The remainder of lunch was punctuated by moments of awkward politeness and Abbey's sarcastic attempts at humor, which would have been funny if not for her thinly veiled resentment. Cody was clearly uncomfortable and trying to measure his words, but by the time we were done eating, Abbey had finished three drinks and her attitude lightened. She became casually chatty and seemed willing to put her issues with Cody on the back burner, at least for the time being. It was likely the booze talking, I suspected. Minus the alcohol, her anger would probably return in one form or another. There was no question in my mind that Cody would need to earn her respect and love. I just hoped the process wouldn't be an overwhelming burden for my old pal, no matter how deserving of her wrath he might be.

Other than that, I had no desire to contemplate Cody's late arrival into his daughter's life, or her response to his sudden presence. It would sort itself out in a positive way, I hoped. I certainly wasn't tempted to pass judgment on the situation. A woman once told me I wasn't complex enough for parenthood. Although she was lashing out in a grieving rage, I never forgot those words. They bounced around in my head each time Candi mentioned getting pregnant, which she had done a few times recently.

"I'm staying at the Plaza downtown," Cody said, after we left Abbey at her car. "Why don't you follow me over and check in?"

"Maybe tomorrow," I said, as we walked toward a parking structure behind the casino. "I need to drive to L.A."

"What for? It's a five-hour road trip," Cody said.

"You up for it?"

"No," he said, squinting into the cold, dry air. "I'm gonna go have a chat with whoever at Vegas PD approved Abbey for the perv squad."

"You sure you want to do that?"

"What, you don't trust my diplomatic skills?"

"I didn't know you had any," I said with a laugh, but when I looked at him, the crow's feet spreading from his eyes looked carved by shrapnel.

"It's the responsible thing to do," he said.

"I guess you're right, buddy," I said, patting his massive shoulder. "Just try not to put her in a bad spot, you know?"

Cody didn't respond, and I spotted his car parked outside the garage. "You drove the Hellfire Hooptie?" I said.

"Why wouldn't I?" he replied. The car hadn't changed from when I'd seen it last. It was a maroon 1990's Toyota Camry, paint faded and scratched, rims mismatched, a dent in the driver's side quarter panel. Cody claimed it was the perfect stakeout vehicle for the slums. But the engine, suspension, and brakes had been fully modified for performance, and after nearly wrecking a few times, Cody had gone to racing school to learn how to manage the 450-horsepower beast.

"How's she running?" I asked.

"Like a bat out of hell. Hit one-fifty through the Mojave on the way here."

We reached the Camry and stood gazing at the red rock mountain range west of the city. "I found the murder victim's cell phone," I said. "He met someone at the Port of Los Angeles two weeks before he died. I need to check it out."

Cody continued staring out at the jagged horizon, a grimace on his mug. "You coming back tomorrow?"

"Probably."

He sighed and pulled his keys from his pocket. "What do you think of Abbey?"

"I like her. But I think you got your hands full."

"No shit, huh?" he said, a smile beginning on his lips.

"I'll call you tomorrow."

"Watch out for those L.A. bimbos with the fake boobs," he said.

• • •

Within a few minutes the Las Vegas cityscape was like a mirage in my rearview mirror, the glass facades shimmering like something out of a desperate gambler's dream. Ahead, I-15 bisected two hundred miles of the Mojave Desert. The interstate ran southwest through the stark wasteland, until terminating at the Inland Empire, which always struck me as an odd name for the easternmost section of Southern California's densely populated communities. After that there would be heavy traffic, which would likely add a couple hours to my trip. It would be well after sunset by the time I reached the Port of Los Angeles.

I crossed into California and drove hard, over Mountain Pass and then through Baker and onto the whitened flatlands of San Bernardino County. After a ten minute break to fill my tank in Barstow, I continued south on the sunbaked roadway, cruising at eighty-five and watching for highway patrol cruisers. By the time I reached the 210 and turned due west, the sun was low in the sky and its silver glare was bright on my windshield.

Three hours of commuter traffic later, I stopped at a fast food joint in Long Beach and reviewed my GPS while I ate. The Port of Los Angeles stretched into Long Beach and encompassed an area as large as a small city. I studied the map carefully, then drove off into the night. It was 8:30 and there was only a sliver of moon in the sky.

I found West Ocean Boulevard easily enough, but when I crossed the Los Angeles River I had to either turn off or take an on-ramp onto a freeway. I ended up on a side street parallel to a row of oil silos and hit a dead end. After a few U-turns, I finally found South Henry Ford Avenue, then I turned onto New Dock Street.

The road was straight, deserted, and unlit. To my left was a series of railroad tracks, and about fifty yards out sat an unmoving train stacked with containers. On my right, a cyclone fence topped with barbwire ran the length of the street. I drove slowly, looking for signage indicating berth 207. According to my map, a couple hundred yards beyond the fencing was the Cerritos Channel. I reached the end of the street, and across a vacant yard I saw a row of massive harbor cranes, their white superstructures dimly visible in the scant moonlight.

I turned around and doubled back, peering at the concrete buildings behind the fence line. One sign was for a marine repair business, and another for an oil production pipe yard. For the next hundred yards I saw nothing but a few NO TRESPASSING placards, before reaching a small, weather-beaten plywood sign, which read DOCK 206-209. I stopped, got out of my truck, and walked to a gate in the fence. On the other side was a parking lot scattered with freight containers and big rigs.

I rattled the gate and was immediately startled by a bright light.

"This is a restricted area," a man said, walking up with a flashlight. He wore a beanie with earflaps and an orange safety vest over a thick coat. "What you doin' here?"

"I'm a photographer. I was hoping to go down on the dock and take some pictures."

"You cain't go there. Only authorized persons."

"How about in the daytime?"

"Not unless you authorized. Even then there ain't no pictures allowed."

"Why not?"

The security guard shined the light directly into my face. "Because it's a bidness, and they don't want no one interferin' with the unloadin' and loadin' and such."

"Oh. I guess I'll try somewhere else."

The man shook his head and blew in his hands, then turned and walked back to the small shack from which he'd come. I got in my truck and hung a U-turn, and when I reached a dead end a quarter mile away I turned off my lights and parked with my truck facing outward.

A minute later I was walking along the fence. I wore my dark coat, gloves and a black beanie. A little ways past the marine repair sign, I stopped. It was pitch black and I was a couple hundred yards from where I'd talked to the security guard. On the other side was an empty lot, and further in I saw what looked like a row of concrete highway dividers.

I looked up and down the street, then pulled myself up on the fence and neatly snipped the barbwire with a pair of cutters I always carried when working. I folded the barbed section back and scaled the fence, silently dropping to the other side. The darkness forced me to walk cautiously, until I came to a row of containers. I slipped between them and stood at a second barbwire fence. Above the fence rose a pair of steel pillars, perhaps a hundred feet high, and at the top I thought I could see canisters. It reminded me of lighting systems I'd seen at baseball parks, but whether or not these lights were functional, I couldn't tell.

I cut the barbwire and continued forward. There were more rows of containers and large stacks of steel girders and pipes. I walked past them, staying in the deep shadows, and hopped a waist-high fence. It was only then that I saw the huge black profile of a vessel directly in front of me. I continued forward until I stood within a few feet of the ship's bow. Across the channel to my right, dozens of small craft were docked, and light spilled out over the water. The damp air smelled of brine and oil.

The container ship in the berth was empty, and the hull floated high above its waterline, the paint turning a rusty brown at least twenty feet above the black seawater. Four tall cranes were mounted on its deck, stretching into the dark sky. I walked the length of the boat until I came to a cement block stenciled with number 207. I stared up at a ladder welded to the hull and imagined a man descending and jumping to the dock.

I spent another few minutes in the shadow of the ship, walking under the thick ropes mooring it to six iron bollards on the dock. Could an athletic man climb down one of the ropes to the dock? It was definitely possible.

Ten minutes later I was back at my truck. Nothing I'd seen gave me any hint why Jeff Jordan would have met someone hereabouts at dawn on a November morning. But that wasn't a disappointment; I hadn't expected to learn anything specific from my nocturnal visit. I just wanted to be here, to retrace footsteps, to get a sense of the place, to soak it in. This is something I always do in an investigation. I always put myself at the place of occurrence, even when it seems to serve little tactile purpose.

And every now and then, in the most confusing phase of a case, I'll wake from a night's sleep with a subconscious revelation hovering near the surface. Not long afterwards, I'll have a moment of clarity, and the previously opaque will present itself plainly. This usually occurs when I'm distracted with some mundane task, like tying my shoe or talking to a convenience store clerk.

But I didn't dwell on those abstractions as I drove to the nearest hotel. I needed to focus on more tangible issues, like finding out what boat arrived at berth 207 at 5:15 a.m. on November 16. I needed to know where it came from and if possible, get the ship's manifest. I was tired and not looking forward to the task, but I told myself to stay positive, and maybe the information would be easy to find.

•   •   •

By one a.m. I had a headache and my eyes kept closing. I tried to power down my notebook, but I hit the wrong button and the program froze. I slapped the screen shut and had to catch the computer before it fell off the desk.

My problem was, I couldn't find a way to trace the arrival time and date without knowing where the cargo ship came from. There were numerous websites that offered tracking databases, but none allowed me to search based solely on the arrival date. Frustrated and fighting my temper, I fell into bed, wondering if I could sleep, but within a minute I fell into a dreamless slumber. I must have been more tired than I thought, because I slept seven straight hours before waking.

•   •   •

The next morning brought good news in the way of strong coffee, free and available in sixteen-ounce cups from the Long Beach Best Western hotel lobby. Halfway through my second cup, I was back at my computer, determined, focused, and vowing to be patient. After trying several different search patterns, I ended up routed to a shipping company's website. KTM was a large, global freight carrier, operating container ships serving hundreds of ports. At eleven a.m., after immersing myself in their online database, I finally found what I was looking for. A ship named VMS VIRGO had arrived at POLA on November 16, docking at berth 207 at 5:24 a.m. It came directly from the Port of Freetown in Sierra Leone, Africa. Its previous ports had been Capetown, South Africa, then north to Luanda in Angola, with one more stop at Port Banana in the Democratic Republic of the Congo.

By noon I had the ship's manifest, which I learned is publicly available information. However, it required me to buy a subscription to a site which would provide the document. I printed the manifest on the hotel's printer, and studied the varied cargo, and the names of all aboard the ship. Nothing seemed unusual; there was no gold or diamonds aboard, at least none listed, but I didn't expect there to be. I didn't know exactly how a country would ship precious commodities, but I doubted it was by container ship. I was more interested in the ship's company, which was the term the manifest used to record those onboard, including rank from captain to civilian. The names were all foreign sounding, except for two listed civilians, who could have been British, Canadian, or American. I highlighted those two names.

When I walked outside I saw the overcast had turned dark and thick bands of gunship gray clouds were roiling to the north.

"Storm brewing," I said.

8

BY THE TIME I reached the freeway, the first raindrops were splattering on my windshield. Within five minutes the rain was hammering down, the sound like a roomful of clattery motors. At full speed my wipers couldn't keep up with the torrent. Streams ran across the pavement and traffic slowed to thirty miles per hour.

I drove cautiously, fully aware that most California drivers are in a perpetual hurry and not used to inclement weather. The combination would probably result in an accident shortly, I mused. Resigned that any chance of making time was shot, I turned up my radio and listened for weather and road updates. Sure enough, after a minute the traffic ground to a halt.

For the next hour I crawled along, passing two wrecks, until the downpour finally lightened in Anaheim, and the flow of cars resumed at thirty, and then forty MPH. I drove patiently, and mulled over what I'd learned earlier in the morning.

Jeff Jordan had met an unnamed person near berth 207 at dawn, shortly after the docking of a cargo ship from Africa. The text message had said to park on the street, which made sense since that was the closest an unauthorized person could get to the berth. It was logical to assume Jeff met someone disembarking the ship. Why else would the meeting be near the port? And for what purpose?

I thought about it as I drove, my mind circling and searching for connections. What about the black man who had been one of the intruders at the Jordan's home? There was almost no black population in Cedar City. Could this man have been an African national, arriving in the U.S. on the freighter? If so, it presented the possibility that Jeff Jordan knew his murderer.

The other angle was diamonds. The stones I found in the Jordan's safe, based on the appraisal from the Cedar City jeweler, were possibly worth well over a million dollars. And the stones were uncut, which was something I'd never seen before. I didn't think uncut diamonds were available to ordinary consumers. Which led me to ask, how did a construction contractor like Jeff Jordan get his hands on them? Did they come from Africa, a continent known for its diamond mines?

It stopped raining outside of Pomona, just as I turned onto I-15 North. The skies stayed dry as I approached the grade splitting the San Bernardino and San Gabriel mountain ranges, then it started raining again over the pass. The visibility lessened when I drove into a cloud sitting on the summit, and the sleet turned to snow. My phone rang, but the road required my full attention, and it wasn't until I descended out of the hills and onto the high desert floor that the clouds dissipated and the sky turned blue.

Cruising at eighty under a cold sun, I checked my cell and saw it was Cody who'd called. I pushed the callback button, and he answered and began speaking without preamble.

"So, I went over to see the Las Vegas PD and spoke to Denise Culligan, the lieutenant in charge of the sex crimes division," he said. "They recently assigned a few detectives to focus on kiddie porn. Seems there's been an increase in underage prostitution."

"Did you talk about Abbey?"

"Yeah. I told her, look, this is my daughter, for all I know she's a virgin. Why would you let her be part of this?"

"What'd she say?"

"She said her first inclination was to tell Abbey to go elsewhere. But after they talked awhile, she said she sensed something in Abbey, something she doesn't see often in cops."

"Like what?"

"She had a hard time describing it, even though we talked for half an hour. But she was very impressed with her, and said she felt Abbey could make a meaningful contribution, maybe help some people."

"Hmm. Sounds like a positive discussion."

"It was, actually."

"I'll be rolling into town in a couple hours. You want to go get a steak somewhere?"

"Ah, no, I'll be tied up. Denise and I decided to continue our conversation over dinner."

"Really?"

"Yeah. I mean, I think it's a good idea for me to know her, know what Abbey's getting into."

"I see. What does Denise look like, if you don't mind me asking?" I was smiling and trying to keep my voice even.

"Not that it makes a difference, but she's pretty damn cute."

"No, of course that wouldn't make a difference," I said, no longer able to keep from laughing.

"Christ, Dirt, your mind's always in the gutter."

"*My* mind?"

"Yeah, you've always been a horn dog, so don't try to pretend you've changed. So get this—I'm leaving the police station and I run into this patrolman and two detectives I know, back from that incident a couple years ago."

"You mean the time you boned the mayor's daughter and ran into his car when you dropped her off?"

"All right, let's make sure we have this straight, once and for all. She was about thirty, and she latched onto me while I was just trying to enjoy a drink. She literally wouldn't let go of my arm until I took her to my hotel. She was insatiable, a complete nympho, and once she wore me out, I asked if she wanted to spend the night. She said, 'Hell, no, it's only midnight,' and she wanted to go back to the bar. Being the responsible citizen I am, I thought it would be better to take her home. But right when we pulled up she started groping me, and my foot slipped while I was trying to park."

"Thanks for the clarification. I always thought you were getting ripped and hopped into bed with a loose woman and then drove her home drunk."

"I did not drive drunk. All the exercise sobered me up before I drove her home."

"Well, that's good to know."

"Anyway, I'm walking through the main reception area and I hear my name, and these three cops are snickering like a pack of jackasses, so I stop and look over. One says, 'The man, the myth, the legend,' and I ask what that's supposed to mean. They got these shit-eating grins, and one of the beat walkers asks if I'm there to fill out an application. I tell him, 'Sorry to disappoint you, but I'm not interested.' Then the other patrolman says, 'Just keep it in your pants.' They start laughing like this is high comedy. But I got more important things to do than deal with those bozos, so I start walking away, and the patrolman says, 'Hey, Gibbons. This is Las Vegas, not San Jose. Don't even think of stretching the law.' What do you make of that crap?"

"Sounds like they're pissing on the fire hydrant."

"Why lay it on me?"

"Your reputation precedes you."

"And I thought I was keeping a low profile."

"I wouldn't worry about it," I said.

•   •   •

The Plaza Hotel and Casino was north of The Strip, right off Fremont Street in old downtown Vegas. I got there late in the afternoon and checked into a room on the tenth floor. I set up my notebook computer and got online, but then I stood in the dark interior and stared out the window. The sun was setting and the clouds over the jagged horizon were streaked with orange and red.

I'd reached the point in my investigation where I needed to identify suspects, or at least people who could provide information pointing to suspects. All my work to this point now felt preliminary. Learning about the crime and discovering Jeff Jordan's secret caches of gold and gemstones were no doubt important pieces of the puzzle, but I still didn't have any real idea what I was dealing with.

If I was back in Cedar City, I'd interview everyone I could find who knew Jeff Jordan. That would be a standard investigative approach. With luck, I'd come across a scrap of information, maybe from a work buddy or a bar friend who Jordan boasted to about his treasure. Most people can't resist saying something to someone when they've run into good fortune. No matter how secretive you vow to be, all it takes is a moment of weakness.

For a minute I seriously considered getting in my truck and driving straight back to Cedar City. If I chose to stay in Vegas for any length of time, I'd need to justify it. To that end, the logical angle was the Jordan's missing ten-year-old daughter. If Mia Jordan wasn't buried in a shallow grave somewhere, it was possible she was in the clutches of someone who wished to use her to make money. If that was the case, Vegas was a good place to begin searching.

I walked back to my computer haltingly, trying to fathom an excuse to delay the task at hand. I'd dealt with kiddie porn twice before, and in both cases my disgust and anger had resulted in violence followed by heavy drinking. I stared off, seeing nothing, and finally muttered, "Screw it, I'll do it later." I sat at my keyboard, deciding to instead do some general research on Africa's diamond trade. Fortunately, the data on this subject was abundant and easy to find.

Beginning in the early nineties and still reportedly happening on a smaller scale, billions of dollars of rough diamonds were illicitly exported out of Africa, primarily to finance civil wars in countries along Africa's west coast and interior. It was a bloody business involving immeasurable human suffering. Families were ripped apart, children were forced into militias or slave labor, and malnutrition and infectious disease were rampant. Among the most egregious participants was a rebel group called the Revolutionary United Front in Sierra Leone. Their signature atrocity was the amputation of limbs by machete, which they imposed on both adults and children, as a means to terrorize the population. They were also prolific rapists, sometimes forcing entire families to watch while they gang-raped mothers, sisters, and daughters. If they ran low on victims, they'd even victimize elderly women and small boys.

The civil war in Sierra Leone ended in 2002, and while the current government promotes democracy and capitalism, corruption and limited freedom of speech remain in place. The most recent Sierra Leone news to make global headlines involved the deadly Ebola breakout of 2014, which killed thousands.

I spent half an hour researching Sierra Leone. The existence of large diamond mines in a poor, corrupt African country piqued my interest. If one was willing to bribe, I had no doubt arrangements could be made for a bagful of uncut diamonds to be smuggled into the U.S. Probably not on a plane, but on a cargo ship? Easy to imagine.

I continued scouring the Internet, saving pages and taking notes. Liberia, just south of Sierra Leone, had its own civil war in the nineties, which crossed the border and exacerbated the conflict in Sierra Leone. The atrocities endured by the people of Liberia were similar to those suffered by their northern neighbor. Liberia also has diamond mines, although not as rich as those in Sierra Leone. But, more recent discoveries of large Liberian gold deposits has spurred a resurgence of mining.

Liberian gold. A possible connection?

Next I read up on the Democratic Republic of the Congo. The unfortunate history of the Congo made the difficulties of the two countries I'd researched previously seem minor in scale. After fifty years of exploitation by the Belgium government, the Congo gained its independence in 1960, which immediately resulted in civil war. Leaders took office, followed rapidly by coups, executions, and more war. Starvation, malnutrition, and deadly diseases, including HIV/AIDS, typhoid, malaria, and hepatitis, were ubiquitous.

In 1971, President Joseph Mobutu renamed the country Zaire. Mobutu was anti-communist, and was able to maintain power with the backing of the United States. Under Mobutu's dictatorship, Zaire became a poster child for human rights violations, political repression, and corruption. Mobutu's massive personal theft of tax dollars and international aid funds caused Zaire's infrastructure to crumble to an estimated 25% of what had existed in 1960.

When the Soviet Union collapsed and the cold war ended in 1991, the U.S. no longer saw it politically expedient to support Mobutu, and in 1996 rebel forces overthrew his rule. If the citizenry hoped that the elimination of an evil despot would bring peace and prosperity, they were sorely disappointed, for what followed was a six-year conflict sometimes referred to as the African World War. Nine African countries participated, their weaponry often bought with smuggled diamonds. Although the savagery and genocide were on a grand scale, the biggest killer was disease and starvation. Over five million people perished during the war and its aftermath.

Although its diamonds are reportedly no longer used to fund bloodshed, the Congo is still struggling to realize the economic benefit of its diamond mines. Much of its diamond supply is provided by artisanal mining, the career choice of thousands of unregulated workers who are routinely robbed, cheated, and murdered by ragtag bands of soldiers, some of whom simply never turned in their uniforms and weapons after the war ended.

South of the Congo is Angola, a former Portuguese colony. Rich in oil, iron ore, and diamonds, Angola was ravaged by civil war from 1975 to 2002. The fighting was primarily between two rival factions that wanted control of Angola's abundant natural resources. One group was backed by the Soviet Union, the other by the United States. Still recovering from the political fallout over Vietnam, the U.S. was reluctant to send troops to Angola. Instead, the CIA operated in the shadows, enabling a flow of arms and money and providing military training and intelligence.

Soviet and U.S. funding of the Angolan conflict continued to increase into the 1990s, until a ceasefire was signed in 2002. Although the combatants agreed to disarm, pockets of rebel militias continued terrorizing the population for years. CIA operatives remained in place, ostensibly to monitor the fragile peace. The KGB was also in no hurry to leave, for while post-Soviet Russia was no longer motivated to defend communism, they were very interested in financial gain. And certain members of the CIA felt the same way, for Angola was ripe to be plundered.

The revenue from smuggled Angolan diamonds sold to fund the war has been estimated as high as $10 billion. The fighters supported by the U.S. relied heavily on blood diamonds, and employed thousands of diamond miners who were underpaid and forced to suffer harsh work conditions. Toiling in riverbeds in only their underwear, these workers clawed diamonds from the earth by hand, under the close scrutiny of armed guards.

It was seven p.m. when I stood and stretched. I'd wanted to avoid the grim prospect of researching child pornography, and had instead wandered into the modern history of Africa, which read like a script from a horror movie. But my labor had not been without benefit, for now I was convinced that the uncut diamonds in the Jordans' safe were likely smuggled onboard the freighter in either Sierra Leone, the Congo, or Angola, and then passed to Jeff Jordan by someone from the ship. I still didn't know by whom, or why, but at least I had a premise from which to move forward.

The skies outside my window were dark but a few miles away the lights on The Strip glowed brightly. I left my room and took the elevator down to the ground floor casino, to the ever-present melodies of the slot machines. I walked past the food court and out the main entrance. The night air was dry and cold, and I zipped my jacket while waiting to cross Main Street, into the pedestrian-only section of Fremont Street.

The party on Fremont was in full swing. Crowds lined the sidewalks and spilled out onto the main drag, where a man on stilts in a silver Elvis costume sang into a microphone. I walked past the former Glitter Gulch strip club, which had closed and was being converted into a casino. I continued past souvenir shops, restaurants, more casinos, a live band, and street bars selling beer and liquor in plastic cups. A pair of men, one who bore an uncanny resemblance to actor Robert De Niro, and the other an Al Pacino lookalike, were taking pictures with tourists. Thirty feet up, four teenagers, hooting and hollering, rode by on a zip line. Above the zip line, the LED canopy flashed brilliantly.

Looking for a restaurant, I came to an intersection and saw a scattering of colorful cards lying in the street. I picked one up, then went into an uncrowded diner. The waitress seated me at a booth in the back.

The card was an advertisement for escorts. On either side were pictures of young women in bikinis who were obviously call girls. I stared at the card and the phone number, wondering if this outfit would traffic in underage girls. After a minute I realized I was frowning. It was day twenty-nine of my sobriety.

I ordered a cheeseburger, fries, and a non-alcoholic beer, and sat in the quiet restaurant with my fist against my mouth. A sudden pang of loneliness and yearning struck me, and I sat there for a minute before I shook my head and called Candi. I felt remorseful that I hadn't spoken to her for a couple of days. I hadn't called her after Melanie Jordan's nude excursion into my bedroom, nor had I told her I'd met Cody's daughter. She was also totally unaware that I was in Las Vegas with Cody.

The call went to voicemail. I left a message, then texted her. The key to maintaining a relationship is communication, a woman I knew before Candi once told me. To some this may sound obvious, but I don't always find it intuitive. I have to sometimes push myself to open up, to make conversation. I always felt better after talking to Candi, so I don't know why I was prone to go silent. She never failed to brighten my spirits and push my dark thoughts to the sidelines.

Shortly after we got married, my ex-wife said that when I immersed myself in a case, there was nothing left of me for her. That's not what killed our relationship, though. I drove her away with a drunk binge, one that I used as an excuse to deal with my fatal shooting of a pedophile.

I slouched forward on the yellow vinyl upholstery, my elbows on the white table top, and wished the florescent lighting wasn't so bright. But what I really wished at that moment was to be either at home with Candi, or in the friendly confines of a dark bar, tilting back a shot of Canadian whiskey followed by a draught beer in an ice-rimmed glass. After a few rounds, a calming euphoria would come over me, and my concerns and guilt would temporarily melt away. And sometimes, in that state, I would see things more clearly, as if the alcohol released subconscious insights that were tightly bound by my sober mind.

Or maybe that was just a lame drunkard's rationale, a preposterous twist of logic I'd created to justify the drowning of my thirst.

I was halfway done with my dinner when Candi called back. We talked for half an hour, and I told her everything about the case, including the situation in Vegas with Cody and his daughter. She listened and asked a few questions, and then the conversation turned lighthearted, then flirtatious. She only made one request, and that was that I stay safe, which was something she always said when I was away working, especially if Cody was around. When we hung up, I was smiling so broadly my jaw hurt. I swore to myself I'd get home as soon as I could and take her to dinner after an afternoon in our bedroom.

• • •

It was almost nine o'clock when I got back to my room at the Plaza. I began searching porn sites online, looking for escort services or strippers servicing Las Vegas. I found several links, but when I tried to narrow the search to young girls, I hit a dead end.

Back when I was barely a teenager, the Internet was in its infancy. I remember an older kid in our neighborhood, a nerd with prolific acne and a penchant for technology, talking about what the Internet would eventually become. Cynical for my age, I asked him how it was currently being used.

"Mostly pornography," he said.

I rejoiced smugly, thinking that surely more mainstream businesses would have already embraced the World Wide Web if it had so much potential. I mean, how valid could it be if only smut peddlers used it?

Within a couple years, I learned two things: First, I'm not a technical visionary, and second, uninformed skepticism is the domain of fools.

As I sat scanning through what seemed like dozens of sites in the sex trade, I had a third revelation: pornography is a business like any other, and it's a big business, one that makes millionaires out of savvy marketers. It's also not an industry where the purveyors would be foolish enough to advertise anything as blatantly illegal as prepubescent prostitutes.

I entered a variety of keywords, hoping to find a backdoor to a hidden site where pedophiles might lurk. I knew these sites existed, sometimes in the form of chatrooms or forums. A few links I found looked promising, but firewalls blocked my access. I kept searching, but most of what came up were stories of men arrested for possessing child pornography. None lived in Las Vegas.

An hour later I gave up. Want to visit sites promoting terrorism and racism, maybe join the Islamic State? No problem. Feel like hooking up with cannibals, necrophiliacs, or Satanists? Piece of cake. In the mood to view an unending stream of vile and abhorrent videos, including real snuff films? Easy to do. But child porn? It's a sure ticket to a long stretch in prison, and I couldn't find anyone dimwitted enough to advertise it.

I closed my computer screen and sat in the dark. I wasn't surprised by my lack of success in finding direct links to kiddie porn, but I'd hoped to find something that would point me in the right direction. The only thing I'd found potentially useful was numerous sites offering call girls. A few of these sites used the term, "barely legal."

I stood and crossed my arms. Prostitution, the world's oldest profession, is usually a victimless crime. In many countries, and in states like Nevada, it's legal within certain guidelines. But that status applies to women of eighteen years or older. Anyone under eighteen is legally a child. As for Mia Jordan, at ten years old, her appeal wouldn't be to lecherous middle-aged men who craved sex with a teenager. Mia would appeal to only hardcore pedophiles.

My lips tightened, and I felt my nostrils flare. I hadn't yet truly accepted the likelihood that Mia Jordan had been kidnapped by those who knew no boundaries. That, I admitted to myself, was because up to now I'd avoided steering my investigation toward something I consider unspeakably sordid. But sordid barely scratches the surface in describing individuals who defile and exploit innocent children. You could add deranged, perverted, and immoral to the list, but that still doesn't really cut it. Actually, I didn't think any words were adequate to describe how I felt about this unfortunate subset of humanity.

I tried to swallow a lump of anger rising from my gut. In a fistfight, when a brawler reaches his boiling point, he'll often attack head-on with a blizzard of punches. This may be effective against a weak opponent, but it's a losing strategy against an adversary who knows how to box, and will usually result in the aggressor waking up on the floor and wondering what hit him. I pressed my knuckles to my forehead and took a deep breath. I couldn't afford to get knocked out this time; not with Mia's life at stake. I needed to take the emotion out of it and think clearly.

Of course, that was assuming Mia was still alive. I sat on the edge of the bed and slumped forward, staring at the floor. There was no evidence she'd been kidnapped, no ransom demand. There was also no evidence she'd been killed, and no motive I could imagine, other than a psychopath's rage. Given the nature of Jeff Jordan's gruesome murder, I couldn't discount that Mia was killed solely for being in the wrong place at the wrong time. But, if she was killed, why wasn't the body left at the scene, the same as her murdered father's?

I went back to my computer and found one of the sites advertising barely legal call girls. I called a number and spoke to a woman who asked what I was looking for.

"Younger is better," I replied.

"I have an eighteen-year-old I bet you'll like."

"How about fifteen?"

She hung up on me.

I punched in the number for a second site and spoke with another woman, who said I could have a buxom eighteen-year-old blonde knocking on my door in twenty minutes. I checked my wallet for cash, then gave her my room number.

The hooker arrived promptly at eleven p.m. She wore silver heels and white pants and her peach-colored top left her midriff bare and was form-fitted to highlight her breasts. Her makeup was too heavy, her eyes dark and her lips cherry red. She didn't look like she was in her teens, but that may have been because of the jaded expression on her face.

"What kind of party you looking for?" she asked, standing next to the bed.

"No party, I'm working."

Her eyes sharpened, and she looked at me suspiciously. "You a cop?"

"Nope, private investigator."

She shook her head and muttered, "Waste of my time," then turned toward the door.

"Wait a minute. Don't you want to be paid?"

"Damn right. Room call is two hundred."

"Take a seat then, and keep your clothes on."

She hesitated, trying to decide if staying would be in her best interest. I opened my wallet and pulled out a handful of twenties. Once she saw the money, she lowered herself into the second chair in the room. Like all call girls, she was coin-operated.

"I'm looking for a ten-year-old girl who may have been kidnapped. I'm looking for pimps who deal in young children, or local child pornographers. Any ideas?"

"Ten years old? That's sick."

"You know anybody who deals in children?"

"This is Vegas," she said. "You can get anything you want here."

"I'm sure you can. But I need to know where to find a ten-year-old."

"How much you got there?" she asked, eyeing the wad of cash I'd set on the desk.

"Two hundred. But you need to earn it."

She looked away, and I wondered if she was formulating a story, something that would get her paid and out of here quickly. Then she said, "The McGillicuddy Man."

"Who?"

"He works the Greyhound station most nights, right next door. Runaways get off the bus, hungry and broke, and he takes them in. Then they owe him. And he owns them."

"He's pimping a ten-year-old girl?"

"No, I didn't say that. Maybe fourteen is the youngest he's ever had in his stable."

"Then how can he help me?"

"McGillicuddy talks big, like he's the badass pimp of North Vegas. He never shows his face on The Strip because the heavyweights would crush him. But he knows the business, so if anybody knows about a ten-year-old, he would."

"What's McGillicuddy look like?"

"Black, tall, six-five maybe. Scarecrow skinny. Gray beard. About forty-five." She stood and took a step toward me. "Good enough?" she asked.

"One more question. What's his real name?"

"Who knows? I think his first name starts with a J, like Jacob or Joshua or something like that."

I handed her the cash. "Easy money, huh?" I said.

"You could have both got laid and got the info," she said, showing a sly smile.

"Not in the market," I replied.

•   •   •

It took only five minutes to go from my room to the bus depot next door. I walked in right after a bus arrived, and the disembarking passengers were milling about. There was no line at the ticket booths, but about fifty people were sitting in the rows of seats bolted to the scuffed tile floor. It was a little before midnight, and most of the folks looked tired and disheveled. I walked the perimeter, passed a closed cafeteria and restrooms, and then went out a side door to a parking lot. When I came back in, I stopped and looked at a board showing departures and arrivals. Then I took a seat a couple of rows behind two white teenage girls.

They looked unwashed, their hair braided and matted, their tattoos blurry on their wan skin. One was dark-haired, the other blond, and both wore the same tired, blank expression, as if stoically resigned to whatever became of them. A stained, army-green duffle bag lay at their feet. As for their ages, I estimated somewhere between fourteen and seventeen.

Fifteen minutes passed, and most in the terminal left to be picked up by cars that stopped along the sidewalk. The girls remained, silent and uninterested in the activity on the curbside. My guess was they'd been here for a while, had nowhere to go, and would spend the night unless they were told to leave.

A tall black man came from the parking lot door into the station. He wore embroidered bell-bottom jeans and a black leather coat. His shoes were pointy and the cap on his head was tilted at a jaunty angle. A sharply trimmed goatee was gray against his dark skin. In his hands was a pizza box, and when he came closer, I could see a wisp of steam rise from the cardboard.

"Evening, ladies," he said to the girls. "My name's Jimmy G, and I'm an advocate for the homeless here in Vegas. May I interest you in supper tonight?" He opened the box, and the aroma wafted into their faces. He sat next to them and laid napkins on their laps, all the while maintaining a friendly patter. Both girls ate ravenously, responding with only grunts and nods.

"You may find winter nights in our great desert very cold. Even the coyotes and jackrabbits hole up this time of year. You don't want to be campin', that's for sure. You're welcome to spend a warm night in my shelter, with a few other friendly people."

I kept my head down, pretending I was immersed with my smartphone. When I glanced up, I saw McGillicuddy's profile, his face welcoming and friendly, but when he cut his eyes toward me they had a sharp edge, as if a separate persona hovered just beneath the surface.

I looked down and continued fiddling with my phone. A minute later he closed the pizza box and stood. "I got more food in the shelter, and you can shower and wash your clothes too. My car's right out here, just this way."

The girls began following him to the exit leading to the parking lot. Their movements were almost robotic, as if they were in a trance. I let them get a four-step head start before I followed.

When they reached the door, McGillicuddy held it open for them. His smile vanished when he saw me coming quickly.

"What do —" he started, but the words froze in his throat when I grabbed his arm and cranked it hard behind his back. I shoved him out the door, into the dark night. "Go back to your seats," I said to the girls, as the door swung shut.

"You take your hands off me, you bitch motherfucker," he said, right before I slammed him against a concrete pillar. Standing behind him, I punched him hard in the lower back, right in the kidney. He gasped, and a cry escaped his lips.

"Your night's taken a turn for the worse, pimp."

"That right?" he said, and then I heard a click and saw a switchblade in his left hand. He threw his right elbow at my face, but I moved laterally, and before he could turn I hit him in the back of the head with my palm. His face bounced off the concrete, then I hit him again in the kidney. His knees buckled, and I stepped back to let him fall.

I thought I'd taken the fight out of him, but I'd underestimated the man, because he rolled to his feet and lashed out with the knife. He had long arms and I felt the blade nick my elbow. I kicked at his hand, but he was quick and my foot caught nothing but air. Then he sprang forward, jabbing at my gut.

I jumped back, watching as he crouched and moved toward me. He was bleeding from the nose, and his eyes had a murderous gleam. I could have thrown a right cross, probably knocked him out, but in doing so I'd leave my ribs undefended, and would likely get stabbed. As we circled each other he jabbed, catlike, at my midsection. He had a significant reach advantage, and I had to continually back up to avoid his thrusts, but now I was up against a wall.

He lunged once more and this time I anticipated it and grabbed his wrist. He had a split second to realize he was in trouble, then I threw a snap-kick, the heel of my boot driving into his solar plexus. His eyes went round, his jaw fell open, and he staggered back. I kicked his hand, and the knife went flying behind him.

Temporarily unable to breathe, he was defenseless. I tripped him to the ground and dropped a knee onto his back. After cinching a zip-tie around his right ankle, I yanked his left arm back and zip-tied his wrist to the ankle.

A young couple walked past and stared, openmouthed. "Police business," I said. "Keep walking." They went into the terminal and I knew I had to finish quickly. I dragged the pimp behind a row of cars, his clothes skidding and tearing on the pavement.

"What do you want?" he hissed. He lay face down on the coarse tar and gravel surface.

"A ten-year-old girl's been kidnapped. Who has her?"

"How the fuck would I know?"

I pulled his wallet from his back pocket and found his Nevada driver's license. His name was Jerome Glincey.

"You're in the business, Jerome. You pimp out children, you know all the angles."

"I never dealt with nobody that young."

I straightened and stepped on the side of Jerome Glincey's face. Then I lifted my other foot and balanced my weight on one leg, my boot tread crushing into his skin. He tried to yell, but all he could manage was a muted garble. I counted to five, then stepped off.

"Start talking or this will get worse. You're smart enough to figure that out, right?"

His lip was cut and a frothy dribble of blood ran through his beard. His eyes were squeezed shut and when he opened them, he blinked hard, as if trying to comprehend his pain.

"The Russians," he croaked. "They're the only ones take on girls too young to breed."

I felt my brow crease. "Russians? I need names."

He paused, and I put my boot on his neck, pivoting the sole into his flesh.

"Don't! The Volkovs, damn it."

"Where do I find them?"

"There's a Russian restaurant in the Mandalay Bay. Another one off Tropicana."

I opened his wallet again and removed a thick stack of cash. A couple hundreds and some twenties.

"Here's the deal, Jerome. Your career in Vegas is finished. It's time to relocate. You don't get to abuse women here anymore, not on my watch."

"Who the hell you think you are?"

"Wrong answer," I said, and reared back my leg and kicked him as hard as I could between the buttocks, my steel toe ramming into his testicles. He screamed, and a moment later a puddle of urine spread from beneath his body.

I cut his ties, and he curled into the fetal position. I dropped his wallet onto his face.

"I'm serious about you hitting the road, Jerome. I'd hate to have to tell the Volkovs you sold them out."

He didn't reply, which was the smartest thing he'd done all night.

. . .

After giving Jerome's bankroll to the two teenage girls, I drove them to a decent hotel away from the casinos. I didn't ask them about their circumstances, and they didn't offer to explain how they ended up in a Vegas bus terminal near midnight in the dead of winter. I only imparted one bit of advice, and that was to be wary of men offering help, unless they were interested in a career in the sex trade. When they didn't respond, I added, "By that I mean becoming a whore." Neither appeared shocked or very interested in my warning. That made me a little sad, and made me wonder about the nature of what they were running from. It also served as a reminder that I can't solve the world's problems. Best I focus on doing my job and solving my own.

. . .

When I got back to my hotel, I sat in my truck for a minute. Even though it seemed a long time since I had woken in Long Beach, I didn't feel tired in the slightest. Not only was I wide awake, I was energized, because the altercation with the pimp had produced a real lead. Ordinarily I wouldn't have felt enthusiastic about a coerced scrap of information from a career criminal, but as soon as the pimp said, "The Russians", I remembered Melanie's comment about her attacker's Eastern European accent.

I headed to the freeway and drove five miles south on 15, skirting The Strip until I exited on Flamingo and turned south on Las Vegas Boulevard. I drove by the Bellagio and Paris, and then past the CityCenter and

Cosmopolitan, the two newest additions to Las Vegas's mega-hotel-casino industry. At the Tropicana intersection I waited at the stoplight and looked up at the 150-foot tall Statue of Liberty in front of the New York-New York's faux cityscape. A rollercoaster weaved through the hotel's superstructure, the red tracks brightly lit.

Mandalay Bay was at the far southern end of The Strip. It was a massive complex with two hotel towers. I found a spot on the second story of the parking structure and went into the casino. Most of the restaurants, including one called Red Square, were right off the main casino floor. A five-minute walk took me to a statue of a headless man aside a rectangular portico supported by square gold columns. Above the columns was Russian lettering.

I walked through the doors and past a hostess. The interior was brown and red and had a brooding feel, but the dining tables were packed and lively, even though it was past midnight. Waitresses in skimpy black dresses attended to the patrons, some whom would no doubt be partying and gambling until dawn. The music from the bar was loud, and I wondered if those dining could hear each other.

I walked the perimeter, looking for a hallway leading to a back office. I came to a door where a man stood at a podium.

"What's in here?" I asked.

"It's our vodka vault. It's full now, but I can put your name on the list. Here," he said, handing me a leather bound folder. I opened it and looked at prices for 360 different vodkas, sold by the bottle or in shots. The paragraph above the price list described the interior as zero degrees Fahrenheit, and assured patrons that fur coats and hats were provided to those willing to pay thirty dollars for an ounce of common vodka. It also mentioned that the statue out front was that of Vladimir Lenin, and his missing head was kept preserved in the vault. Visitors were invited to 'Come "join the party" and do shots off Lenin's head.'

I moved on, past the kitchen and to the bar. A large hammer and sickle symbol above the shelved bottles overlooked a row of barstools and a dozen cocktail tables. There was nowhere to sit, so I stood off to the side, looking around as if waiting for someone.

The crowd was mostly under thirty and in nightclub attire. Most of the men wore button-down shirts with thin neckties, or tight V-neck short-sleeved shirts to show off their physiques. The women strutted on high heels, and their short skirts or pants looked painted to their figures. Three bartenders poured drinks and were hustling to keep up with the demand, as were a trio of cocktail waitresses.

Two couples in their early forties came into the room, searching for open seats. They went to the bar, the men frowning and trying to get the attention of a bartender, while the woman chatted obliviously.

I stood against a wall for another few minutes, trying to play the role of a man waiting for his date, but feeling increasing conspicuous. Then two men entered the bar.

The first wore a dark wool coat with buckles. The coat was thick and so was the body beneath it, but the bulk was fat, not muscle. The man was perhaps fifty, and his torso was shaped more like a pear than a barrel. He had a full head of black hair going gray, and his heavy jowls were unshaven. His face looked puffy, and I may have discounted him for a harmless tourist, except for his half-lidded eyes. They were still and hard, and when he spoke I was reminded of men who gave orders that were rarely disobeyed.

The second man was taller and twenty years younger. He wore a suit that fit his musculature poorly. His facial features were blunt; the nose flat at the tip, the jaw square. He looked classically Slavic, except his hairline was unusually low on his forehead, which made his face seem oddly out of proportion. But it was his eyes I paid more intention to, for they were cold and uncompromising, the same as his counterpart's.

They came my way, and I made a pretense of playing with my phone while I took their pictures. When they reached the bar, one of the harried bartenders immediately climbed a ladder and took a bottle from a glass case. He poured a pair of shots, set them on a tray, then came around and served the two men, bowing slightly.

I moved away from the bar and stood behind some folks who were waiting for a table. Within a minute the two men tossed back their vodkas and headed toward the exit, apparently having fulfilled the purpose of their visit. Whether they had stopped in solely for a quick drink, or for something else, I didn't know. I fell in behind them, walking out of the restaurant and into the casino. They strode the opposite direction from which I'd come, and we crossed the casino floor and entered the hotel lobby. They went through the front doors and out to the sidewalk where valet attendants and bellhops milled about. A white Cadillac limousine promptly arrived at the curb, and the driver got out and opened the rear door.

I waved for a taxi parked outside the reception circle, but the cabby either wasn't looking or chose to ignore me. The pair I followed got into the limo. I managed to take a picture of the license plate as they pulled away.

"Need a cab?" an attendant asked.

I watched the limo exit the resort and disappear.

"Not anymore," I said.

• • •

When I got back to my truck, I drove out to The Strip and turned right on Tropicana. Once I passed the airport entrance and crossed Paradise Road, the neon glow from Las Vegas Boulevard was swallowed by the abyss of the desert. Away from the casinos, the night was dark and silent.

I found the establishment I was looking for a mile up the road, to my left. The Café Leonov was a standalone building with stucco facing and shuttered windows. An unlit sign over the entrance was badly weathered and needed repair. The restaurant was definitely closed for the evening. The parking lot was large, and empty except for three vehicles. Two were sedans, and the third, parked parallel in front of the building, was the white limousine.

I drove by, tapping my steering wheel. The pimp had fingered a Russian crime family as involved in prepubescent girls, and told me where to find them. Of course, he might have named the Volkovs solely because it was the first name that came to mind as he lay with his face ground into the pavement. But Melanie claimed she heard an accent that could have been Russian. And now two men in a white limo show up at both restaurants named by the pimp. It definitely was worth looking into.

I hung a U-turn and drove past the Café Leonov, then turned off my lights and steered into the office complex next door. I backed my truck into a dark area aside the building, stepped out, and removed a few items from the steel box in my truck bed. The limo was fifty feet to my right. I blew out my breath, hopped a short fence, and sprinted forward, sliding to a stop at the limo's rear bumper. I shimmed under the gas tank, holding a flashlight in my teeth, and attached a magnetized tracking device to the frame behind the rear axle. When I pushed myself from beneath the car, I held my stun gun at the ready.

Seeing no one, I repeated the procedure on the second car, a black Dodge Charger. The third car was an older Ford, but I only had two tracking units. I grimaced, mad at myself for being unprepared. The devices were expensive and top-of-the-line, and once deployed they usually were not recoverable. But that was no excuse for not having at least three on hand.

I quickly took photos of both cars' license plates, then ran back to my truck and drove across the street to an apartment complex on Tropicana. I was able to find a spot in the shadows, directly across from the Café Leonov.

It was a little past one a.m. I sat staring at the restaurant through binoculars. It was too dark to make out much detail, but little things like the untrimmed shrubs and litter near the front steps made me question whether the place was actually in business. No light shone from the windows, and I hadn't heard any sounds from the interior when I was close to the building. But people were definitely inside, including the two men and the limo driver.

I set down the binoculars and spent a few minutes making sure the app on my cellphone was syncing with the tracking devices. My screen showed a map with two blinking lights. The next time either of the cars were driven, I would receive an alert and I could follow their movements. The batteries on the devices would last for roughly seventy-two hours.

I refocused the binoculars on the dark restaurant, expecting the front doors to open at any moment. After an hour I started wondering if they planned to spend the night there. I became drowsy to the point that I got outside and stood in the cold and jogged in place until my heart rate quickened. When I returned to my driver's seat I turned the radio up loud and did isometric exercises. When nothing happened by 2:30, I was ready to pack it in.

The front doors opened just as I was reaching to start my engine. The same two men I'd seen earlier walked out with the limo driver, followed by three women in furry jackets, short skirts, and high heels.

They all got in the limo and took off toward The Strip. I tailed them, lights off, until we neared Las Vegas Boulevard. But they didn't turn toward Mandalay Bay, like I suspected they would. Instead, they continued through the main intersection and got onto northbound I-15.

I followed them for five miles on the freeway, until they took the 95 exit, less than a mile from where I was staying at the Plaza. Then they drove east for another five miles, before turning into a tract of apartments and duplexes. It wasn't as bad as some neighborhoods I've seen, but it was worse than most. The darkness couldn't hide the dismal quality; graffiti scrawled on fences, parked cars that obviously weren't operable, dead lawns, and iron security bars on windows. This was a place where rents were cheap and the standard of living was somewhere between ghetto grade and lower middle-class. Gang activity and a high crime rate were a given.

The limo stopped in front of a duplex and the three women climbed out and went to the front door. From my spot down the street, I could see them in the porch light. One had long, curly, orange hair, definitely a wig, and looked middle-aged. The other two were younger.

After the women went inside, the limo drove back to the freeway and I followed it all the way back to The Strip. At three in the morning there was still plenty of traffic on the main drag, and I didn't have to worry about being spotted. I tailed them to the reception circle at Caesar's Palace and watched the driver open the door for the two men, who went into the lobby. Then the limo driver had a quick conversation with an attendant, passed him a few bills, and pulled forward and parked in a temporary zone.

I considered if there was anything to be gained by chatting with the driver, and quickly decided against it. My mind was dull with fatigue and I didn't want to do anything rash. If these men were the Volkovs, alerting them to my presence would be a dumb move. Staying in the shadows made far more sense for now. Besides, I could easily pick up their trail tomorrow.

"Goodnight, assholes," I muttered, and hit it back to my hotel.

9

T HE PIERCING RING OF my cell phone jolted me from a dead sleep at nine the next morning. When I saw it was Lillian McDermott, I declined the call and tried to fall back asleep, but a minute later she called again.

"Hello," I mumbled, lying on my back, eyes closed.

"Good morning, Mr. Reno."

When I didn't respond, she said, "I was expecting you to email me an update, as we discussed."

"Been busy," I croaked.

"And I'm sure your bill will reflect that. However, if you expect to get paid, you need to let me know exactly what kind of progress you're making."

I sat up on the edge of the bed. "Fine. I'll send you something by noon."

"Make sure you do."

"Anything else?"

"I'm sorry, did I wake you?"

"Yeah."

"What, if you don't mind me asking, are you still doing in bed at nine a.m.?"

I felt a surge of impatience in my chest, and for a moment I held the phone away, trying to resist the temptation to answer with a string of profanities.

"Mr. Reno?"

"I was sleeping. I was up until three-thirty last night."

"You weren't drinking, I hope."

I stood, gripping the phone tightly. "No, I wasn't, not that it's any of your goddamned business."

"It is my business. You are in my employ. If your billable hours include your time drunk or hungover, I will not pay you."

"For Christ's sake, lady, I haven't touched a drop since I began working your case. All right?"

"I suppose I have no choice but to take you at your word. I look forward to your report."

"Hey," I said. "How's Melanie doing?"

"We took her to see the specialists who cared for her during her coma."

"And?"

"Their test results are inconclusive, but you needn't concern yourself. Please focus on what I hired you to do."

"Is she there?"

"Good bye, Mr. Reno." The line went dead.

I tossed my phone on the bed, stretched, and rubbed my eyes. "Next time, you can leave me a voice mail," I muttered. Then I went to the lobby, gulped a cup of coffee, brought a second back to my room, and got to work on her damned report.

An hour later I was still sorting through the details, and I realized I was compiling a case log bloated with meaningless minutia. It wouldn't do for a client status report, but I kept at it, trying to capture every bit of data I'd come across. By noon I had three single-space pages typed. It took fifteen minutes to pare it down to a single-page version, which I then emailed to Lillian McDermott.

The task complete, I called Cody Gibbons, to see if he wanted to head out to Fremont Street and get lunch. When he answered his voice sounded groggy.

"You're still in bed?" I asked.

"I didn't get to sleep until four. I just woke up."

"Why were you up so late?" I asked, but even before the words left my mouth, I was thinking, *don't tell me you bedded down the LVPD woman you took to dinner.*

"Denise and I had a late dinner, and ended up talking for a long time."

"With clothes on, or off?"

"Dirt, you really do have a one-track mind. Is it that hard to believe we spent a few hours together, talking like mature adults?"

"Is that what happened?"

"For the most part, yeah. We started off over at this fancy joint at the Wynn, where the cocktails are twenty bucks a pop. We didn't get out of there until one o'clock, after I dropped about two bills on dinner."

"And then?"

"I mean, Denise and I have a lot in common. I felt like I'd known her all my life."

"Like a sister?"

"Ah, no, not exactly. To be honest, I haven't felt this way about a woman in a long time. So we ended up back here in my room, and I told her we shouldn't do anything foolish, and she kept saying I'm absolutely right. She's sitting at the desk and I'm on the bed, and she gets up and comes over, and I say no, and then I get up and go to the desk and she says no, and I swear we did that until we were freaking exhausted. When she finally left I felt like my schwantz was cast in concrete. Seriously, I was ready to explode."

"Wow. What next?"

"We're going to dinner again tonight."

"What's Abbey gonna say when she finds out?"

"Abbey? Why?"

"Seems a little awkward, you starting a romance with her boss."

"Why should it matter? Look, we're consenting adults, and we didn't just go jump in the sack. There's nothing to apologize for."

"Well, good."

"Damn right, it's good. Man, talk about chemistry."

"You want to get some grub?" I asked.

"Yeah, meet me in the lobby in fifteen."

• • •

We walked down Fremont Street, looking for a restaurant that offered lighter fare, because Cody claimed he wanted to lose a couple pounds. His weight ranged from 280 to 315 or so, but I could never tell the difference. He was wearing the huge army green winter jacket I'd bought him a few years ago after we nearly froze to death during an unfortunate encounter with a corrupt sheriff in South Lake Tahoe.

"I wonder what it'd be like to live here," he said, his hands shoved deep in his pockets.

"You'd consider moving from San Jose?"

"Why not? You moved from San Jose to Lake Tahoe, of all places. Besides, what's keeping me there? The traffic sucks, and they keep jacking up my property tax."

"Yeah, but you get plenty of work there, right?"

"I'm sure there's enough work to be had in Vegas."

We walked until stopping at a bar and grill with an empty patio out front.

"Does Abbey plan on staying here?" I asked.

"Maybe. If her internship goes well, Denise said LVPD might bring her aboard."

"She really wants to be a cop, huh?"

"It runs in her veins. Isn't that what you said?"

"Something like that," I replied, as we waded into the dark joint. Yellow light from the soffit illuminated the bar's glasslike mahogany surface. The stools were covered in leather and the chrome beer taps glowed with a promising sheen.

We sat at the far end, deep in the place, and Cody said to the bartender, "Bring me a light beer and a couple menus."

"Diet Coke," I said.

"Still punishing yourself?" Cody asked.

"You know I never drink until sundown."

"Your thirty days are up, right?"

"I might stay dry until my case is finished."

"What's the deal with that?"

I arched my back and flexed my shoulders, then exhaled and leaned forward on the bar. "I'm tailing some dudes I think might be Russian mobsters. Supposedly, they traffic in young girls, like the ten-year-old I'm looking for."

"Russian, huh? So, let's have a few shots of vodka and take the cleats to them."

"I don't even know who they are yet. All I've got is their license plates."

"Why do you think they deal in children?"

The bartender brought our drinks. Once he left, I gave Cody a rundown on my encounter with the pimp known as the McGillicuddy Man, and the results of my visit to the restaurant in Mandalay Bay and the Café Leonov.

"You captain-hooked him so hard he pissed his pants?"

"I guess I found his attitude a little annoying," I said.

"I imagine you did. Text me the license plates."

"Why?"

"Because I'll have Abbey run them. Then I'll ask Denise if they're on the radar."

A minute later our food arrived, and I watched him drain half his beer in a single swig, and take a bite out of a cheeseburger so big he could barely hold it with one hand. Cody's version of lighter fare.

"Look, you don't need to stick your neck out for me, Cody. I don't want you to."

"What? Running plates is nothing, and you know it. That look on your face, I don't know whether to laugh or worry about you." He patted me on the shoulder with his huge hand, causing some of my soft drink to splash onto the bar. "You're wound so tight you look like you're trying to crap out your penis." He laughed, then waved his hand at the bartender. "Bring me a shot of J.D. No, make that vodka, Stolichnaya."

The bartender placed the shot glass on the bar, and Cody held it up to the light and rotated it in his fingers. "Now, here's the deal, Dirt. I'm gonna help you on your case, and you're gonna lighten up. And once everything is a done deal, we're gonna go get hammered, because not only is that your inalienable right, but goddamn, you look like you need it."

I closed my eyes and sighed. "Okay, buddy," I said.

· · ·

When I got back to my room, I double-checked my cell to see if I'd missed an alert from the tracking devices. The Dodge Charger hadn't moved since I'd bugged it, and the limo was parked back at the Café Leonov. Apparently the owners of these vehicles kept a nocturnal schedule. That alone didn't mean they were involved in organized crime, but it did suggest they didn't have ordinary day jobs.

I moved to the desk and reviewed the notes I'd typed for Lillian McDermott, then I took the cargo ship manifest from my backpack. My eyes went to the two names I'd highlighted: Steven Castle and Brent Pederman. These were the only civilians listed on the manifest, and the only two American-sounding names.

I Googled Steven Castle and found references to over a dozen people by that name. I looked at Facebook profiles, Twitter accounts, and a website for a physician and a professional photographer. The ages ranged from nineteen to sixty-four and the online white pages listed addresses in seven different states.

Next, I typed Brent Pederman into Google. When I didn't get a single match, I clicked around but still couldn't find anything. Scratching my head, I logged onto a subscription people finder service and searched for Brent Pederman, and again found no one by that name. I then entered Steven Castle, and found seventeen separate individuals, most with phone numbers listed.

I began calling the numbers, introducing myself as an investigator looking for Brent Pederman. This aroused the curiosity of those who answered and resulted in some conversation, but it wasn't until the eighth call I found the right Steven Castle.

"Yeah, we were on that godforsaken ship together," he said.

"You returned from Africa to the U.S. on a cargo ship?" I clicked on his name and saw he was twenty-six years old and had an address in Irvine, about an hour east of Long Beach.

"I was lucky to get out of there, period, after I got fired and lost my passport."

"What were you doing in Africa?"

"I worked for an oil company. It was a great job until the boss's girlfriend tried to jump my bones. I resisted her, even though she had a rack that wouldn't quit, but it didn't make a difference. When he found out about it, he fired my ass on the spot. So I tried to get a flight out of there, but my passport was gone. I think the bastard might have taken it from my room."

"He was that pissed, huh?"

"Hell, he was drunk and threatened to kill me. I've already contacted an attorney about a lawsuit."

"So you paid the freighter to take you to Los Angeles?"

"Cost me two grand cash, but I made it."

"Even without a passport, huh?"

"Dude, it's Africa. Money talks."

"Do you know a Jeff Jordan?"

"No, who's he?"

"How about Brent Pederman?"

"Yeah, he was the only other white guy on the ship. He came aboard at Angola."

"Can you describe him?"

"About fifty. Big guy, around six-two and two hundred. Completely bald, not a hair on his head. You know who he looked like? That old time actor, Yul Brynner. You know him?"

"He was in The Magnificent Seven, right?"

"I think so. Anyway, he was the only guy onboard who spoke much English, so I tried to hang with him."

"Tried?"

"Yeah, he wasn't real friendly. Not a jerk, just distant. I'd ask him something simple, like what he did for a living or where he was headed, and he'd never answer. Sometimes he'd say philosophical stuff, like he was some kind of mystic. Once he said 'It's better to be silent than to speak for the sake of speaking.'"

"Kind of a conversation killer."

"You got that right."

"I'm trying to find him. Any idea how I can reach him, or where he might be?"

"No idea. That dude never said where he was coming from, or where he was going."

"Did he ever talk of friends or family?"

"Not a word."

"How about diamonds, or gold?"

"Nope."

"Anything else about him you can remember?"

"Not really. When we reached port, I was gonna say goodbye to him, but I never saw him, which was kind of weird. But, hey, I think I got a picture of him, if that'll help."

"He was okay with you taking his picture?"

"He never knew. I was taking a picture of the sunrise near the Panama Canal, and he ended up in it."

"Can you text it to me?"

"Sure."

We hung up and a minute later I looked at the photo. The sun was brilliant on the horizon, the ocean sparkling with bursts of silver. On the right side of the picture, a man in a T-shirt was leaning against the railing. His arms were muscular and his waist thin. His face was caught in profile, and it was true he bore a resemblance to Yul Brynner. I stared at the picture for a long time, hoping for an epiphany, but none came. I had no idea what role, if any, this man played in the death of Jeff Jordan.

After a minute, I dialed Walter McDermott's cell number.

"Yes, hello?"

"Walter, Dan Reno. May I speak with Melanie, please?"

"Yes, but she'll call you as soon as she gets out, if that's okay."

"Gets out of what?"

"She's having a follow up with her neurologist."

"Oh."

"It might be another half hour or so."

"Are you at the hospital?"

"Yes, we're at the University Medical Center."

"How about if I meet you there?"

"That'd be fine, I suppose. Come to the neurology waiting room."

• • •

I found Walter McDermott sitting cross legged in a white-walled room on the second floor of the hospital. A middle-aged woman and a teenage boy were speaking in hushed tones to a reception nurse at a desk in front of the room. The boy stared vacantly, and when he reached to scratch his arm, his movement looked awkward, as if his muscles were out of sync with his brain commands.

"Afternoon, Walter," I said, sitting beside him.

He closed the magazine resting on his lap and moved it aside. "Hello, Dan." He wore corduroy pants, purple socks with an argyle pattern, and leather sandals.

"I have a picture I'd like to show you," I said, opening my computer. I turned the screen toward him. "Do you recognize this man?"

He adjusted his spectacles and peered at my notebook. "No, I don't," he said. "Should I?"

"I don't know," I said.

"What does he have to do with your investigation?"

"I think Jeff Jordan may have met him, about two weeks before Jeff was killed."

"But you don't know who he is?"

"He goes by Brent Pederman. Ever hear the name?"

"No."

"I doubt it's his real name, anyway."

"Intriguing."

I closed my computer and looked at my watch. "Will Melanie be out soon?"

"She should be."

Neither of us spoke for a minute, until Walter said, "Dan, I want to thank you for your patience with Lillian. Ever since the crime, she's not been herself. Please understand, she's a good woman, but I think she needs somebody to project her anger upon. It used to be me, but now, apparently, you're serving that role."

"I don't deserve it."

"I know that, of course. But it's not about deserving, is it? I've suggested she see a therapist to help her deal with this."

"What did she say to that?"

"You might be surprised to know she agreed. She actually may see the same psychiatrist Melanie has seen."

"Melanie's seen a head-shrink?"

Walter chuckled briefly, then said, "Yes, her neurologist works closely with the head psychiatrist here."

At that moment a door opened, and Melanie walked out, followed by a slight, balding man in a white lab coat. Walter and I stood as they approached.

"Melanie's recovery seems to be going well," the doctor said without preamble, looking down at his clipboard. His voice was very soft, and I had to strain to hear him. "I see nothing to be alarmed about. Understand, full recovery from a traumatic brain injury may take many months, or even years."

"So, we should expect little deviances in her functioning moving forward?" Walter asked.

"Yes, that would be normal," he said.

Melanie stood with her hands clasped in front of her thighs. Her jeans were low cut and tight on her curvaceous hips, and I thought they were probably new. Her face was framed by her long, shiny hair, which fell to the sides of her cheeks and onto her chest.

"Your prognosis is optimistic, then?" I said.

"The brain is a dynamic organ," the doctor replied, his tone shifting to one of rote recital. "It has an innate ability to adapt and change with time. After injury, the brain recovers by forming new connections between neurons. We call this 'plasticity.' It occurs naturally in everyone; it's how our brains evolve as we react to varying stimuli over time. This dynamic is more pronounced when recovering from an injury. In Melanie's case, her exposure to stimuli has shifted her plasticity into overdrive. This is a healthy sign."

Melanie waited patiently, eyes downcast, while the doctor referred to her in the third person. When she looked up, her expression was both timid and hopeful.

The doctor turned to leave, and I followed him to the door.

"Excuse me, doc," I said quietly, handing him a card. "I've been hired by the family to find out who harmed Melanie."

He looked up at me, his eyes quizzical. His skin was pale, and he struck me as a man who spent little time outdoors. "Yes?" he said.

"I'd like to speak with the psychiatrist Melanie has seen. Can you help me arrange it?"

He hesitated, then said, "It would probably be best to get Melanie's permission."

I looked to where Melanie and Walter stood together. "That's okay," I said. "I'll talk to them and we'll get back to you."

The neurologist left us and I asked Melanie to take a seat while I pulled my computer from my backpack. I brought up the photo of the man on the boat.

"Have you seen this man before?" I asked.

She took my PC and balanced it on her lap, then tilted the screen back and stared down at it.

"Melanie?" Walter said.

It took ten seconds for Melanie to raise her head. "I think this person is related to Jeff," she said.

"Why?" I asked.

"Look," she said, pointing at the man's profile. "His face—it's older and thinner than Jeff's, but the nose and the chin. If Jeff was twenty years older, twenty pounds lighter, and bald, with a suntan, this is what he would look like."

I looked over her shoulder and watched her fingers trace the image on my screen. The only pictures I'd seen of Jeff Jordan were postmortem shots shown to me by the Cedar City detective. None that I remembered showed a clear view of his profile.

"Do either of you have any pictures of Jeff we could use to compare?"

"Possibly, back at home," Walter said.

"I do," Melanie said. She handed me my computer and pulled a cellphone from her purse. "Just got it yesterday. All my files were backed up on the cloud, so I didn't lose a thing."

"Your old phone is gone?" I said, feeling stupid as it occurred to me I'd never seen Melanie with a phone in her hands.

"I never saw it again after I was knocked out."

While Melanie looked through her photo gallery, I considered the likelihood the intruders had taken Melanie's phone. Since I'd searched the house and found only Jeff's phone, it was a reasonable assumption that Melanie's had been stolen. But what value would it be to the intruders, if any?

"Give me your number," I said.

"Okay," she said, then she held up her phone. "Here's a good one."

I looked at a photo of a smiling Jeff Jordan. He held an electric drill in one hand and in the background I recognized their land in Cedar City. It was only a partial profile, and his face was a little too small to see clearly.

"Here," Melanie, expanding the image with her fingers. "Hold it next to your picture and tell me you don't see the resemblance."

I did as she said, noting the shapes of their heads, the jawlines, the eyes, the ears. There was some similarity, but not enough to indicate the two were blood relatives. I handed her phone back.

"You don't see it?"

I shook my head. "Not really."

She scanned through more pictures in her gallery, then said, "Here we go. Look at *this* one."

She had expanded the image to show only Jeff's face. It was a clean, unsmiling profile. I compared it to the image on my computer, and this time there was no doubt.

"Jeff's older brother?" I said.

"No, I've met him and he looks different."

"Who, then?"

She shrugged. "His father?"

•   •   •

We walked out of the hospital and I watched them get into Walter's car, then I went back inside and returned to the second floor reception desk.

"I was just speaking with the neurologist here," I said to the attendant. "I'd like to make an appointment with the psychiatrist he works with."

"That would be Doctor Marques. You'll need to contact him directly." She handed me a business card.

"Is he here, at the hospital?"

"Not today. He usually sees patients at his office, over on Sahara."

I looked at the address on the card. "Thanks," I said, and went to my truck and got on the freeway. The temperature had risen to nearly seventy, but the dry air felt brittle, as if it might shatter and be invaded by harsh cold at any moment.

Ten minutes later I parked at an office complex and found the suite for Doctor Felix Marques. I went into the carpeted lobby and asked the woman at the desk if the doctor was available.

"He's with a patient now. Would you like to make an appointment?"

"Actually, I'd like to speak with him about a murder case involving one of his patients." I handed her my card.

She looked up at me, a cynical smile beginning on her face, as if she'd heard everything and wasn't impressed by my request. But then she said, "Take a seat if you like. He'll be done in fifteen minutes. I'll let him know you're here."

The décor in the lobby looked like it was designed to soothe patients with frazzled nerves. It was done in earth tones, from the green carpet to the tan walls and the painted landscapes on the walls. The couch and four chairs in the room were matching pieces with orange cushions. After a minute, I noticed the sound of waves and birds chirping, coming from invisible speakers and set at a volume so low it was almost indiscernible.

As I waited, I wondered if the shrink would grant me an audience, or if I was just wasting time. All casework involved this type of fundamental challenge; deciding who was worth talking to, and what actions would deliver results. If I made the right choices, I could conclude cases in a timely manner and provide good value to my clients. That would enhance my reputation and result in more business. Conversely, billing clients for unproductive hours would ultimately hurt my ability to make a living. This was not a subject I took lightly, because Candi had mentioned having kids, and in the back of my mind I had no doubt the conversation would be recurring. I also knew that parenthood meant she would stop working, at least temporarily, and I'd need to work more consistently.

I closed my eyes and reminded myself that my job requires the ability to wait with a purpose. Lack of patience is a trait that separates amateur investigators from pros. But patience is only a virtue if the waiting is worthwhile. And I was beginning to question my reasons for being here. There were many other things I could be doing.

I pushed my doubts aside, opened my computer, and reviewed my case notes, trying to immerse myself in the two separate investigative lines I was following; first, the who and why of Jeff's meeting at the Port of Los Angeles, and second, my effort to find Mia. Hopefully, these paths would soon intersect. If not, I'd need to quickly recalibrate.

The door at the far side of the room opened and a woman who looked anorexic beneath her long overcoat came out and walked past me to the exit. The receptionist went through the door and closed it behind her.

"Mr. Reno?" she said a minute later, holding the door open. "Doctor Marques will see you now. He has fifteen minutes until his next appointment."

I went in and stood before an oversized antique desk with scrolled, ornate woodwork, but the man behind it seemed all wrong. Perhaps I subconsciously expected a Sigmund Freud lookalike, or maybe a heavy-set, scholarly type, but Doctor Felix Marques was no older than me, and looked younger, mainly due to facial skin that was so smooth I doubted it had ever been touched by a razor. His complexion was quite fair, almost milky white, in stark contrast to his jet black hair, which was long and combed back. He wore a blue knit sweater with yellow stripes across the chest.

On the wall behind the desk hung a number of diplomas. Among them I noticed not one, but three PhDs: psychology, psychiatry, and sociology.

"That's one hell of a desk you got there," I said, smiling.

He stood and offered his hand. "It's been in my family for three centuries. What can I do for you, Mr. Reno?"

I blinked. He had pronounced my name correctly. But I was more curious about his credentials. "Three PhDs?" I asked.

"Yes. I began college in Spain, at twelve years old. Please, take a seat."

I sat across from him. "I've studied criminology as well," he said, "so my natural curiosity couldn't resist when I saw your card. What is it you'd like to discuss?"

"Your patient, Melanie Jordan, and the crime committed against her and her family."

"Ah. She has told me of it, but those details are bound by doctor-patient confidentiality."

"Let me ask this in a very general way, then, Doctor Marques. Is there anything she said suggesting she might have any idea who killed her husband?"

He shook his head. "She's said nothing of the sort. That much I can assure you."

"How about regarding her missing daughter? Any insights she's shared that might help me find her?"

"She's obviously distressed by the disappearance of her daughter, as any parent would be. But she has said nothing to indicate any particular suspicions."

I leaned forward and noticed his fingernails looked professionally manicured. "If she's said anything you think might help bring her husband's murderer to justice, would you reveal it?"

"Certainly, with her permission. But I think she's fully cooperating with you, isn't she?"

"As far as I know."

"She says she trusts you."

I paused and leaned back. The doctor seemed willing to cooperate, and didn't seem at all full of himself, despite his academic achievements and obvious intellect. He also had a certain androgynous quality that was a distraction, although I didn't think he was gay. But it did make him hard to read.

"Let me share with you something that happened at her house in Cedar City, doc," I said. "I was staying in her guest room, and in the middle of the night she comes in, her face all done up, stark naked except for high heels, and tries to jump in bed with me. While doing this, she referred to herself as Sasha. I fought her off, and the next morning she was back to being Melanie, with no recollection of what happened."

The doctor stared at me, his quick brown eyes scrutinizing. "This really happened?"

"Yes, sir."

"Fascinating. It could be a sign of trauma-induced multiple personality disorder."

"I've never heard of such a thing."

"It's rare, or more accurately, theoretical. The precursor to MPD would need to exist prior to the injury, from childhood experience. The question is, how does a brain trauma interact with latent MPD? This is a largely unstudied topic."

"So, Melanie likely had MPD brewing before she was struck?"

"Almost certainly. Brain trauma can cause many problems, but there is no known case of it being a sole cause of multiple personality."

"It sounds like you're suggesting she must have had some horrible sexual experience as a child."

"Given the emergence of Sasha, yes. But horrible is a subjective term. What's important is she perceived something so negatively that she couldn't consciously accept it. So she suppressed it deep in her subconscious. This is the dynamic that results in the manifestation of a secondary personality."

When I didn't respond, he said, "I'm sorry if this isn't the feedback you're looking for."

I took a deep breath in an effort relieve a knot of unease that had taken hold in my gut. I exhaled slowly and decided to change the subject.

"Here's another angle," I said. "Melanie's husband believed in conspiracy theories, and thought a secret society of powerful people were plotting to bring about anarchy, and then take control of the world. He thought the economy would collapse, the dollar would become valueless, and the masses would fight for food and energy. He felt so sure of this he was storing enough food to last for years, and had built a home powered by natural energy. His goal was to be totally self-reliant."

"A doomsday prepper," Marques said.

"Right. But I don't think Melanie really bought into it. I'm thinking, maybe the stress of being forced into an alternative lifestyle might play into her mental issues."

Marques shook his head in disagreement. "As I said, the genesis of MPD is always from childhood. While Melanie may have felt stress about her living situation, that alone is not a significant causal factor. More likely, the death of her husband, along with the disappearance of her daughter, would have preempted the incidence of a secondary personality. But again, the root cause must be traced further back, to traumatic events in her younger years."

"Are you aware of any of these events?"

"No, but Melanie has not come to me for psychoanalysis."

"Well," I said after a moment, suddenly regretting my visit. I began to push myself out of the chair, then stopped.

"Just out of curiosity," I said, "these doomsday preppers and their conspiracy theories. What do you think about it?"

The doctor looked at his watch and clasped his hands. "Before the Internet, the common man relied on mainstream media for the information that forms our values and cultural norms. While network news stations, newspapers, and print magazines are not wholly unbiased, for the most part they adhere to traditional journalistic standards. That means these media make an effort to draw a clear line between factual reporting and editorial content."

"That doesn't apply much to the Internet, does it?"

"No, Mr. Reno, it does not. The Internet is an unfiltered forum for information of every conceivable sort. In many ways, it's wonderfully beneficial to society. But there is another side to the coin. There are those who use it for nefarious purposes; a blatant example is the recruiting of terrorists by ISIS. But perhaps just as harmful are sites that peddle fake news, which guides the unsuspecting populace away from truth and reality."

"I'm not sure how all this applies to conspiracy theories."

"Please forgive my prolixity, I'll do my best to be succinct. There are a plethora of sites that seek to convince us of notions commonly called conspiracy theories. These sites often present their claims as irrefutable and disbelievers are characterized as sheep or lemmings. They insist that the data upon which they base their assertions is factual, but what they usually do is take a small collection of facts, and then add a gross amount of supposition in an effort to make the facts fit their preconceived narrative. The conclusion reached by all conspiracy theories is the same: a clandestine group of ultra-rich businesspeople, politicians, and intellectuals is conspiring to tear down society, and then rebuild it in their own vision, and under their full control."

"What kind of people buy into this stuff?"

"There are a few different profiles, but in every case the ego is at play. Take ex-cons, for instance. They may be unhappy with their lot in life, and thus adopt a mindset that says, "Well, my life's bad, but we'll all be doomed soon enough, so no one is really better off than me." This is the ego's way of combatting feelings of inadequacy. Next, consider the man who has failed in his career. He may buy into conspiracies, based on a general distrust of those in power, as he feels they are responsible for his failings. Again, the ego is being appeased, this time by claiming higher understanding, as in, "I've been victimized by evil forces, but I know what they're up to." And sometimes, even relatively successful and prosperous people become doomsday preppers. They do so not only because their life experiences have taught them to distrust others, but also because they are instinctively distrustful, or even paranoid. In this case, embracing the conspiracy narrative elevates the individual's sense of security, and also superiority and rightness, which is a drug the ego can never resist."

"Kind of bizarre, huh?"

"Not really, when you consider the human psyche. I should also add that education level is a factor. Those who have a college degree tend to be more trusting of institutionalized power, as they've been successful within the system. So they gravitate away from conspiracy theories. Likewise, those without the advantage of higher education are more prone to distrust our institutions, since they've not benefitted from the system. These people also at some level need to validate their intelligence and worthiness. Subscribing to conspiracies allows them to feel they have inside information that only a privileged few are savvy enough to understand."

The door opened, and the receptionist said, "Doctor, your four-thirty is here."

"Thanks again," I said, standing.

"My pleasure," he replied. "I feel sorry for Melanie, and I like her."

"So do I."

"I hope in some small way our conversation will help you with your case."

"Hard to say," I said.

• • •

My phone rang just as I reached my truck.

"Hey, Cody," I said, leaning against the fender.

"Abbey ran the plates. She wants to discuss it with you."

"Why?"

"Because the owners are soulless douche bags someone should have made into fertilizer a long time ago."

"Sounds promising. Are you at the Plaza?"

"Yeah."

"I'll be there in ten minutes or so."

We hung up, and I stood at my bumper and looked at where the sun was sitting low on a distant ridge. The doctor's lecture on the psychology of doomsday preppers hadn't been particularly helpful, but his comments about Melanie gave me reason for pause.

Might it be possible that whatever occurred in Melanie's childhood somehow played into the crime against her and her family? It seemed like a stretch, and I told myself it was an unlikely notion, and to resist the temptation to call the McDermotts. But my job required turning over every stone, and not doing so would be a sign of laziness, or worse, incompetence. So, despite my reservations, I tapped their number into my cell. I was hoping Walter would pick up. No such luck.

"Yes?" Lillian said.

"It's Dan Reno, Mrs. McDermott."

"Yes, I know. What is it?"

I hesitated, then said, "There's no easy way to ask this, so…"

"Get to the point, please."

"I have reason to believe Melanie suffered some sort of sexual trauma as a child. That could mean any number of things."

"What are you suggesting?"

"She may have witnessed a rape, or simply saw someone close to her having sex. Or maybe it was something worse."

"Why on god's green earth would you think that has any relevance to what I've hired you to do?"

"I like to know what I'm dealing with."

When Lillian replied, her uppity diction was replaced by a hard, southern twang that shocked me. "Melanie's childhood has nothin' to do with your case, you nosey son of a bitch. So quit wasting my fuckin' time and pull your nose out of your ass and find my granddaughter. I hope that's plain enough for you."

The line went dead before I could reply. I stared at my phone and said, *"Lady, what's your problem?"*

But maybe I should have asked myself the same question, because she was probably right; I was almost certainly off on an irrelevant tangent. By calling her, I'd admitted as much, and had foolishly walked into a stiff backhand.

I kicked at the dirt edging the lot and vowed to not let Lillian McDermott get to me. I couldn't tell if I was angrier at her or myself. My mouth was suddenly flooded with a sour taste, and I hawked a stream of saliva into the weeds. I stood there for a minute, trying to discount her verbal attack. Slowly, as I mulled the abrupt transformation of her voice, my ire receded. When she started cursing, it was as if another person was speaking. I could only assume the English professor with the deprecating attitude came from a far different background than she'd been portraying.

As I got in my truck and drove off, I wondered what Lillian McDermott would think when she saw my next case update and learned I'd spoken to the shrink she planned to see. She'd probably take exception to it, but that was her problem, not mine.

. . .

When I got to the Plaza lobby, I looked toward the food court, but then spotted Cody sitting at the casino bar with his daughter. I walked over and saw they were both drinking highballs, probably gin or vodka tonics.

"Cody, Abbey," I said.

"Dirty," Cody exclaimed eagerly, "pull up a stool, over there next to Abbey."

Abbey wore tan slacks and polished black shoes with a steel toe and thick tread. They looked like standard issue footwear for patrolmen. I didn't know if a female version was available, but apparently that didn't concern Abbey. Her shirt was blue, and the sleeves were cut short. The muscles in her shoulders were more pronounced than I was used to seeing in a woman.

I sat next to her and watched while she hit off her drink through a straw. When she set it down, she said, "What's your interest in the Volkov family?"

"The cars are registered to them?"

"You got it."

"A lowlife pimp told me they deal in underage girls."

"They run an escort service, but that's probably just the tip of the iceberg. They're also suspected of money laundering, extortion, human trafficking, and of course, drugs."

"Why not bust them for the escorts?" I asked.

"Prostitution is quasi-legal in Nevada. LVPD mostly ignores it unless it's connected to other crimes."

"I see."

"What's your plan?" she asked.

I crossed my arms and stared at the bottles behind the bar. "Follow them around, see what comes up."

"I'd like to join you."

I laughed. "No, sorry. No."

"Hey, Dan," Cody said. "You got nothing to worry about. Abbey wants to help nail these scumbags."

"That's all well and good, but Abbey, it's not a good idea."

"Why not?" she said.

"It could be dangerous, plus I don't want to drag you into something that could screw up your internship."

"What, are you suggesting you might break the law? Is that how it works for you private dicks?"

I took a breath and exhaled. "My rule book might be a little different than any police force's. Let's just leave it at that."

"That's well put, Dan," Cody said, a grin on his face, and it occurred to me he'd probably been sitting at the bar for a while. "Very well put, indeed!"

At that moment my cell beeped, and I looked down and saw an alert indicating the black Charger was on the move. It was a little past five p.m.

"I need to get going," I said.

"Bullshit," Abbey said, her eyes ablaze. "Listen, I'm not a cop, I'm just doing a part-time internship. You want to bring the Volkovs down, I'll look the other way if things get a little rough."

"My job is not to bring the Volkovs down. I'm only looking at them as possibly holding a kidnapped girl. I want to recover the girl, nothing else."

"I've got no problem with that. I want to be part of it."

I rubbed my forehead. "Would you excuse me for a minute, Abbey? I'd like to speak to your father privately."

She rolled her eyes. "Whatever."

I eased off my stool and walked behind Cody. "Come on," I said. He followed me deeper into the casino until we found two chairs at a vacant card table.

"What's up?" he asked.

"I'm following the Russian mob, hoping to track down a kidnapped girl, and your daughter wants to tag along?"

"Hell, she wants to do more than tag along. Give her a gun and she'll start blasting away."

"Would you be serious, please? Can't you talk some sense into her?"

He put his hand on the back of his neck and looked at me sheepishly. "I've been trying to impart my fatherly advice, but she's really not interested. I guess I can't blame her."

"Well, I'm gonna go tell her thanks, but no, thanks."

"Hold up, Dirt, think this through for a minute. Abbey is gung-ho to learn the business. Plus, she has access to police databases. She can give you the skinny on the Volkovs, save you a lot of time and energy. She's already pulled their files."

I shook my head. "Bad idea."

"Look, what have you got planned for tonight? A little surveillance, right? Bring her along, as a favor to me, okay? Just one favor. What harm can come of it?"

For a moment I was stunned, as the realization set in that I could not turn down my best friend, a man who'd saved my life and had actually taken bullets meant for me. Then I suddenly thought, why not sidestep the issue, take the night off, just say, *forget about the Volkovs for now, let's go to the bar and have a few drinks.* For an instant it sounded so tempting I felt the words ready to burst from my lips. But I swallowed the impulse, and it hit my stomach with a hollow thud.

"All right," I said, hearing the defeat in my voice. "Get your gear and let's go."

"Me? Are you nuts? I've got dinner with Denise tonight."

"What?"

"I really appreciate this, Dirt. Text me and let me know how it goes. I'm sure you and Abbey will be great together!"

•   •   •

Fifteen minutes later Abbey and I were in my truck. She wore a dark blue jacket that was free of insignia but looked police issue none the less.

"You need to lose the coat and shoes," I said.

"Why?"

"Because you're trying to look like a cop, and that's a problem."

"What, are we going undercover?"

"If you want to call it that. I don't want to give the people I'm following reason to suspect they're being watched."

"Until when?"

"Hopefully never."

"Well, you'll need to take me to my place, then."

I drove five miles south, toward the UNLV campus, and parked in front of a nearby apartment building. "Make it quick, please," I said.

She went inside, and I checked my phone. The black Charger had returned to the Café Leonov. My app showed it had traveled down the block to a strip mall. The trip had only taken twenty minutes.

Abbey returned promptly. She had traded her polished black shoes for low heels and wore a brown jacket that was stylish but not flashy.

"Good enough?" she asked.

"Yeah, fine," I said, pulling from the curb. "The license plate numbers I sent—give me the rundown."

She removed a pad of paper from her purse. "The limo is Serj Volkov's. Twenty-nine years old. I pulled his record."

"How about the other two?"

"The Dodge Charger is also registered to Serj Volkov. The Ford belongs to Lexi Voronin. He's on parole, has a long record."

"You took their files from the squad room?"

"No, but I took pictures of every page, then printed them out. Here," she said, holding up a manila folder.

I raised my eyebrows. "Nice work."

She didn't respond, but when I glanced over her eyes were smiling.

We drove a mile to the Café Leonov and parked across the street. It was nearing 6:30, and the restaurant was lit up, the parking lot scattered with cars. The limo, Charger, and the older Ford were parked off to the side.

"I'd like to know who owns this joint," I said. "I'll do a search when I'm in front of my computer."

"I bet I can find out quicker than you," she said. "I can probably do it on my phone."

"I doubt it," I said, but five quiet minutes later she said, "I got it. It's owned by a company, no individual listed."

"Figures."

"Why?"

"Organized crime members always try to hide their property from the government. They hide behind dummy corporations. It helps them launder income and stay off the radar."

"I'll see if I can find out more about this company."

"Do it later. Instead, tell me everything you've learned about the Volkovs and Lexi Voronin."

"You could try asking politely."

I looked over and tried to smile.

"How familiar are you with the Russian Mafia?" she asked.

I stared at the restaurant, watching another car pull in. "Not very," I admitted.

"Lucky for you, I'm writing a paper on the subject, so I've been studying their history. You interested?"

"Go ahead," I said.

"All right. The Russian mob never achieved the pop culture status of the Italian Mafia, but the scope of Russian organized crime make the Italians look like small potatoes. The Russian crime families go back to the seventeen hundreds, but really developed during the Soviet era, which began in

1917. Lenin, the original leader of communist Russia, tried to wipe out the gangs, but he died in 1924. Stalin took over, and his solution was to send millions of suspected criminals to the gulags. It was there the gangs became better organized, forming into regimented groups with bosses and ranks."

"Okay, and then?"

"So, check this out: when World War Two started, the Russians needed more soldiers, so they offered the millions of crooks in the gulags their freedom if they'd fight for the Soviets. But this was against the anti-government policy of the *Bratva,* which is what the crime gangs called themselves. It means brotherhood in Russian. Many of the *Bratva* couldn't resist the opportunity to leave the gulags, but Stalin royally screwed them by sending them back after the war. The hardline mobsters who'd stayed in the gulags saw them as traitors, and labeled them *cyka,* Russian for bitch. The *cyka* were forced to the bottom of the gang food chain, and eventually they banded together and formed their own families. This resulted in eight years of prison warfare between the original families and the upstarts. The gulag guards encouraged the daily killings, as they saw it a convenient way to keep the prison population under control. Nice, huh?"

I shrugged, keeping my eyes on the restaurant.

"When Stalin died in 1953, Khrushchev became the Soviet leader, and he released eight million inmates from the gulags. The gangs hit the streets and soon realized the communist government was so corrupt it made more sense to work with them rather than against them. Then Brezhnev became the Soviet leader in 1964, and the corruption grew even worse. The criminal underworld became so entrenched in Soviet commerce that they basically ran Russia jointly with government officials. By the 1980s, the Soviet economy was predominantly a black market."

"But the Soviet Union collapsed in the early nineties, right?" I said.

"Right," Abbey said, her voice growing more animated. "And that's when the shit really hit the fan. The end of communism and the emerging capitalism basically awarded the Russian economy to the mobsters. Ex-KGB goons and Afghan war criminals went to the crime bosses for jobs. Ever since, Russia has been, for the most part, a criminal state."

"But what about Russia's current leader, Trump's buddy, Vladimir Putin? Has he done anything about it?"

Abbey laughed sarcastically. "He's ex-KGB and has been running the show there for the last eighteen years. His personal net worth is hard to verify, but some estimates put it at somewhere between forty and eighty billion dollars. Draw your own conclusions."

"He ain't making that much on a politician's salary."

"No kidding. Putin may be the richest crook in the history of the world."

"That's somebody else's problem. How about filling me in on Serj Volkov and Lexi Voronin?"

She put her folder on her lap and licked a finger. "You might think I'm appalled by the history of Russia," she said. "And while that's true, it really hits home when you learn two guys like this are running around our streets."

"Hold on," I said, as the three men I'd followed the night before came out of the Café Leonov. I grabbed my binoculars and handed them to Abbey. "Recognize them?"

"The older one, no," she said, as they walked toward the white limo. "The tall guy with the crew cut looks like Serj Volkov. The dark-haired one is definitely Lexi Voronin."

"Looks like Lexi's the driver," I said.

"That's odd," Abbey said.

"Why?" I started my truck.

"He did a year in state prison for computer fraud, related to money laundering. It says he has an accounting degree."

"Someone's got to do the driving," I said.

"He was also suspected of two murders, and arrested for one, but there wasn't enough evidence to prosecute."

"Bean counter, killer, driver. He wears a lot of hats. Anything in his jacket involve prostitution or child porn?"

"No."

"How about Serj?"

"He has two arrests for assault. Both times the charges were dropped. The victims and witnesses all recanted their statements."

"That's not an encouraging sign."

"Get this: I knew one of the victims, Chris Towne. He was a student here. His family owned a junkyard, and the Volkovs wanted the business, but the family wouldn't sell. So, Serj Volkov attacked Chris with a baseball bat. Broke his arms and legs. He was on the UNLV tennis team, but now he'll be lucky to walk normal again."

"Did the Volkovs get the junkyard?"

"The family sold out and left town. But when I checked, the business wasn't registered to the Volkovs."

"It's called 'fronting points.' Like I said before, mobsters try to avoid legal ownership of their businesses, especially if they're hiding cash flow from the IRS, as they always are. So they get someone they can control to sign the paperwork. This makes it more difficult for prosecutors to trace their income."

"I know what fronting points means," Abbey said.

The limo turned onto the boulevard, and I gave them a hundred yards before following. When we reached The Strip, they turned left, and a minute later they turned onto the road leading to Mandalay Bay. I turned off my headlights and tailed them at a distance.

"They're heading to the main entrance," I said. "When we get there, I'll get out and keep an eye on them, and you go park my truck. I'll text you where to meet me."

"Why don't I follow them and you park?" Abbey said.

"Have you ever tailed anyone?"

"How hard can it be?"

"Following someone is easy. The hard part is not being made."

Abbey didn't look happy about it, but before she could reply we came around a bend and I saw the limo stopped at the brightly lit reception circle. The pear-shaped, bearded man and the crewcut blond Abbey thought was Serj Volkov climbed out.

I stopped on the side of the road. "Go park and come to the casino," I said, then hopped down to the street.

The two Russians went through the glass doors, and I quick-stepped, catching up to them as they reached the end of the lobby and entered the casino. I had no doubt they were here to conduct business of some sort, but I wasn't particularly optimistic about tailing them around this joint. If they were truly dealing in underage girls, this seemed an unlikely place to learn about it. They might be just heading over to the Red Square for a free dinner and drinks. For me, that would mean sitting around for a wasteful hour or two.

Or not, I reminded myself. *You don't know what you don't know,* my first boss used to say. He was an older man, a friend of my late father's, and of all the lessons he taught me, that one sentence is what I most often remember. His approach to investigative work was stealthy, methodical, and infinitely patient. When less disciplined investigators hit dead ends, he would persevere, probing from different angles until something cracked. He rarely failed to solve a case.

We traversed the gaming floor, but instead of heading across to the Red Square, the two men stopped at a circular bar in the middle of the casino.

At the bar were three women. Two of them could have been sisters; they both were large breasted blondes. Their big hair might have been phony, but they had the same prominent chin and deep set eyes.

I sat at a slot machine. The two blondes were quite pretty and had a distinctive look I thought was definitely Eastern European. The other woman was a dark Latina with flowing locks of black hair. All three wore short skirts and spiked heels. They were obviously prostitutes, which struck me as strange, because the upper echelon of Vegas casinos had banned hookers from their floors years ago. While this wasn't a law, it had been communicated plainly to those in the trade, who, for practical reasons, gravitated elsewhere.

Serj Volkov and his older counterpart, who acted like he was in charge, stood talking to the call girls. The conversation appeared civil but not necessarily friendly. One of the women handed an envelope to Serj. He peeked at its contents and frowned, then said something to the pear-shaped man. He shook his head and spoke to the ladies, who became stone-faced.

My phone buzzed, and I saw Abbey's text message: *where are you?*

I texted her back, but when I looked up, the men were on the move.

The casino floor was somewhat crowded but not as congested as it might be later in the evening. The flow of meandering people made it easy to follow the men without risk of being spotted. When we reached the far end of the floor, I texted Abbey: *red square restaurant.*

I was leaning on a counter next to a ticket office outside the restaurant when she showed up a minute later. Her face was flushed from the quick walk.

"They're inside," I said, nodding toward the Red Square.

"Why don't we go in?"

"All right."

She took my arm. "We'll pretend to be a couple."

"I'm old enough to be your father."

"Just barely. And I look mature, so don't worry about it."

We walked past the hostess and into the bar. Every seat in the room was taken, but a couple right at the entrance stood to leave as soon as we entered. "Here," I said, and quickly sat at the small cocktail table. Abbey took the chair across from me. We had a view of the bar, where the two men stood, sipping what I assumed were shots of top shelf vodka.

"What are they doing?" she asked.

"Standing around like they own the place."

"What do you mean?"

"It's their demeanor. They might have a stake in the ownership."

"I'll look into it." She began poking at her phone.

"I'm sending you a picture of the older man," I said.

"Should be easy enough to identify him," she replied.

"Here they come," I said. They began toward us, but veered right, into a dark alcove where a waitress had just been. When they didn't reappear after a minute, I said, "I think they've gone into the kitchen."

Abbey looked up just as a cocktail waitress approached.

"Two Smirnoffs and two waters, please," I said.

"Got it," she said, and hurried away.

"I prefer my vodka with tonic," Abbey said.

"It's not for you to drink. Pour it in your water glass."

"What a waste."

When I didn't respond, Abbey said, "You think the Volkovs have an office in the back somewhere?"

"I don't know. But they definitely do at the Café Leonov."

"Well, they've got to know someone here."

"Either an associate, or someone they're extorting," I said.

"You want to go back and see what we can find out?"

I shook my head. "No."

"What, then?"

"I'm gonna follow them. It'll probably be a late night. If you're not up for it, I understand."

"I'm not going anywhere," she said. "You should stop frowning. Smile, look like you're enjoying yourself."

I sat back and let my face go slack, then I laughed as if she'd said something funny. "Good point," I said.

"My dad said you could be a little intense."

"Let's talk," I said. "About anything. Tell me about your school." Filling the space with chatter would be less conspicuous than sitting in grim concentration, which I realized was my current state of mind.

Abbey started talking, and I smiled and asked questions and tried to behave as if I were on a date. Her chatter was light and friendly, and after a while it struck me that despite her tough exterior, she was really just a young girl, barely out of her teens. Some of the things she said were silly in a teasing way, as if she was hoping I'd respond in kind. I began finding it hard to resist the temptation. Then the waitress brought our drinks, and I snatched her shot glass.

"Hey!"

I guzzled my water and discreetly poured both vodkas onto the ice cubes.

"I thought you were the hard drinking P.I."

"Cody said that?"

"He told me a few stories."

"Well, everything has its time and place."

Thirty minutes passed, and it became increasingly easy to chat with Abbey. She kept trying to mock me, but I found it entertaining rather than offensive. Her tone was flirtatious, but not seriously so.

"So, just curious, how do you get your jobs?" she asked.

"Mostly by referral."

"The family that hired you, they're from Utah?"

"No, San Jose."

"Is that where they are now?"

"No. Melanie Jordan, the victim, is staying with her parents here in Vegas."

"Is that right? Could I meet her?"

"Why?"

"Well," she said, clicking her nails on her water glass. "It's a girl-girl thing. Maybe she would tell me things she wouldn't tell you."

"I doubt it."

"What have you got to lose?"

I scratched my forearm. "I don't want to muddle things."

"Where are they staying?"

"A hotel near the airport," I said.

"Which hotel?"

I shook my head. "Forget it, Abbey."

"Fine, be that way."

I ignored her comment, and said, "I'm hungry, and who knows how long we might wait for these guys. Let's go get a bite and wait out front."

We stood and walked out of the restaurant. "Tell you what," I said, handing her a twenty- dollar bill. "There's a food court that way. Go get a couple sandwiches and meet me back here. If they show up, I'll text you."

Abbey left me at a row of slots that provided a view of the Red Square entrance. The possibility that the Volkovs were involved with the Red Square management was not surprising. It also wasn't particularly relevant unless it provided a link to child pornography. I couldn't imagine how it could, unless they kept incriminating records on the premises, which I felt was unlikely. Smart mobsters only keep written records when absolutely necessary, and they keep them well hidden. Of course, not all mobsters were smart, and even some highly successful crooks were sometimes imprudent.

Fifteen minutes later Abbey hadn't returned, but the two Russians had. They'd been out of sight for almost an hour, and now they strode purposely across the casino, back toward the hotel lobby.

I texted *front exit* to Abbey and fell in behind them. I didn't know what was keeping her, but then she responded: *had to go to coffee shop, just got food.*

When we reached the hotel lobby they walked straight out to the reception circle. I watched from behind the glass doors as they waited at the curb. Just as Abbey walked up, the limo came around, and the driver got out and opened the back door. The Russians disappeared into the interior, and the limo drove off into the night.

"How'd we let that happen?" Abbey asked.

"Let what happen?" I said.

She looked at me with widened eyes. "We lost them!"

"You have much to learn, child."

•   •   •

Once we got to my pickup, I handed Abbey my phone.

"See the red arrow? That's the limo."

"How'd you do that?"

"Tools of the trade. I'll show you later if you behave yourself."

"Oh, so that's how it's gonna be, huh?"

"Navigate for me."

"They're heading north. Turn left and get on the freeway."

I gunned the engine and covered five miles in a little over three minutes.

"Take ninety-five east," Abbey said. I swerved to the exit and took my phone from her hand.

"They're heading to the same place as last night," I said.

"Where?"

"They just stopped. It's a duplex where some of their whores live."

"You don't have to call them that."

"Why not?" I said, blowing through a yellow light.

"Because you don't know what their circumstances are. They could be so desperate for money that it's the only choice they have. Or, they could be victims of forced prostitution. Have you heard of those scams?"

"Yeah."

"It's very common in Southeast Asia and Eastern Europe. Poor girls without much hope for a decent life answer ads to come to the U.S. for real jobs, and maybe to find a husband. Then they get here, and the nightmare begins."

"You think the Volkovs are involved in that?"

"I don't think they'd hesitate if they could make a buck."

"Can't argue that," I said, hitting a green light.

"Turn here," Abbey said.

I entered the same decrepit neighborhood I'd visited the previous night and saw the limo parked in front of the same duplex where they'd dropped off the three women who'd been keeping them company at the Café Leonov. The limo's driver's seat was empty. I switched my lights off and parked a few units away on the opposite side of the street.

"What now?"

"We wait," I said.

Five minutes passed, and though the street was lined with parked cars, none drove past us. The night was dark and still.

"You think there's a chance that little girl is inside?" Abbey said.

I rubbed the stubble on my jaw. "Anything's possible."

We sat in silence for another few minutes until I said, "I'm gonna do a little recon. Text me if you see anything."

"What do you mean, recon?"

"Just wait here." I got out of my truck and walked behind it, then darted across the street. I moved past two duplexes before reaching the limo, then I crept to a wood slat fence aside the unit where the Russians had entered. I looked over the fence into an alley where two plastic garbage cans sat next to the stucco wall. Above one of the cans was a square of yellow light coming from a small bathroom window.

I went through the gate and crouched below the window, then peeked in. Seeing the bathroom empty, I lifted the hinged top to one of the containers and used my cellphone to illuminate the contents. Brown paper bags overflowed with frozen food packaging, tissues, a shampoo bottle, and a broken wine bottle. I reached in and picked through the trash, looking for anything that might suggest a ten-year-old girl was being kept here. I was hoping to see a peanut butter jar, or maybe a fast food happy meal box, or, if I was really lucky, an article of children's clothing. But I found nothing of the sort, and I gave up after my hand hit a reeking mess of rotted food.

I eased the lid shut and was looking for something to wipe my hand on when I heard a sound from the bathroom. Then I heard a muted voice. I pressed my ear against the stucco, my head just aside the window.

"It's time to test your cranial ability," a man said. His voice had a sharp pitch, deep but piercing. I could easily hear his thick Russian accent.

The woman's voice that replied was too quiet to discern. I heard some moving about, and when there was no conversation for a minute, I risked a glance inside.

The young woman was sitting on the toilet, performing fellatio on the limo driver. Her head moved back and forth rapidly. He stared down at her, his pants bunched around his ankles.

I ducked down and moved deeper into the alley. When I reached the corner of the building, I saw a concrete patio and a weed yard. The view into the duplex through the sliding glass door was obscured by vertical blinds. But there was light coming from around the imperfectly hung slats, and from my angle I could partially see into the room.

Serj Volkov was sitting on a couch next to two women while his older partner stood speaking with an older woman wearing a red wig. She had been with the Russians the previous night and given her age I assumed she played the role of a madam. I watched the room for a few minutes and saw nothing to suggest a young girl was being held here. The duplex was probably leased by the Volkovs and used as an inexpensive home for their call girls. The madam would handle incoming calls and send the girls out for jobs. The Volkovs would come by to pick up cash on a nightly basis. Whether these girls worked for the Volkovs by choice or under duress, I couldn't tell.

If the Volkovs were holding Mia Jordan, it would have to be somewhere secure and secretive, with little traffic. I doubted this duplex fit the bill.

On my way out, I took a quick look through the second garbage receptacle, and found nothing of interest. I eased the gate open, slid through, and jogged back to my truck.

"What's that smell?" Abbey said as soon as I sat.

"I rooted through their garbage cans."

"That would explain it."

"I was looking for any sign a child was there."

"Find anything?"

"Nope."

"Did you see anything else?"

"Lexi the limo driver was sampling the wares."

"Huh?"

"He was getting a blow job in the bathroom."

"Oh, that's wonderful. Thanks for sharing."

"This place is just a nightly cash stop for the Volkovs."

"Those women in there, are they there on their own free will?"

"Hard to say. They could probably just leave if they wanted to."

"That's not how it works," Abbey said. "The Volkovs could hold their passports, tell them they owe thousands of dollars until they pay off their debt, and threaten to harm their families back in Russia if the debt isn't paid."

When I didn't respond, Abbey said, "You think they should be allowed to get away with that?"

"No," I said. "But I've got other priorities."

Abbey shook her head. "You know, Cody said, at your core, you despise criminals. But I'm not really feeling that."

"Is that why you want to be a cop? Because you despise criminals?"

"That's part of it. Maybe a big part. What about you?"

"I try to keep the emotion out of it," I said.

She blew her breath out. "Good luck with that. So, what now?"

"We hope they take us somewhere meaningful."

"And what if they don't?"

I looked away from the duplex and Abbey's eyes looked reptilian in the shadows.

"Then I need to decide if this is a dead lead, or if there's reason to take it up a notch."

"I was hoping you'd say that. This surveillance stuff is like moving in slow motion. What have you got in mind?"

"I could plant bugs, maybe in the limo, or maybe at the Café Leonov."

"The café would be easy. Probably be tough getting into the limo."

"Not really."

"You know what would be really cool? To get our hands on one of their cell phones, see who they're calling, read their messages, listen to their voice mail."

"How would you do that?" I asked.

"Get one of them alone, mug him. You're a bad ass, no problem, right?"

I shook my head. "If the Volkovs suspect they're being watched, they'll get ultra-cautious. We need to operate in the shadows. The goal is to not alert them."

"Right," Abbey said, as the duplex front door opened. The three men came down the walkway and got into the limo.

"Let's hope they go somewhere interesting," Abbey said.

"Patience," I replied.

The limo drove away, and I had to wait until it reached the corner before pulling from the curb. Then I gunned it, lights off, and regained sight as they turned onto Decatur Boulevard. I suspected they'd head to the southbound freeway and go back toward The Strip, but they turned north. I tailed them at a distance for two miles until they took the on-ramp for 215 east.

"Not much out this way," Abbey said. "Nellis Air Force Base, and that's about it."

To the left of the freeway was a barren stretch of desert, and to the right there were only sporadic lights. We were approaching the junction for Interstate 15 when the limo slowed and exited on North Lamb. The road was dark and there was no traffic. I again turned off my headlights.

We drove for half a mile and there was nothing on either side of the road, no buildings, no lights, no turn-offs. I fell back and gave them plenty of room. When they finally reached an intersection they turned right, and I accelerated and saw they had turned onto the gravel shoulder. They were stopped at a chain-link gate, illuminated by their headlights. Lexi got out, pulled free a padlocked chain, pushed the gate open, then returned to the limo and drove it through. After he stopped and re-locked the gate, the limo rounded a bend behind a single story structure and was no longer visible.

I drove forward and looked for a concealed place to park. Finding nothing suitable, I hung a U-turn and stopped near the gate.

"What is this place?" Abbey asked.

"There's a sign over there. Wait here," I said, then left my truck and jogged over to where a plywood sign rose slightly above the fencing. The wood was rotted, the paint dim. I shined my cell light at it and read the faded lettering.

"Towne Auto Salvage," I said when I returned to my truck.

"That's the junkyard they took over. They didn't even bother changing the name. Chris Towne was the student Serj Volkov sent to the hospital."

"They're probably using it to launder money."

"Why are they here at ten p.m.? A little late for cooking the books, isn't it?"

"They keep late hours."

We sat staring at the front gate. "Look at this place," Abbey said. "All fenced off and remote. How much you want to bet there're dead bodies buried in there?"

"Are there any unresolved killings they're suspected of?"

"I already told you Lexi skated on two murder charges. One of the bodies was never found."

"What do you want to do, get a warrant, dig up the place?"

Abbey looked at me out of the corner of her eye. "Not if there's an easier way. Any ideas?"

"Yeah," I said. "If Mia Jordan is being held captive, this could be the place."

"So what do we do about it? I'd need probable cause to get a warrant."

"That's the advantage of being a P.I.," I said.

"What?"

"I don't need probable cause. At least not the legal version."

•   •   •

It wasn't until around midnight that the Russians left the junkyard. They drove back across town to the Cafe Leonov, then an hour later headed to a high-end Vegas strip club. Apparently that revved them up, for at 2:30 a.m. they drove back to Mandalay Bay and picked up the three call girls they'd talked to earlier in the evening. They herded the ladies into the limo and took them to the Café Leonov.

Abbey fell asleep in my passenger seat as I sat watching the café from the parking lot across the street. I finally called it a night at 3:30 and drove Abbey to her apartment near the college.

I shook her shoulder. "Go get some rest," I said.

"I'm sorry. I don't know how you stay awake."

"You didn't miss anything."

"Okay," she murmured, trying to blink the sleep from her eyes. I watched her go into her unit before I drove off to my hotel. When I got there, I wondered if Cody was shacked up with Abbey's boss in a nearby room. I would have bet on it, but I was too tired to care, and I fell into bed and slept fully clothed until the gray hues of dawn invaded my room and woke me from a dreamless slumber. That gave me the opportunity to make sure my cell phone was off, and then I didn't wake again until eleven in the morning.

10

SOMETIMES, AFTER A LONG sleep, I'll awake with a newfound clarity, as if my subconscious has sorted through the prior day's events and drawn ready conclusions. But when I got out of bed and peered out the hotel window, the sunless skies were pallid and the distant ridges were obscured by a wintery haze. My mind felt the same way, sluggish, my thoughts blurry and listless.

I showered, brewed coffee, and went downstairs to buy a couple of energy bars. It took until noon for my head to clear. Then I sat at my computer and began updating my case file. Fifteen minutes into it I stopped and dialed Melanie's cell number.

"Hello?"

"Hi, Melanie, it's Dan. How are you?"

"Fine," she said haltingly. "Do you have something good to report?"

"Not yet, but remember when you said the picture I showed you could have been Jeff's father?"

"Yes?"

"Do you know how I can reach him?"

"Hmm, that's a tough one. Jeff hadn't spoken to him in years that I knew of."

"How about Jeff's mom?"

"They were divorced."

"Maybe his brother or sister would know," I said.

"Yeah, maybe."

"You told me you thought Bur Jordan worked for the government and might have been a spy."

"That's what Jeff told me."

"Do you have phone numbers for any of Jeff's family?" I asked.

"No. I mean, we never had any contact with them. Except for Kenny, Jeff's brother. He called a couple times, about a year ago, trying to borrow money."

"Thanks. I'll be in touch," I said, walking to where my duffle bag sat in a corner of the room. I found Jeff Jordan's cellphone in a zipped pocket and plugged it into my charger. When the power came on, I began searching through his contact list. Within a minute I saw phone numbers and email addresses for Jeff's mother, Elaine, his brother, Kenny, and his sister, Janice.

Elaine Jordan's number had a San Jose area code. I called her first.

"Hello, who's calling?" a whispery voice said.

"Mrs. Jordan, my name's Dan Reno, private investigations. I've been hired to look into your son's murder."

"Hired by whom?"

"Your daughter-in-law's parents."

"So, what do you want from me?" Her voice was hushed and barely audible.

"I believe Jeff may have been in touch with his father shortly before he was killed. Do you know how I can reach Bur Jordan?"

"I haven't spoken to him in years."

"I understand he worked for the government as a spy," I said.

"He worked for the CIA," she replied. "I have no idea if he still does."

"Do you have a phone number or address where I might find him?"

"No."

"I'm trying to find the men who killed Jeff, Mrs. Jordan. They need to pay for their crimes."

"Good luck," she whispered, and hung up.

"Really?" I said, tilting my head. Her lack of interest in her son's death and her brusque end to our call made me curious about the severity of her mental health issues. Melanie had said Elaine Jordan suffered from depression and never left her darkened house. It was possible she kept her voice low as a mechanism to minimize her engagement with the outside world. Maybe she felt speaking at a normal volume would invite people to intrude on her fragile state. In that light, I was fortunate she took my call, and even more fortunate she'd revealed that her ex-husband worked, or had worked, for the CIA.

Next I dialed the Denver area code number for Kenny Jordan.

"Yo, Kenny."

"Hi Kenny, Dan Reno, investigations."

"Great, it's about time. Have you got the probate thing figured out yet?"

"The what?"

"The will and all that probate crap. Russ Gilmore from the state department said you'd be calling."

"Kenny, I'm a private investigator hired by Melanie Jordan's family to find out who killed your brother, and possibly his daughter."

"You're not with the state department?"

"Afraid not."

"Ah, crap. I've been waiting almost two months now."

"Waiting for what?"

"For the paper work to get sorted out so I can get my inheritance."

"From Jeff?"

"Jeff? What are you talking about? Jeff didn't leave me anything. It's from my dad."

"Bur Jordan died?"

"And you call yourself an investigator? Don't you read the obituaries?"

"I've only been on the case for a week. When did your father die? How did he die?"

"He was shot in November. They caught up to him in L.A."

"Who caught up to him?"

"Who knows? Whoever he was spying on over in congo-bongo land."

"Bur Jordan was working for the CIA in Africa?"

"Most recently, yeah. Before that it was Russia."

"I see," I said slowly. "Do you know who his boss was at the CIA?"

"Nah. He never talked about that."

"So, you think your dad made enemies in Africa?"

"He was an agent of the U.S. government, a white man, working in a black man's land that happens to be rich in resources. You tell me."

"Was your father murdered before Jeff?"

"Three days before. The same bastards killed them both."

"How do you know?"

"They both were shot and had one of their arms hacked off. That's about all the CIA has told me."

"The CIA's investigating both murders?"

"Don't act so surprised. These people take care of their own. They'll get to the bottom of it."

"I'd like to speak to them if I could. You got a name I can contact?"

"The only guy I have contact info for is Russ Gilmore, but he's not CIA. I did talk to one CIA guy, but that was only once, and it was pretty brief. He quizzed me on a few things, and said if we needed to talk again, he'd call me."

I squinted out the window. The clouds over the eastern ridgeline had become darker. "Kenny, I'm gonna text you a picture. Can you confirm it's your dad?"

"Go ahead."

"Are you the executor of your father's will?" I asked.

"It was originally Jeff, but now it's passed to me. That's part of the delay. Hold on, I'm pulling up your pic. Yeah, that's him. He was a good looking guy, I'll give him that."

"Did your dad have a big estate?"

"I don't know. I hope so."

We hung up, and I began typing the details of the two calls into my case log. Then I stopped and considered Kenny Jordan's remarks, or more so, his attitude. He didn't express the slightest remorse his father and brother had been killed. He didn't even make a pretense of it. His interest was solely in an inheritance. It was hard to imagine a person could be so emotionally detached from the recent murders of two members of his nuclear family. Regardless of how minimal his relationship had been with them, I expected he would convey some sense of shock, anger, or maybe fear, if not outright grief. His cavalier tone seemed pathologically deviant, but if he was somehow involved, he surely would have been more guarded with me. I shook my head. Maybe he was just extremely self-centered.

I finished typing, then contemplated the prospect of contacting the CIA. I knew an agent in California, from a case a year ago. I had been of value to him, and he'd admitted as much, but that didn't mean he'd help me or even take my call. Before calling him, I needed something to barter with.

I stood and started toward the door, then sat back down and Google-mapped Towne Auto Salvage. I clicked on the *Earth* tab and zoomed in until the entirety of the business filled my screen. The aerial view showed three buildings, two near the entrance, and one in the back of the property, beyond rows of wrecked cars that covered at least ten acres. I expanded the images until they became fuzzy, looking for anything out of place.

Five minutes later I was at my truck in the parking garage. I unlocked the box behind my cab and fitted my lead sap into my jacket pocket. Then I removed my coat, strapped on my bulletproof vest, and checked the load on my .40 cal Beretta automatic. I slipped the shoulder harness over my head and put my jacket back on, feeling the weight of my pistol on the left and the sap to the right. After grabbing a few lighter items, I got in my truck and started the engine, but before pulling out, I texted Cody: *Hey, Lance Romance, how was your date?*

It took fifteen minutes to get to Towne Auto Salvage. I drove through the open gate and parked in their customer lot. I could see the rows of wrecked cars behind a chain-link fence, but to gain entrance I had to go into the main building first, a single story structure with a tar and gravel roof. The room was unheated and the three employees wore heavy coats. An overweight white woman sat aside a U-shaped counter, collecting entrance fees, while two Latino men behind the counter quoted and charged customers for parts they had pulled.

To my left was an adjoining room, which I could see into through two large sliding windows. In the room were metal filing cabinets and two desks. At one of the desks sat a middle-aged man, punching the keys of an old fashioned adding machine and penciling numbers onto a ledger.

"Three bucks entry," the woman said as I approached. Her jowls were deeply creased, and she had dark circles under her colorless eyes. She smelled of unwashed clothes and cigarette smoke. I paid her and proceeded out the opened rear of the structure, into the yard.

I walked by two green outhouses and looked over the wrecks. I started down one row, then retreated and walked further out. The cars were organized by brand; Fords, GMs, Plymouths, and past the American models were acres of Japanese junkers. I kept walking toward the back of the yard, and found a European section where Audis, Mercedes Benzes, and BMWs had found their final resting place.

It was a cold, sunless day, and there were perhaps a dozen customers scattered about the place. They wore coveralls and had their own tool boxes, and some lay in the dirt wrenching on rust bucket wrecks, trying to remove suspension pieces or brake calipers or axles. None of the cars were late models; most were from the eighties and nineties. It was hard to imagine the demand for these parts could keep a business afloat. At best, they might pull in a few thousand a week.

I was nearing the rear fence line when I saw the third building on the property. It sat in the corner farthest from the entrance, and when I'd seen the overhead view on my computer screen, I thought it might have been a storage unit. But it was an old Streamline trailer, resting on cinder blocks and two flattened tires. Its rounded shell was coated in peeling white paint dotted with rust spots. Two propane tanks were mounted to a V-shaped trailer hitch beneath the front window. From the window I could see a dim glow of light.

I crouched behind the battered hulk of a Mercedes sedan and took a few pictures of the trailer. Maybe it was the residence of a watchman, although I doubted there was much here worth stealing. But what other purpose would a trailer out here serve?

I walked toward the back fence, keeping my eyes averted until I reached the end of the row nearest the trailer. I was now within ten yards of it. The windows were screened and opaque, but didn't appear reinforced. The door between the windows looked rickety, and the lock was one that could easily be broken by a crow bar or even a firm kick.

I continued staring at the trailer. If Mia Jordan was being held against her will, this would be an unlikely place. Even a ten-year-old girl could break out, or at least break a window and scream at someone. But my gut told me something wasn't right about this decrepit old trailer, an eyesore even in a place as dismal as a junkyard. Add in that the Volkovs coerced the junkyard from its former owners, and the potential was something I couldn't ignore.

I turned and looked back toward the front of the yard. The nearest people were almost a hundred yards away.

There are moments in every investigation where certain choices must be made. In this case that meant risking a move from the shadows and into plain view. So far, the Volkovs had no idea I was watching them. Once that changed, my investigative tactics would need to adapt, and rapidly.

I walked to the trailer and stood at the two wooden stairs before the door and rapped my knuckles on the aluminum frame. I was hoping no one would answer, and then I'd break in and search the place. As a second choice, if someone answered and provided a reasonable and benign explanation for their presence, I could leave with no harm done.

I heard a sound, and as soon as the door opened, I knew neither of my choices were options.

The man looking down at me was about my height and few years older. He was black, and the deep tone of his skin showed no hint of racial mixing. He wore slip-on loafers, yellow socks, and his red pants were too short. His belt was beaded and colorful, and square-knotted in the front. His sole concession to the near freezing weather was a camouflage army jacket.

"What you doing here?" he barked. His fingers were scarred, the knuckles gray, as if the pigment had been scraped off over a long period of time.

"Uh, looking for a bathroom?"

His eyes flashed, and he glowered at me, his thick lips flattening against the sharp contours of his face.

"Back there, stupid boy," he said thrusting his hand outward.

But before his arm reached full length mine was already moving forward. I grabbed him by his knotted belt and pulled forward, then slammed my right fist into his gut. The uppercut blow knocked him off his feet, and I jumped up and shoved him through the doorway before he could fall onto me. The door swung shut behind us.

He lay gasping on the floor. I tried to force him flat on his stomach so I could zip-tie his hands, but he fought back, his elbow clipping my mouth and bringing blood. I countered with a strike to the neck with the meat of my hand, and that stunned him long enough for me to hogtie him. Then I tied a black strip of cloth over his eyes.

"What is this?" he hissed.

"I'm going to ask you some simple questions. You'll give me simple answers. I don't have a lot of time, so we'll have to make this quick. What's your name?"

"Allassane Ouattara."

"Nice try, but isn't he the president of Nigeria? Or is it the Ivory Coast?" I rose from my knees and began searching through a set of drawers next to his bed. I pulled out all his clothes and threw them on the mattress, looking futilely for a driver's license or a passport. I didn't find a single scrap of paper.

I went back to him and checked his pockets. No wallet or keys, but I did find an inexpensive cell phone in his coat pocket. It was the type commonly available at discount stores, and probably had service through a prepaid provider, which meant it could be used anonymously and was mostly untraceable. I stuck it in my coat, then continued searching him, and felt a square object in his chest pocket.

It was a pack of cigarettes. The brand was Pacific Blue.

"You're not a citizen of this country, are you, buddy?" I asked pleasantly. "Why don't you tell me about it?"

He laughed and said something in a foreign language. I ignored him and went into the kitchenette and found a trash bag under the sink. I spilled it on the floor, carefully picked out a few cigarette butts, and placed them in a plastic baggie. Then I emptied the drawers, and removed every plate, bowl, cup, and glass from the cupboards. The area to be searched was small, and it only took a minute. Finding nothing, I stepped over him and stripped the sheets from the bed, then flipped the mattress. I doubted I'd find paperwork, but I was hoping to see a large knife, perhaps a machete.

There was no blade under the mattress, but I did notice a torn section about four inches long that had been sewed shut. I ripped it open with my finger and felt a plastic bag. When I removed it I saw it contained a stack of Polaroid photos. Some had blurry ink notations on the flip sides.

"I'm gonna ask you once more," I said. "Your name, and what you're doing in this country. Give me the wrong answers and you'll regret it."

"Soon you'll regret being born."

I kicked him in the ribs, hard enough to make him seriously consider his next answer.

"Where's the little girl?"

His body stiffened, and he spat, "You gonna die."

"You like cutting people, don't you, dirt-bag? Tell me about the people whose arms you hacked off in L.A. and Utah."

"You can learn yourself, when I do it to you." He was flexing against his restraints, and his teeth were clenched.

"I've got to go soon, good buddy. So I've just got one more question, and if I don't like your answer, I'm gonna stomp on you until I break every one of your ribs. One will probably puncture your lungs, then you'll suffocate on your own blood. Is the girl alive?"

When he didn't say a word, I kicked him in the same spot as before. This time saliva sprayed from around his teeth.

"She's alive," he said.

"Where is she?"

"I don't know."

"Do the Volkovs have her?"

"I have nothing to do with her."

"Last chance," I said. "Where's the girl?"

He took a deep breath, then bellowed from deep in his lungs, loud enough for anyone within a hundred feet of the trailer to hear.

I kicked him again and his yell turned into a cry as a rib cracked. Then I pulled the lead sap I called 'Good Night Irene' from my coat and slapped him behind the ear. His body went limp.

He lay sprawled across the dirty floor, unconscious. He'd wake to a massive headache and a searing pain every time he took a breath, but I had no doubt he was deserving of far worse. As I peeked out the window to make sure no one was watching, my main regret was that I couldn't take him with me and subject him to a full interrogation.

I stood over his inert body and dialed Cody's number. "I need you to call your lady friend from LVPD," I said.

"What? Abbey's coming to the Plaza. Why don't you meet us here?"

"Cody, listen to me. I'm at Towne Auto Salvage, out in north Vegas. I found a man I believe is an African national, probably here illegally. He says the little girl is still alive, which means the Volkovs kidnapped her."

"How do you reach that conclusion?"

"The Volkovs own this business. They're letting the African stay here. He also basically admitted he was involved in Jeff Jordan's murder, and Bur Jordan's too."

"Who?"

"Jeff Jordan's father. The police need to pick this guy up right away. I can't wait here."

"Why not?"

"Because, goddammit, I busted him up, and I also don't want the Volkovs to know who I am. They got that little girl."

"Okay, calm down. I'll call Denise. Where is this guy?"

"In a trailer in the far corner of the yard, back behind the European cars."

"I'll tell her to send a car right away."

I left the junkyard, trying to move swiftly without drawing attention. I made it to my truck without incident and drove down the street, then hung a U-turn and parked about a quarter mile away on the opposite side of the road.

Ten minutes went by and no police car, marked or unmarked, arrived. My eyes were glued to the front of the junkyard. As soon as the man in the trailer regained consciousness, he'd take off, if he was thinking clearly. But I'd left him hogtied, so he'd be stuck there unless he could get free on his own, or get some help.

Another ten minutes went by and the only car I saw was one leaving the junkyard. It was a compact pickup truck, and when I viewed it though my binoculars, I could see there was only room in the cab for the two men inside, and no person was in the gateless bed.

I called Cody again.

"What's up?" he asked.

"What did Denise say?"

"That she'd send a couple of plainclothesmen."

"When?"

"As soon as she could."

"That could mean maybe today, maybe tomorrow."

"Look, Dirt, these murders didn't happen in Vegas, so this is not an active case here. There's only so much Denise can do. You want me to drive over and we'll make a citizen's arrest?"

"Let me think about it," I said.

We hung up, and I went to my address book and found the cell number for the Sacramento-based CIA man I knew. Greg Stillman was everything I expected a federal agent to be; patriotic, professional, disciplined, wound tight, and disdainful of all outside his world. But in our brief interaction some months ago, I'd provided information helpful to him, and he'd shown a begrudging respect. He'd even made a call on my behalf and helped me out of a sticky situation with a San Jose assistant district attorney.

I was sure I could raise Greg Stillman's interest by telling him I knew who killed Bur Jordan. The CIA would be here within an hour or two, and they played by their own rules, which meant they could use whatever interrogation tactics they wished. The problem with that was, once the Volkovs knew the noose was tightening, they'd view Mia Jordan as a liability. If they were caught with her, that meant a kidnapping charge, and implication in at least one murder. Rather than risk that, they'd kill her and bury the body where it would never be found, out in the boundless desert.

My mouth went dry, and I stared out the windshield. I'd just worked over the African, and Vegas PD was on the way. I don't know why I was worried about the CIA rousting the Volkovs. The damage was already done.

Of course, I was assuming the Volkovs still had Mia. That was blind hope on my part. They could have already sold her to the highest bidder. She could be on a boat in the middle of the ocean, on her way to stock a sheik's harem. Or, she could be shackled in some rich pervert's basement, where she'd be subjected to abuse that would ruin her for life, if she survived it.

I squeezed my eyes shut and clenched my teeth. "Think," I said out loud. Then I opened my eyes and saw a car approaching. It slowed at the entrance to Towne Auto Salvage. It was a tan, late model American sedan. Before it could turn in, I flashed my lights twice.

The car stopped, then drove forward. It came up alongside me, and the passenger window lowered. Inside were two men wearing button down shirts, their eyes hidden behind sunglasses. The passenger flashed a badge at me.

"Dan Reno, private investigations," I said. "I'm investigating a kidnapping and two murders, one in Utah, the other in California. Looks like the Volkovs are involved."

"Why?" asked the passenger. His face was beefy and red, his nose bulbous. Curly gray hair grew from his ears and tufts protruded from his collar. When he talked, I saw white food particles jammed between his teeth.

"Because they're housing a man I think is an African national. Both the victims had their arms hacked off, and when I questioned him, he didn't deny doing it."

"Arms hacked off?" said the driver, a gaunt man of indeterminate race. He removed his sunglasses and leaned forward to stare at me.

"That's right. It's a trademark of African militias."

The driver blinked and squinted as if the sun was in his eyes. "The FBI know about this?"

"Not that I know of."

"Sounds like their jurisdiction," the other cop said.

I took a deep breath and tried to swallow a surge of impatience rising from my gut. "He's an illegal alien suspected of two murders. I can give you the details. Don't let him slip through your fingers. Bring him in, then you can call the Feds."

The passenger window whirred, and I watched it close. The two detectives spoke for a minute, shaking their heads and frowning. Then the window lowered again, and the beefy cop said, "Tell us exactly where he is."

•   •   •

After watching the cops drive into the wrecking yard, I called Cody.

"Cops show?" he asked.

"Yeah. After they grab the African, I'll need to go with them and provide a statement."

"Right. Abbey wants to talk to you."

"Put her on."

"Hi, Dan," she said.

"What's up?"

"The fat Russian is Igor Volkov. He's Serj Volkov's uncle. He's been in the U.S. for five years. He's got a green card, but he's not a citizen."

"Any arrests?"

"Just one, for tax fraud. But the government couldn't make it stick, and the charges were dropped."

"Huh," I said.

"But get this—in Russia, they called him Igor the Butcher, because he and his crew firebombed an enemy's house and ended up killing three women and five children."

"That was in his jacket?"

"Yup. I also tried to find links to real estate ownership, but couldn't find anything for the Volkovs. Then I looked at Cafe Leonov and Red Square. They're both owned by corporations."

"No surprise," I said, hearing the disinterest in my voice.

"Are you going to follow them around this evening?"

"Maybe."

"What time?"

"I don't know yet," I said. "Could you put your dad back on, please?"

"You're welcome for the info," she said.

A moment later, Cody said, "What's the deal?"

"You got plans again tonight?" I asked.

"No, I don't think so. Probably not. I'll tell you about it later."

"You in the mood for Russian food?"

"I don't know. Is it any good?"

"Probably not," I said.

"Call me when you're done at the police station."

I sat in my truck, watching the entrance to the auto wrecker. I figured the LVPD detectives would have to bring the African in if he couldn't provide identification papers, or otherwise prove he was here legally. As an illegal alien, he would have no rights, which meant he could be held indefinitely without charges. The police would have no obligation to grant him a phone call. It could be a few days before the Volkovs realized he was missing.

"Wrong," I muttered, chiding myself for the fallacious assumption. Someone at Towne Auto Salvage would surely call the Volkovs and tell them the African had been apprehended. My main concern was the middle-aged man I saw working the adding machine in the adjoining room. If he was dealing with numbers, he was likely a Volkov operative.

I still didn't understand the links between a Russian crime family, an African national, a CIA man who worked in Africa and Russia, and his son, a building contractor with fringe political beliefs. I didn't yet know how the two murders, uncut diamonds, gold coins, and the kidnapping of a young girl fit together. But there was one thing I was sure of, and that was the clock was now ticking faster for Mia Jordan. If the Volkovs were still holding her captive, and decided to dispose of her, her blood would be on my hands.

I turned on my radio and tried to relax, then switched it off. It had been fifteen minutes since the detectives entered the wrecking yard. It was a long walk to the trailer, and it would probably be another five or ten minutes before they reappeared, after which I'd follow them to the police station. Once we were in route, I could call the FBI, or the CIA, and apprise them of the situation. They could meet us at the station and conduct a full interrogation of the African. In a best case scenario, he may even know what happened to Mia, and hopefully where she was being held.

At that moment I saw the tan sedan emerge from the parking lot. I grabbed for my binoculars, but they turned toward me, and as they got closer, I could see the back seat was empty. I stepped out of my truck and waited for them.

The man with the curly gray hair opened the passenger door and stood looking at me. His torso was bearlike, the shoulders rounded and massive. He had no neck and his head was shaped like a squat pumpkin.

"No one was there," he said.

"At the trailer?"

"That's right."

"Did you find any clothes?"

"Nope. Dishes, cups, silverware, but no clothes."

I looked past him at the fence along the street. "I've been sitting here since I visited him. He didn't come out."

"What did you say your name is?"

"Dan Reno."

"Well, here's a tip for you, Reno. Sometimes, crooks use back doors." He brought his meaty hand down hard on my shoulder and chuckled. "Got to always remember the back door."

The driver climbed out of his seat and stood grinning at me over the roof. "Aren't you partners with Cody Gibbons?"

I didn't reply, and his grin faded. "I've heard you two are a real circus act," he said. "Like something out of the freak show."

"Don't waste our time again," the burly cop said, as he got back in the car. His partner did the same, then he revved the motor and dropped the shifter into drive. The sedan jolted from the shoulder, the tires spitting dust and gravel and leaving me in a cloud of dirt. I walked out of the cloud and watched the car grow smaller on the long, straight road, until it was no longer visible.

"Thanks a lot, guys," I said.

I got back in my truck, spewing curses, and hit the ignition. Then in a sudden flash, without my permission or forethought, my temper erupted. Adrenalin surged in my chest, and I could feel my face distort as if in a windstorm. I flexed my arms and legs and brought my fist down on my padded dashboard and heard something break. Then I stomped the gas pedal and roasted my tires off the dirt, my fingers clamped like a vice on the steering wheel. I roared down the highway, hitting a hundred before I eased off the pedal, then I punched it again up to 110, my mind blowing steam like a locomotive on its last run, as the pressure of my job and sobriety finally erupted like a dormant volcano.

After a minute I blew out my breath and let off the gas. I smiled crook-edly, and I was sure if anyone witnessed me at that moment they would have thought I was a lunatic. I slowed to a normal speed, but I felt loose and unhinged, as if I was careening down a rutted trail, brakes failed, suspension shot, bouncing off the walls, demolishing whatever lay in my path. It was a feeling I recognized from certain episodes in my past; when I destroyed my marriage after first killing a man, when I ran into a burning house and found only corpses, and when I was thrown in jail for running over a San Salvadorian gangbanger who nearly killed Cody.

I pulled over and skidded to a stop. My first instinct, and what I'd always done after a meltdown, was to run to a whiskey bottle. I could always regain myself after a few drinks. Besides, I was a good drunk, a happy drunk, and I hadn't really abused the privilege since my divorce. I was younger back then, less self-aware, less mature. When I first became a private investigator, I had thought there was something noble and ro-mantic about swilling eighty-proof in dive bars, as if the nature of my profession justified it. It was a great rationale for the fact that I just plain liked to drink.

I sat with my eyes closed. I could be in a bar in ten minutes, and five drinks later my commitments to Walter and Lillian McDermott and Melanie Jordan would seem like a distant abstraction, something that could surely be postponed for a day or two. I could call the FBI and CIA from the bar and they'd take care of the African and the Volkovs. And Mia, she'd already been missing for almost two months, so why sweat another couple of days?

I got out of my truck and stared northward. The air was dry and a cold wind kicked up a plume of dust. I could see past a hardpan field to the freeway, where the cars looked small and insignificant. Beyond the interstate was hundreds of miles of nothing but high, mountainous desert, barren and blown with tumbleweeds. I stood staring into the horizon for a long minute. There was a stark, foreboding beauty to the land, elemental and unforgiving, as if a reminder that we were all just temporary visitors.

When I dropped my head, I saw a tiny, solitary desert flower next to my boot. It had an orange center and purple petals and was no larger than a quarter. How it survived this long into the winter, I had no idea, for there were no other flowers nearby. For some reason, it lived while the others died. I bent down and studied it.

"Resilient damn thing," I said. I went and got a plastic bottle from my truck and carefully poured water around the flower's base. I watched the water sink into the dirt, and when it quickly dried, I poured some more. Once the earth absorbed the last of it, for reasons I didn't contemplate, I felt calm again.

I returned to my driver's seat and ran my fingers over the small dent my fist had left on top of the dashboard. Then I checked my GPS. The African had escaped and probably had help. He was likely still at the wrecking yard, maybe hidden in the backroom with the bean counter. If not, and he had left through the back of the lot, he would have had to climb a fence and walk almost half a mile to the next road. Doing so with a broken rib would have been very difficult. But not impossible.

I drove until reaching an intersection, then made a couple of lefts until I was behind the wrecking yard. This would be the 'back door' street the LVPD detectives alluded to. It was a nothing road, long and narrow, its only purpose to link two busier streets. To either side were desolate fields, no buildings, no trees, no obvious places to hide. There was no traffic on this road, not a single car. I drove its three-mile length, then back again, and saw no one.

•   •   •

It was 3:30 by the time I made it to my hotel. I went up to my room and called Cody.

"How'd it go?" he asked.

"It didn't," I replied. "The cops said the African had bailed."

"Shit. I should have come out there."

"Don't worry about it. I'm gonna go do some Dumpster diving. Want to come along?"

"Where at?"

"The Café Leonov."

Cody was waiting in the lobby when I came downstairs. He wore a gray UNLV sweatshirt that barely fit his massive torso, and his beard was trimmed to the point that it looked like only a few days growth.

"New look?" I asked, touching my face.

"It'll grow back."

"Denise's idea?"

"How'd you know?"

"Just a guess."

We walked through the door leading to the garage. "Yeah, she said something about kissing a man with a beard. So I shaved it."

"You got your gear bag in your car?" I asked.

"Yeah, over here." Cody pointed, and I saw his maroon 1990s Toyota Camry parked at the far side of the lot.

"We had dinner at this fancy Italian joint over at the Palazzo. Four or five martinis later, we ended up in my room. I blame the booze."

"For what?"

"It was like we were both sex-starved. A total frenzy. There was no stopping it."

I laughed. "Did you tell Abbey?"

"What? Why would I do that?"

"Don't you think she should know her father's having a relationship with her boss?"

218

"She knows already. I mean, she knows we've gone out," he said, as we walked through the garage. "Christ, we went at it like teenagers, all night long, up against the wall, bent over the chair, looking out the window at The Strip. She's got a great body, and I swear she couldn't get enough."

"But no date tonight?"

"Well, I think she felt a little guilty. The whole time she's saying, 'We shouldn't be doing this', and 'I'm not usually like this.' It got funny, she's panting and moaning and loving it to death, and she's saying, 'Please don't get the wrong impression.' At one point I burst out laughing."

"Did she get mad at that?"

"No, she was having a screaming orgasm at the time, so I don't think she noticed."

"You've always had good timing."

"I'll take that as a compliment," he said as we reached his car. "Where we headed again?"

"The restaurant where the Volkovs hang out. It's over on Tropicana."

"Don't you want to wait until dark?"

"Let's just drive out there," I said. "Where's Abbey?"

"She took off, said she'd call later."

"Let's take your ride. My truck's been around, probably been seen."

I lowered myself into Cody's passenger seat and listened while he started the supercharged motor. Then he deftly worked the gearbox as we drove to the southbound freeway. The suspension and steering felt stiff and precise. Five minutes later we took the Tropicana exit and rolled through the big intersection, past the Excalibur and the MGM. There was ninety minutes of daylight left and the afternoon had become more overcast. As we drove east, the sky grew darker and the heavy air seemed to descend upon us.

"Looks like rain," Cody said.

We turned into the lot next to the Café Leonov. A half dozen cars were parked to the side of the building, including the white limo. Cody left the motor idling as we sat looking at the restaurant.

"It's like the Volkovs live here," I said. "The limo's always here."

"Are they open?"

"Not until five-thirty, the sign says."

"What's the plan?"

"I'm gonna walk behind the place, have a look."

"You want backup?"

"Just keep an eye out, text me if anything happens."

As I left Cody's car, a misty drizzle began falling. I zipped my coat and stepped over the short fence between the lots, then jogged alongside the cafe, toward the rear. When I reached the end of the building, I was surprised to see an extra section extending from the back. It was inset from the main perimeter walls, and invisible from the street. There were no windows in the stucco facing, and when I peeked around the end of the addition, I saw no rear door.

Along the back fence was a large trash bin flanked by scraggly hedges. I ran the fifty feet to the bin and pushed open the lid. It was half full with green garbage bags. I yanked one open and spilled its contents. Large, empty cans that once held olives, stewed tomatoes, and pickled cabbage rolled and clattered from the bag. I opened a second and found head lettuce cores, chicken remains, and other unidentified rubbish, all coated in a mess of thick, lumpy gravy. I was reaching for a third bag when I heard a sound from the building.

I lowered the lid and darted to the rear corner of the Dumpster. Crouching, I heard wheels crunching over gravel. The sound drew closer, then the lid was thrown open, and a man grunted. There were two thumps, the lid banged shut, and I heard the wheels again. I looked around the trash bin and saw a man pushing a dolly back toward the building. He went to the far side and disappeared around the corner of the extended section.

I waited a minute, then opened the lid again. This time I saw a smaller, white garbage bag on top. I pulled it open and shook out some of the contents. Crumpled tissues, a rolled toothpaste tube, and a few toilet paper rolls fell free, and then a larger item, an empty Froot Loops cereal box. I felt the skin around my face tighten. I jammed the items back in the white bag, cinched it shut, and carried it at a jog to where Cody waited in his modified Toyota.

"Find any good stuff?" he asked.

"I think Mia Jordan is inside," I said.

"What's in the bag?"

"Fruit Loops box. Plus, there's a back section that looks added to the original structure. They could be holding her there. I'm betting her DNA or fingerprints are on something in this bag."

"You want me to bring it to Denise?"

"There's no time for that."

"Gear up, then?"

"Yes, sir," I replied.

Cody reached into the backseat and grabbed his bag, while I tightened my bulletproof vest across my chest, secured my shoulder holster, and made sure my sap was in place in my coat pocket.

"Should I bring this?" Cody asked, adjusting his vest. The single barrel of his sawed-off Remington ten gauge lay across his thigh.

"No. Just your handgun." I watched him check the cylinder of his .357 Magnum revolver and fit it into the holster on his rib cage.

"Front door or back?" he asked.

"Back."

We set out and Cody followed me as I retraced my footsteps to the back of the Café Leonov. The rain was now falling in a light patter. The asphalt was cracked and muddy puddles were forming in the dirt creases. When we reached the end of the building, I led us to the far side, where the man with the dolly had emerged from an unseen door.

Now we stood directly in front of the door. It was a stout, metal unit, providing passage into the main building, not to the section I thought was likely an add-on.

"The door probably leads to the kitchen," I said. "But we need to get into this area." I pointed at the wall ten feet to our right.

"Let's do it," Cody said.

I pulled on the handle and we entered a hallway stacked with boxes on one side. As we walked forward, I could smell boiling meat, but it was over-powered by an odor that reminded me of sour milk. We turned into the kitchen, where the man nearest us was chopping carrots and mushrooms with a French knife. Behind a counter another cook tended to pots on a stove while a third pulled a tray from a large oven.

The man with the knife looked up. It was the same man who'd taken out the trash. He was of medium size and unshaven.

"Could we get a table for two?" Cody said.

The man blinked and looked confused, then he muttered something in a thick Russian accent. I stepped forward and brought my hand down on top of his, pinning the knife against the cutting board.

"Don't do anything stupid," I said. "Where's the girl?"

He yelled out, and the other two cooks turned and stared openmouthed.

Cody pulled his big pistol from his holster. "Make a sound, I'll blow you to hell," he said. "On the ground, now."

The chef at the oven dropped to his knees, but the other cook had a cocksure, defiant gleam in his eyes. He shook his head and smiled, then began walking toward a doorway that led to the dining room.

Cody ran forward and cut him off, and the cook had a brief moment to regret his misunderstanding of the situation before Cody swung the pistol barrel down and clubbed him behind the ear. The man collapsed to the floor in a heap.

"I won't be as easy on you," I said to the prep cook. "Where is she?"

He tried to yank his hand from my grasp, and I punched him with a straight right to the nose, not hard enough to break it, just enough to stun him and make his eyes water. His face puckered, the skin pinching and creasing, then he lashed out with his free hand. I ducked, but his finger grazed my eye, which prompted me to smack him with a full backhand across the mouth. When his knees buckled I grabbed him by the neck to keep him upright, then threw him up on the counter, his head banging the wall.

"Last chance," I said. His eyes were unfocused and dull, but then he spit a mouthful of blood at me. I hit him with another straight right, and this time I didn't hold back. My fist slammed into his chin and he slumped over unconscious, then slid off the cutting board and onto the tiled floor.

"Worthless piece of shit," I said.

"Dirt, Dirt," Cody said, shaking his head. He came around the counter, pushing the chef who'd been at the stove. The man was in his early twenties and the scowl on his face looked like an exaggerated attempt to hide fear and vulnerability. *He's low man on the totem pole, an underling, not a thug,* I thought. His right arm was pinned behind him and he was grimacing in pain. Cody's left hand held the man by the back of the collar, while his right maintained the police arm lock.

"My friend has no subtlety," Cody said into the cook's ear. "But I'm different. If I crank your arm up another inch, the tendons will start tearing. But I won't stop there. I'll ruin your shoulder so your arm will never work again. You'll go through life as a cripple. So you get to make a big decision today, douche bag. Take us to the girl."

His eyes were squeezed shut and his teeth clenched. He gestured with his free hand. "They'll kill me," he said.

"You're screwed either way, pal," I said. "But at least we'll let you get a head start out of town." When Cody jerked his arm, the man cried, "The cooler!"

Cody pushed him forward, and I followed them around to the left. "Open it," Cody said, as we approached the door to a walk-in refrigerator. He pulled the latch, and we walked to a second latch handle in the back of the cooler. He opened that one to reveal a hallway running perpendicular. There were three doors, one in front of us and one to either side.

"Which one?" I said.

He nodded to our left. "Last question," I said. "What were the plans for the girl?" I saw the beginnings of a lie on his face, but it vanished when Cody pushed him against the wall and reapplied pressure on his shoulder joint.

"Sell her," he whined. "I had nothing to do with it, I swear. You're just in time."

"To who?" I asked.

"A man with a lot of money."

"Why did they wait so long?"

"He's coming from the Mideast. Lots of plans, details."

I sighed, then dropped him with my lead-weighted sap.

"Good night, Irene," Cody said, looking down at the unconscious body. "I'd say his career here is done."

We moved to the door on the left. I tried the locked door knob, then drew back my leg and slammed my heel below the knob. The door didn't give.

"Son of a bitch," I said. "It's reinforced."

"You're weak," Cody said. "Stand back." He yanked on the knob with both hands, once, twice, and the third time the knob broke off in his hand. He tossed it aside and kicked the door, but it didn't budge. Then he pulled out his revolver.

"No," I said. "She's in there."

I could see Cody's ears turn red, before he drove his foot into the wall next to the door. The sheetrock caved in and he continued kicking, the hole widening below a crossbeam. When the opening was wide enough, he dropped to his butt and pounded his heels into the opposite wall, kicking through, his huge legs pumping like pistons. He moved in a frenzy, exerting his brute size and strength against a problem that required a solution that was not only urgent, but also obvious if one possessed the physical attributes.

When he paused, I heard the cry of a tiny voice.

Cody gave a final kick, then rolled out of the way. "Go," he said.

I ducked down and wedged my body through the jagged hole, pushing away bands of fiberglass insulation and trying not to breathe in the thick dust. When I got my shoulders past the second wall, I looked up and saw a small table and a bed. On the corner of the bed against the wall, a little figure sat huddled, a blanket pulled over her head, as if to shield her.

"Mia? It's okay, I'm here to help you," I said. I walked myself into the carpeted room on my hands until my feet were free. Then I stood and said, "I'm going to bring you back to your mom."

The blanket slowly lowered until two large brown eyes stared at me. The little girl had short, dark hair that looked like it had recently been styled.

"My mommy and daddy are dead," she said. Her voice was tiny but defiant.

"Mia, I was hired by your mom to find you. She's alive, I promise."

"They killed her, and they'll kill you, too," she said, her voice breaking. She held the blanket just below her eyes, clutching it in her little hands. Her fingernails were painted red.

"We have to go now," I said, but then I heard a sound from outside, a door opening, then the unmistakable hiss of a silenced round fired, followed by the thunderous boom of a large caliber gun shot.

I leapt forward, scooped up Mia Jordan, and moved to the side of the door opposite where Cody had kicked through the wall.

"Stay behind me," I said, training my Beretta on the hole. "Cody!" I yelled.

"Son of a bitch shot me," he replied. "But I put a round through his hand."

"How bad?"

"Kevlar saved my ass. Come on out."

"Where's the shooter?"

"He scurried back into his room. He comes out again he won't be as lucky."

"She's here, Cody. I'm passing her through."

Mia was still clutching the blanket around herself. Her eyes were big and round.

"You don't need to be frightened now," I said. "My friend, Cody, is waiting out there. He won't let anyone harm you, I promise."

Mia dropped the blanket. She was wearing yellow pajamas. She went to the hole and crawled through, and I followed her, chafing my forearms on the broken sheetrock. Once my shoulders cleared, Cody reached down, grabbed my hand, and pulled me to my feet.

"Back through the cooler," I said, stepping over the punk I'd knocked out. I held Mia by the hand, and with the other I grasped the cooler handle.

"Wait a minute," Cody said. "I want to pull that guy out of there." He pointed to the door at the end.

"Not now," I said. "Call Vegas PD. Or your girlfriend."

"Crap," Cody muttered. But he followed us through the cooler. When we walked into the kitchen, the prep cook had regained consciousness. He was on his feet and holding his jaw. He looked in pain and disoriented, but when he saw us he snatched up his French knife. I reached for my pistol, but Cody brushed past me.

"You're not too bright, are you, comrade?" Cody said. The man took a step back, then his eyes became focused and he let out a yell and ran at Cody, his arm locked, the blade held before him as if it were a bayonet.

Cody sidestepped and brought his fist down on the man's arm. The knife clattered to the floor, then Cody picked him up by the crotch and the neck and held him high in the air.

"Time to fly, shit-bird," Cody said, and launched the man over the counter and into a wall lined with pots and pans. It caused a huge racket, and amid the clatter I heard the distinct sound of a bone breaking.

"Let's go," I said.

We hurried down the hallway and out the back door. When we reached Cody's car, I buckled Mia into the backseat. She was weeping silently, tears streaming down her freckled cheeks.

"We're going to take you to your mom soon," I said. I closed the door and looked across the hood at Cody, who had his cell pressed to his ear.

"Denise isn't taking my call," he said.

"Call nine-one-one."

"I think she might be regretting last night."

"Would you call nine-one-one?"

"I shouldn't have let it happen."

"Christ," I said, yanking my phone from my pocket. I dialed the police emergency number and gave the address to the 911 operator.

"Yes," I said. "There's been a shooting, so get a couple cars over here pronto."

"Are you in danger now?" the operator asked.

"No. But there's a wounded gunman holed up inside. Send an ambulance if you want."

"Please wait for us, but stay clear of anywhere that might put you in danger."

I hung up and said, "Let's drive across the street and wait for LVPD."

Cody was typing a text message, and I waited patiently for him to finish. When he looked up, I said, "What did the guy you shot look like?"

"A middle-age fat slob with sagging jowls."

"Nice work," I said. "You shot Igor the Butcher."

"Who?" Cody asked, as we got into his car.

"Igor Volkov. He's the boss."

Cody swung out of the lot and crossed over to the apartments on the opposite side of Tropicana. "I think his hand is toast," Cody said. "I'm packing hollow points."

"You always do. Park facing the restaurant."

"He could go out the back. But I don't see him climbing fences, even if his hand was good. You want a smoke?"

I looked back at Mia. "Are you okay? The police are coming. Then we'll go to your mom."

She sniffled and nodded, and I got out and walked a few steps to where a tree provided refuge from the drizzle. I called Melanie's cell, and when she didn't answer I left a message telling her I'd found and rescued her daughter. After I hung up, Cody handed me a Marlboro, and we stood watching the front of the Café Leonov.

I blew a stream of smoke into the wet air and tried to not think about what Mia Jordan had endured, and what it would mean to the rest of her life. I suspected Cody had the same concerns, for the expression on his face when he first saw her was one I'd seen before. Though we never spoke of it, I knew of Cody's soft spot for defenseless female victims. It was this dynamic that prompted some of his more extreme moments, like when he once threw a rapist off a roof.

"I wouldn't worry about Denise," I said, hoping to keep the mood light. "You didn't do anything wrong."

"Yeah, but somehow I always get blamed."

"Don't rush to conclusions."

Cody squinted into the darkening afternoon and touched a spot on his midsection. "Ouch," he said. "I think it was a thirty-two round, fortunately. Probably leave a bitch of a bruise though."

"Here's what you should do, Cody. Send Denise a big flower bouquet. Send it to her home, not to the station where it will embarrass her."

He looked at me with doubt etched across his face.

"I'm serious, man. Flowers are like magic to a woman. Most guys think, who gives a shit about flowers, right? But to women, it's a big deal."

Cody pointed at me, his cigarette smoking in his fingers. "You know, Dirt, every now and then you say something halfway intelligent." He smiled broadly. "I think I'll take your advice. I'll send her the biggest freaking arrangement they got."

I smiled and patted him on the back. "Life doesn't have to be so complicated, old buddy."

"Here comes the heat," he said, flicking his butt into the gutter. I looked down the street and saw a flash of light from a police cruiser about a quarter-mile away. Then I looked back at the restaurant and saw Igor Volkov come out the front door. He wore his buckled overcoat and his hand was wrapped in a white towel stained with blood. He scurried to the limo and opened the driver's side door.

"He's alone," I said. "His henchmen must be somewhere else."

"We need to stop him," Cody said, climbing into the Toyota.

"Wait, we can't do it with Mia inside."

"Take her, then."

The limo backed up and Igor Volkov started turning toward the street. The squad car was still a couple blocks away. The light bar on the roof was flashing at full tilt, but the patrolman didn't seem to be in a hurry.

"Hold up," I said, and ran to the curb. I yanked my Beretta from its holster and got down on one knee. The limo had begun pulling onto Tropicana. I took aim and fired at the left front tire. The rubber sidewall collapsed with a hiss and the limo dropped onto its rim. I could see Igor's face in the windshield, his features contorted in pain. He stomped on the accelerator and the back tires spun on the gravel, and before the car lurched forward, I put a slug in the radiator.

The limo bounced onto the boulevard, smoke and steam rising from the hood. The engine howled, and the car careened toward oncoming traffic, which consisted of a single eighteen wheel big rig. The truck driver blasted his air horn, and at the last possible second the limo veered back to the right, rocking crazily on its springs, then it ran up over the curb, hit a fire hydrant, and jolted to a stop. Water spewed from beneath the car, spraying and gushing into the street.

The LVPD squad car skidded to a stop a moment later, its bumper facing the driver's side of the limo. Two patrolmen jumped out, pistols drawn. They shouted commands and Igor Volkov climbed out, scowling, hands raised, his half-lidded eyes black in his skull.

"We'd best go introduce ourselves," Cody said.

"Let me do the talking."

He shrugged. "Fine by me."

We got into the Toyota and drove across the street and parked in the lot next to the restaurant. The limo and the policemen were about a hundred feet away. I unclipped my holster. "Wait here," I said, setting my firearm on the seat. I began walking toward where Igor Volkov and the cops stood at the back of the limo, away from the path of the water, which flowed in a torrent and was creating a puddle in the street.

An unmarked four-door pulled up as I approached, and I could hear the wail of more sirens. Two plainclothes detectives got out of the sedan and flashed their badges at me. The driver was a tall man wearing a hardened, weary expression. His partner was an attractive brunette about thirty. Her hair was cut short and her black slacks didn't hide the curve of her hips.

"I'm the one who called it in," I said. "Dan Reno, private investigations."

"What happened here?" the male cop demanded.

"I suspected the Volkovs kidnapped a ten-year-old girl. I found her, hidden in a room in the back of their restaurant. She's been missing for almost two months. The restaurant is a crime scene. You need to get in there and shut it down."

"The Volkovs, huh?"

"That's right. That's the kingpin, Igor Volkov," I said, pointing to where a uniform was searching the mobster, who had assumed the position, legs spread, his hand leaving a smear of blood on the limo's trunk lid.

"Were you involved in the shooting?"

"Nope, I only took out his tire."

"Where's the girl?" the lady detective asked.

"Over there in the maroon Camry, with my partner."

"I'll take him," the tall cop said, nodding toward the limo.

"Listen, don't let Volkov out of your sight," I said. "He was in a room next to the girl. He took a shot at my partner, and would have killed him if not for his body armor. He's a crime boss, a kidnapper, and a killer. I'll come to the station and make a full statement."

The detective nodded and strode away, leaving me with the pretty brunette.

"Tell me about the kidnapping," she said, as we walked to where Cody and Mia waited in the car.

"The Volkovs and an African national, here illegally, took her from a home in Cedar City, Utah. They killed her father and nearly killed her mother. They intended to sell her to a rich pedophile."

"What's her name?"

"Mia Jordan. Her mom is Melanie Jordan. She's staying at a hotel here in Vegas, with her parents."

"We'll need to bring them both in, get their stories, and have a doctor check the little girl out."

"I'll call Melanie and tell her to meet us at the station," I said, as we reached the Camry.

Cody had seen us approaching in his mirror and he climbed out promptly. "Hello, detective," he said, smiling. "I'm Cody Gibbons, nice to meet you."

She looked past him at Mia, who sat round-eyed in the back seat. Then she turned to Cody, her face quizzical. "Your name sounds familiar," she said.

Cody shrugged. "I'm based in San Jose. I'm here visiting my daughter." He paused. "And my buddy, Dan."

"Weren't you with San Jose PD once?"

"That was a long time ago."

She snapped her fingers. "I got it—the Russ Landers case. You testified, right?"

"Yeah, I did," Cody said. "I worked for him too, and he was as dirty as they come."

She shook her head, an impish grin on her face. Cody started to say something, but I interrupted him. "We should get Mia to her mother," I said. I tapped the redial button on my cell, and again it went to Melanie's voicemail. I left a message telling her to meet us at the police station on Las Vegas Boulevard. Then I texted the message to her.

The lady detective opened the Camry's back door and knelt. "Hi Mia," she said. "I'm Anna with the police department. Here's my badge. You can hold it, okay?"

Mia took the badge in her little hands. "We're gonna go to the police station and your mom will meet us there. Are you ready to take a ride in a police car?"

"Will you turn the flashy lights on?"

"Sure, we can do that."

I looked across the lot and watched Igor Volkov climb into the back of the ambulance, followed by a uniformed cop. "I'll try the McDermotts," I said to Cody. I tapped their number and Walter answered.

"Walter, could you put Melanie on, please?"

"She's not here at the moment. Why don't you try her cell?"

"She's not picking up. Walter, I found Mia."

"You, you did?" he stammered. "Is she all right? Where is she?"

"She's here with me. The police are here too. She looks fine, or uninjured, anyway. Where's Melanie?"

"She went out to a restaurant with a young policewoman, about an hour ago."

"What?"

"Did you not hear me?"

"What did the policewoman look like?"

"Tall, reddish-brown hair, green eyes."

"You got to be kidding," I said.

"Excuse me?"

"Hold on, Walter," I said, and muted my phone. "Cody, would you call Abbey, please?"

"What's up?" he asked.

"I think Abbey is out with Melanie."

Cody cocked his head and raised an eyebrow. "Really?"

"Melanie's not answering her cell. Call Abbey, would you?"

"Did you tell her where Melanie was staying?" Cody asked, tapping his phone.

"No," I said, shaking my head. "She must have figured it out." I unmuted my phone. "Walter, what restaurant did they go to?"

"I'm not sure. They were just going for coffee. She said somewhere nearby."

I heard a sound, then Lillian McDermott came on the line.

"You have Mia?" she asked, but it sounded more like a demand.

"That's right. We're all ready to head to the police station. Can you get a hold of Melanie and meet us there?"

"I just called her. She's not answering."

I looked over at Cody. After a moment, he took his phone from his ear. "Went to voice mail," he said.

"Shit," I said.

"I beg your pardon," Lillian said.

"Did they say anything about what restaurant they went to?"

"When they left, they were still discussing it. We were all in the lobby. Melanie mentioned Applebee's. There's one a couple miles away. We ate there the other night."

"Go to the police station, Mrs. McDermott. And keep calling your daughter."

When I hung up, I saw the ambulance pull from the curb, then a squad car swung around and stopped next to us. The lady detective helped Mia into the backseat.

"Follow us, please," she said, before she ducked into the car and sat next to Mia.

"We'll be there in a bit," I said to the vehicle as it drove off. I tapped my phone screen, then opened Cody's passenger door. "Applebee's is over on Warm Springs. Go up a block and take a right on Eastern." Cody smiled uncertainly and got behind the wheel. When he turned onto the boulevard, I said, "Let's try to make some lights. I don't want to be too late."

Cody shifted into second gear as a work truck swerved by us. "Step on it," I said, but when he did, he didn't account for the large puddle in front of us. He drove straight into it, accelerating, throwing a four-foot high wall of cold water to our right, which happened to be where two patrolmen were walking around the front of the disabled limo. They jumped back but were pinned against the fender, and I watched the water splash off their uniforms and soak them from the chest down. Behind them, I saw the tall plainclothesman standing near his sedan, shaking with laughter, his tense expression temporarily relieved.

"Oops," Cody said.

"No big deal. Just a few more members of your fan club."

"I always wanted to be popular," he said, blowing through a yellow light. We were going sixty in a thirty-five zone.

"Why would Abbey want to meet with Melanie?" Cody said, passing a motorcycle on the right.

"She said something about wanting to interview her, maybe a girl-to-girl thing. Like she could find out more about the case than I have. I told her to forget it."

"Huh. Doesn't sound like she's too big on orders."

"Gee, I wonder where she got that?"

"Hold on," he said. We were approaching the light at Warm Springs. It was a stale green, and sure enough, it turned yellow just as Cody mashed the accelerator. We were doing ninety before Cody stomped the brakes, and then he let off when we entered the intersection. The light turned red as we power drifted around the corner, all four wheels sliding. He hit the gas at just the right moment and we launched forward.

"I said make a few lights, not get us killed."

"You know my rules: don't wet your pants in my car."

A minute later we drove under the 215 freeway, then bounced into the Applebee's parking lot and went inside. We quickly walked through the dining area and checked the bar. There was no sign of Melanie and Abbey.

"What the…" Cody muttered.

"Let's call them again," I said. We sat at a table in the bar and worked our cell phones. Neither Abbey nor Melanie answered, or had responded to our text messages.

"This don't smell right," Cody said. "Abbey doesn't always take my calls, but she always responds to text."

I set my phone on the table and drummed my fingers on the lacquered veneer. If Melanie alone had gone unaccounted for, I could have assumed she was having a mental issue, maybe a migraine, maybe she blacked out. Or, maybe Sasha had emerged, and Melanie had hopped in the sack with some oblivious fellow who thought it was his lucky day.

But Melanie wasn't alone; she was with Cody's daughter, who had not had a brain injury. The situation didn't add up, and my concern was increasing with every minute that passed.

Then my phone beeped, with the standard chime programed for a variety of application updates. It was also the same alert for the tracking devices attached to the limo and the black Dodge Charger.

I stared at my screen in disbelief.

"What's up?" Cody asked.

"Serj Volkov's Dodge is heading northeast on fifteen. Just crossed the Arizona state line."

"Give me that," Cody said, snatching my phone. After a moment he looked up and our eyes met. "It's heading to—

"Cedar City," we said simultaneously.

11

THE SKY WAS DARKENING, but the storm clouds dissipated as we drove, and the road turned dry. That was fortunate because Cody was reeling in the desert highway at 120 MPH. The Hellfire Hooptie's suspension was tight and every tiny bump was a jolt, but the car did not sway or bounce. Within a few minutes there were no buildings or signs of civilization, save for the strip of graded pavement growing dim in the twilight. Cody took it up to 135, steering into the southbound lane when necessary to pass cars and trucks traveling at half our speed.

"I can't believe they kidnapped Abbey," Cody said. "If they harm her—no, even if they don't harm one hair on her head, it doesn't matter—I'll settle their hash for good." His face was the color of raw granite, his brow furrowed, the crow's feet around his eyes etched deeply.

"We don't know for sure if anyone was kidnapped."

"What are you saying?"

"She could have got away, or maybe just lost her phone... "

Cody blew out his breath. "Call Denise and ask her if Abbey's been in touch. Get the number from my cell. Dial it from your phone—she probably won't take my call."

"All right." I found the number on Cody's phone and tapped it into mine.

"Culligan," she answered.

"It's Dan Reno, Miss Culligan."

"Cody's friend?"

"That's right. Has Abbey been in touch in the last hour?"

"No, why?"

"Because we think she's been kidnapped by members of the Volkov family."

The line went silent for a moment, then she said, "Based on what?"

"She was with Melanie Jordan, who's also missing. I put a tracking device on Serj Volkov's car, and he's heading north on fifteen, in Arizona right now. I think he's got them both."

"Excuse me, I'm not connecting the dots."

"Cody and I just found Mia, Melanie's missing daughter, at the Volkov's restaurant."

"Yes, Mia just got here."

"Abbey and Melanie aren't answering their phones. I think the Volkovs snatched them."

"What for?"

"They think Melanie has gold and diamonds at her house in Utah. They invaded her house a couple months ago, and now they want to finish the job."

I heard her fingernails click on her desktop. "You have a make, model, and license plate?"

"Black Dodge Charger, maybe a few years old. I've got a picture of the license, I'll text it to you."

"If they're out of state, the best I can do is contact Arizona PD."

"Alert Utah too. They're heading to Cedar City."

"Where's Cody?" she asked.

"Right next to me. Do you want to talk to him?"

She paused for a long moment. "No, not right now."

We hung up, and I looked at the red arrow on my screen. "They've got seventy miles on us."

"Tell me again how you read this." Cody's fists were clenched on the wheel, his knuckles red.

"I blew it, man. I should have been more patient. I didn't have to confront the African. I could have walked away."

"And what if you did?"

"I should have suspected Mia was at that restaurant from the beginning. We could have rescued her before they knew what hit them. They would have had no time to react."

"And you think their reaction was to snatch Melanie because they think the bulk of her fortune is still at her house?"

"They only got a small part of it the first time. Now that I pushed it and the heat is coming down, they want to finish the job in a hurry. Then they'll blow town."

"But how would they know Melanie was in Vegas? How would they know how to find her?"

"She got a new cell phone, but I assume she kept her old number and email address, Facebook page, whatever."

"You think the Russians hacked it."

"Right. Lexi the driver had a computer fraud rap on his sheet. It could have been him, or maybe even that weasel at the restaurant who told us where Mia was."

"Little prick looked like a computer nerd. But how is the African linked to the Russians?"

"I don't know exactly. I think he came to the U.S. to get back the diamonds, or gold, Jeff Jordan's CIA father stole from him, or his clan. But he probably needed help. Once the Volkovs found out there was potentially millions in diamonds to be had, they were more than happy to partner with him."

"If there's one thing that's a given for every scumbag mobster, it's the love of money," Cody said, passing a minivan in a whoosh.

"Yeah, but here's the problem: the Volkovs probably don't know I've already been to the house, and not only dug up the rest of the gold, but also found at least a million in diamonds. It's all locked away in a bank, in a safe deposit box. So, when they get there… "

Cody's leg straightened as he jammed the pedal to the floor.

• • •

The sky was splattered with a confused jumble of clouds, the rolls of dense honeycombed masses giving way to a silky sheen of white wisps that glowed fluorescent in the twilight. The road faded into the dusk, the lane markers rushing by in a blur. Then a series of red rock mesas became visible up ahead, still radiant with the last of the day's sun.

"I'm gonna call the Cedar City PD and tell them to send as many cars as they can to the Jordan house," I said.

"How many cars is that?" Cody asked.

"I don't know. It's a pretty small town."

"You think they can take these guys down?"

"That's their job. They're trained policemen."

"They got a SWAT team?"

"I doubt it," I said, staring out the windshield.

A low flying bird rose above our windshield at the last instant. "I could try the FBI," I said.

"The nearest FBI office is either Vegas or Salt Lake," Cody said. "By the time they arrive, there'll be nothing to do but ask stupid questions and clean up the mess."

I sighed and called the cell number I had for Detective Taylor Humphries, the cop I'd met when I visited the Cedar City police station.

When he didn't answer I called the Cedar City PD main number. After waiting on hold for five minutes, a woman finally came on the line.

"This is a police emergency. Can I speak with an officer?"

"You need to hang up and dial nine-one-one."

"I'm not in town. Please put a policeman on."

"Hold, please."

A minute later a tired male voice said, "Sergeant Wilkens."

I introduced myself and said, "I was hired by the Jordan family to investigate Jeff Jordan's murder."

"Yes?"

"I have reason to believe Melanie Jordan and another woman have been kidnapped by criminals who are driving to the Jordan house now. They should be there within an hour."

"Who are you, again?"

"Dan Reno, private investigator. Listen, these woman are in danger. The kidnappers are professional criminals, and they'll kill them both after they get there. They're driving a black Dodge Charger. Consider them armed and dangerous."

"How do you know all this?"

"Because I've been investigating the case, dammit. Look, if you have questions, call Taylor Humphries, he knows about it. But you need to get squad cars to that house."

"I'll call Detective Humphries," he said.

"You do that. And Sergeant?"

"Yes?"

"Be ready for shooting when you get there. These guys are dead serious."

"Well, so are we."

· · ·

By the time we crossed into Arizona, the Dodge Charger was still forty miles ahead of us. They had to be traveling at between ninety and a hundred miles per hour, which was easy to do in the open desert. We raced across the northwest corner of the state, our headlights panning the red rock formations to either side of the road. Cody stayed hard on the gas through a curvy section, the Toyota hugging the corners as if it was on rails. We slowed when a state cruiser pulled onto the freeway, and lost time for five minutes. As soon as the trooper turned off, Cody buried the pedal and we ran wide open for ten straight miles.

We blasted across the Utah state line under a sky dimly lit by a crescent moon. When we reached Saint George, the Charger was still thirty miles ahead of us, which meant they'd arrive at the Jordan house in roughly twenty minutes.

"We'll never catch them," I said.

"No shit," Cody said, his voice flat. "Go to the backseat. Fill the magazine on my autoloader. It holds eight shells."

I unbuckled my seatbelt and climbed into the back, where Cody's sawed-off ten gauge lay on the seat. I found the big shells in his bag and fed them into the long magazine beneath the barrel. Then I pulled free my Beretta and made sure the eleven-round magazine was full. My hand moved to my left pocket, where I kept my extra clip. It felt cold and heavy in my palm.

We didn't speak much after that, as we sped through the night. The highway was smooth and deserted and Cody ran his souped-up Toyota flat out, the speedometer bouncing off 150. I sat still in my seat, jaw clenched, my hands gripping my knees. I thought briefly about Candi and pictured her inside our remodeled family room, curled on the couch with our fuzzy gray cat. Then I thought of Abbey, cocky and irreverent just like her father, but too damn young and inexperienced to know what she was getting into. And then I thought of Melanie and everything she'd been through.

But I didn't contemplate the three women for very long, because I had more important things to worry about. We were likely heading into a combat situation, one that would probably involve hostages. Distraction could be disastrous. Survival would require a clear mind, heightened senses, and complete focus. And good aim, I reminded myself, touching my automatic. Accurate and quick, without the slightest hesitation.

Cody needed no reminder of combat tactics. As an ex-cop, he'd been involved in many more shootings than me. But I'd had my fair share of experience, and I'd learned that the line between life and death is often a thin one.

We were ten miles outside of Cedar City when the red arrow on my screen showed the Charger moving down the two-mile dirt road leading to the Jordan's house. It could do no more than thirty miles an hour on that stretch, but we'd be at the same disadvantage.

I watched the screen for a few minutes, until I said, "They're at the house."

"What's our ETA?" Cody said. His massive frame was hunched forward, his face inches from the steering wheel.

"About fifteen minutes."

When we reached Cedar City, we were forced to slow to navigate through some light traffic. Cody drove at ninety MPH in the left lane and passed on the right and it didn't take more than two minutes to leave the city lights in the rearview mirror. Then we were out on the desert plains again, and he buried the throttle.

"The turn off is in a couple miles. Better slow down so we don't miss it," I said, peering to the right. The thin moon lit the brush fields and the low hills with an eerie glow. We blew by a big rig pulling a double-trailer, the air pressure buffeting the Camry and pushing it toward the center divider. Cody stayed on the accelerator and fought the wheel until we cleared the truck, and then I said, "Less than a mile. Slow down and get ready."

The shoulder became wider, and up ahead I saw where the dirt and gravel road began.

"Here," I said.

Cody stomped the brakes and steered onto the shoulder. We slid to a stop, the gravel spraying beneath the tires. Then he popped the clutch, spinning the tires and counter-steering as the back end kicked out.

"Go easy," I said. "Throw this thing in a ditch, we're screwed."

"Grab my sawed-off," he said.

I reached behind us and grasped the scattergun. The pistol grip was oversize and had been modified to fit Cody's hands. He was ambidextrous, and could shoot equally well with his right or left.

Cody kept it at thirty, steering carefully around ruts. "Lights off?" he asked.

"Not yet. Keep going."

When the steel gate was in sight, I saw it was wide open. The house was not yet visible, hidden by the low rise to our right.

"Stop here," I said. "The house is just over that hill. Let's go on foot."

He killed the lights and made a couple of Y-turns, until the Hellfire Hooptie was facing back toward the highway. Then we got out and began hiking through the sagebrush, along the same path that I had walked with Melanie on the day I'd first been on the property. There was more snow now, which would make our dark masses easier to spot once we crested the hill.

I stopped. "Smell that?" I whispered.

Cody came up close behind me. "Smoke," he said. "Gasoline smoke."

We continued forward, and then two plumes became visible, rising into the dark sky. It was cold and vapor poured from our mouths. As we neared the crest I said, "Stay low."

A few more steps took us to the spot where I'd previously found the Pacific brand cigarette butt, and then we reached the vantage point.

Crouching, we looked down at the clearing where the Jordans' big house was built. I blinked hard, trying to assimilate the scene before us. In front of the unlit home were two police cars, or what remained of them. They were both on fire, the hulks torn open and charred black, the blue and white paint visible only at the bumpers. In one car I could make out two blackened bodies in the front seats. The roof of the other car was collapsed as if crushed by a boulder, making it impossible to see if anyone was inside. But outside the passenger door a uniformed cop lay face down, unmoving and obviously dead.

"Bazooka," Cody said.

I nodded, then something caught my eye between the house and the barn. The area was shadowed and almost pitch black, but I could make out the shape of a car, and then a second vehicle.

"Down there, next to the barn," I said. "Probably the Charger, another car too."

Ducking low, we scampered down the hill, our boots crunching through the snow. The burning cars cast garish patterns of light and shadow against the dark windows and front door of the house. We reached the far side of the corral and walked behind the horse stalls, guns drawn, until we came to the two cars parked aside the barn. One was the Charger, and twenty feet past it I recognized the older Ford sedan that had been parked at the Café Leonov.

"Someone's in the Ford," I whispered. The Charger was empty.

We crept behind the Ford, Cody aiming his shotgun. I came around the passenger side, my Berretta trained on the figure in the driver's seat. I suspected it was Lexi Voronin, who was both the registered owner and the Volkov's driver. But he also had a long rap sheet and was a suspected murderer. *Maybe your night to pay for your sins,* I thought, as I saw Cody raise his ten gauge. Then, as I moved forward, I caught a glimpse of the occupant's profile.

"Christ, it's Abbey," I rasped.

Cody rushed to the window, and I looked in from the passenger side. Abbey sat, arms outstretched, her hands zip-tied to the steering wheel. She looked back and forth between us with frantic eyes. I tried the door and looked across the roof at Cody.

"Locked," I said, watching him pull on the driver's door. Then he rapped on the window with the barrel of his weapon and motioned with his hand. Abbey turned toward me and ducked her face into her shoulder as Cody broke the window with a loud crunch. He knocked the glass free until the hole was large enough to allow him to open the door.

"Here," I said, reaching over the roof and handing him the wire cutters I always carried. Cody cut her hands free, then Abbey jumped out of the car and into his arms. He held her closely, her frame huddled in his mass, her head against his chest. I looked away, feeling like an awkward witness to a private moment. Instead I focused my attention on the corner of the house. We were aside it, so I couldn't see the front door.

"How many of them?" Cody said quietly.

"Four," Abbey said. "Serj Volkov, Lexi, another Russian, and a black man I've never seen."

"They've got Melanie?" I asked.

She nodded. "I think they're all inside."

"Abbey, listen—"

"Dad, those squad cars were waiting when we got here. Volkov has a grenade launcher. He just stopped and blew them up. One after another, boom, boom. I saw the cops on fire, burning up. I heard their screams." In the moonlight I could see her cheeks were shiny with tears.

"Now, listen, kid," Cody said. "You've got to hold it together. I need you away from here, and quick. My car's parked out on the road, over that hill. You run straight that way, it will only take two minutes, and don't stop for nothing, hear? Take my keys. Drive out to the highway and haul ass to the Cedar City police station. Tell them to send every man they've got."

"And what are you gonna do?"

"Let me worry about that. Now, go!"

Abbey took off at a run, just as I heard a sound. I ran forward until I could see along the front of the house. The front door was open and a man holding an automatic was aiming at where Abbey was running past the corral. I recognized him as the cook from the Café Leonov who tried to disregard us before Cody pistol whipped him. The next instant I dropped into a crouch, arm outstretched, and fired. His gun hand dropped when my first bullet hit him in the gut. His face went slack, his eyes uncomprehending, and he stared at me as if seeking an explanation. He'd die wanting, for my second shot hit him dead center in the chest. He fell forward, then toppled off the porch and lay sprawled in the dirt, staring sightlessly, blood soaking his shirt.

"I bet your cooking sucked, anyways," I said, walking to the body. Cody came up behind me.

"You killed him, and you still need to insult him?" he asked.

"Must be a personality defect. I'll work on it."

We moved to the front door, and I took position against the wall on the near side, and Cody went past me to the far side. "I'll cover you," he said, as I peered into the dark, circular foyer.

I went inside, ducking low. To the left was the unfurnished sitting room and further left a hallway accessed the bedrooms. On my right, a short, curved hallway led to the kitchen, and beyond that was the dining room and the family room, where I had found Jeff Jordan's cell phone wedged in the couch frame.

I could see light from the kitchen spilling onto the tile of the curved hallway. But the kitchen was also accessible through the sitting room, which I felt was a safer approach.

Cody, his shotgun in his left hand and his .357 in his right, followed me as I stepped onto the carpet. My habit is to always stay low in a combat situation, to reduce my target profile. Cody made no such effort. He stood tall, his six-foot-five frame challenging all comers, his weapons at the ready.

A dim light fell onto the carpet from the kitchen archway in the rear of the sitting room. Then a voice called out, "Ilya?"

Cody came alongside me and I pointed toward the light. I crept forward, then stood against the wall and took a quick glance into the kitchen. A single figure stood in front of the refrigerator. It was Lexi Voronin. He wore black jeans and pointy shoes and a white shirt unbuttoned to reveal the dark hair on his chest. In his right hand was a snub nose .32 automatic.

He fired two shots into the wall behind which I stood. One of the rounds blew through the sheetrock above my head and powdered my hair, while the second round must have lodged in a stud. I reached out with my left hand, my body still behind the wall, and rapid-fired three shots. The first shot splatted into the stainless steel door of the refrigerator. The second nicked Voronin's forearm, as he turned to run out the back of the kitchen. I never knew the exact result of my third, because Cody fired his ten gauge simultaneously, and the buckshot blast hit Voronin in the shoulder and neck, and nearly decapitated him. Voronin bounced off a cabinet and slammed to the floor, his pocket-pistol still clutched in his hand. Blood spread from the twitching body rapidly, puddling and flowing along the indentions between the floor tiles.

"I guess he was outgunned," I said.

"Poor planning on his part," Cody replied. "But live and learn."

"Too late for that."

I stepped over the dead man and looked into the family room. The lights were on, but it was empty. I took a few steps toward the couch. Then I dove to the ground as a burst of machine gun fire rang out.

"Hey, bitches," a voice yelled. It wasn't from the kitchen, but farther out, from the front room. I rolled to my feet and returned to the kitchen, where Cody knelt. He pointed his pistol at the archway. We could only see a slim portion of the sitting room from our position.

"You want a shootout? No problem, but I got your pretty girl with me." Another burst clattered, and holes appeared in the cabinets over the stove, the wood splintering. Two rounds came through the archway into the center of the kitchen. One shattered a ceramic jar on the counter above me, and the other pinged off the barrel of Cody's shotgun.

Cody scrambled back to where I crouched. "I'll go around from the front door," he whispered. "Distract him."

I grabbed his arm. "Don't kill him," I said. Cody nodded, then went out the opposite end of the kitchen and turned down the circular hall that led to the foyer. I crept forward until I was at the base of the arch.

"Hey, Serj, take it easy," I said, risking a peek into the sitting room. He stood at the far end, near the hallway to the bedrooms. He held Melanie in front of him, using her body as a shield. In his free hand he held a submachine gun, an HK model with a distinctive 9mm banana clip.

Serj Volkov smiled when he saw me and raised his weapon. But the black man standing behind him in the hallway was not smiling. The grimace on his face was one of pain and anger, and when our eyes met, his smoldered with hatred. He tilted the machete from where it rested against his shoulder and made a hacking motion.

"Don't hurt her, Serj. If you do, you'll never get what you came for."

Serj Volkov pointed his HK and let loose another blast as I dropped to the floor. He aimed low, spraying the kitchen. One of his bullets knocked a piece of rubber off my boot sole, and two slugs plowed into the bloody mess that remained of Lexi Voronin. Then I heard him stitch the walls of the sitting room, shattering the front window.

"You got me, Serj. I give up," I yelled, right before I heard the deep boom of Cody's .357, followed by a shout and a scream. I jumped to my feet and ran through the archway, expecting to see Volkov down. I was hoping to draw on the African and make him surrender. But the African was nowhere in sight, and Volkov was still on his feet, despite a bleeding wound in the meat of his thigh. He staggered to the side, his pants leg soaked red, while Melanie broke free, ran into the hall, and disappeared into a door on the right.

Volkov's face was balled in a mask of agony. His skin on his forehead was bunched and his crew cut hair nearly touched his eyebrows. He tried to raise his weapon, but lost his balance and toppled over. As he fell, I shot at where his right hand grasped the HK. His thumb vanished in a burst of red, and the submachine gun fell to the carpet.

"Keep him alive," I said to Cody, as he came forward, his pistol smoking. He holstered his revolver, released the clip from the HK, and stood frowning over Volkov.

"No guarantees. I think he might bleed out."

"Use his belt as a tourniquet," I said. Then I looked again and said, "You're hit." Cody's dark jacket was wet on the right side, and I saw a tear in the material between his neck and shoulder.

"One of his rounds ricocheted off something, maybe the light fixture. Got me right above the collar bone. Right next to the top of my vest."

"You're bleeding pretty good."

"Don't worry about it," he said, but he looked pale, and then he sat on the floor. "Go get that piece of shit," he said, nodding toward the hallway. "I got your back."

I turned to Serj Volkov and grabbed his shirt from the front, and in a single motion, tore it free of his torso.

"*Po'shyol 'na hui,*" he said, and though I didn't know what the words meant, the insult in his tone was unmistakable. I dropped to my knee, my self-control gone in a rush, and drove my fist toward his face, but I pulled back at the last instant. "I'm tired of hearing your voice, but I need you awake," I said.

Cody lifted his shotgun with his left hand and covered the hallway entrance while I pushed the coat off his shoulders and saw where the bullet had entered his body.

"The round passed all the way through," I said, eying the entrance point above his collar bone. "It's just a flesh wound." The exit hole was in the meat of his trapezius muscle, just over where his body armor covered his back. Blood was trickling from both holes.

"Got any whiskey, doc?" Cody said, trying to smile.

I ignored the question and looped Volkov's shirt under Cody's armpit, then once again, before tying it tight on his chest.

"Hang in there, buddy," I said, standing and pointing my Beretta down the empty hallway.

The four doors were all shut. The first door on the left was to Mia's bedroom. I eased it open, ready to fire if the African slashed at me with his machete. But the room was empty. I quickly checked the closet, then moved back to the hallway.

Across from Mia's room was the den, where Melanie had fled to. I looked at the two remaining doors, one to a bathroom, and the other to the master bedroom at the end. The African could be behind either door. Or, he could be in the den, with Melanie. It was also possible he scrambled out a window in the back and was trying to escape into the cold night.

"Melanie, I'm coming in," I said. "Okay?"

No response.

I took one more look at the other two doors, then I turned the knob and pushed the door open with my toe.

The lights were off, but once the door swung all the way back, I could see the room was empty. I stepped inside and flipped the light switch. I spun in a circle, then my eyes fell on the desk drawer. Inside it was the release for the bookshelf that served as a barricade for the secret basement Jeff Jordan had built to both store food and house his gun safe.

For a moment I considered the possibility that Melanie was down there with the African. I didn't know what had transpired in the fifteen minutes prior to our arrival. Melanie could have already revealed the hidden latch and opened the safe to allow the Volkovs and the Africans to search it. Her best option would have been to stall; tell them that diamonds and gold were buried on the property, but they'd need to wait until daybreak for her to pinpoint the location. But I was sure they had threatened her life and her mind would have been frozen with fear. In that condition, it would be difficult to think strategically.

I went to the desk, opened the drawer, and reached in, searching for the release lever. I was bent over, my right arm deep in the drawer, my automatic in my left hand. My fingers had just touched the lever when a shadow fell over me.

"Freeze or die," a voice whispered.

I stared at the wall, my chin on the desk. I heard the door close quietly.

"Drop the gun," the African said, speaking louder now, "or I'll put a second hole in your ass."

I hesitated. I was in an awkward position, bent over, facing away, and not knowing for sure if the African held a firearm. I estimated the chances at fifty-fifty. I briefly considered a turn and shoot maneuver, but I wasn't willing to risk my life on a coin toss. Especially not with Cody Gibbons, injured or not, in the next room. I let the Beretta slide from my fingers to the carpet, then I slowly straightened, pulling my arm from the drawer.

"Turn around now, so I can see your cowardly face."

I turned and saw I'd made the right call. The African held a .38 revolver. It looked freshly oiled and cleaned, which made a misfire unlikely. He pointed the gun at my face, then lowered it to my crotch.

"You'll die soon, but you will suffer first," he said. His eyes were deep set in his skull, and when he smiled his gums were pink against his dark skin. His chipped teeth looked feral, the lower incisors triangular and sharp. "Too bad I don't have time to cut you to pieces. But you will suffer like the dog you are."

I took a step to my left, turning my hip but keeping my chest square to him. We were only ten feet apart, and if he fired, I hoped to take the round in my vest. Or my hip as a worst case. As long as the shot wasn't immediately disabling, I'd have a chance to get my hands on him before he could pull the trigger again.

"Your knees first, stupid boy," he said, lowering the pistol again. "No more walking, ever, for you." His eyes gleamed with an evil anticipation that seemed almost carnal.

"Don't do it, my partner will take your head off."

"I'll kill him next. But first you die." He straightened his arm, his revolver aimed at my right knee.

"If you want your diamonds—

My sentence was cut short by a thunderous blast from behind. I jumped to the left, startled, my hands outstretched in a defensive pose. The African's mouth puckered into a circle, his eyes round with shock. A crimson stain was spreading from a black hole in the center of his chest. The .38 fell from his hand, then another blast sounded, and a second hole appeared an inch above the first.

The African emitted an odd groan that reminded me of a sound an animal might make, perhaps a mule's bray. Then he dropped to his knees, his head touching the ground for a long moment, before he fell to the side, his sightless eyes locked forever on whatever private hell encapsulated his life.

I turned and saw a wisp of smoke curling from the center of the bookcase. Next came a clunking sound, and the bookcase swung open.

Melanie stepped into the room. In her hands was a Browning .30-06 hunting rifle. She held the big gun at port arms, its length reaching diagonally from her knee to aside her head. She stared at the body on the floor.

"Is—is he dead?"

"Yeah," I said, blinking in disbelief. "Don't look at him. Let's set that over here." I took the rifle from her hands.

"You see the hole," she said, pulling the bookcase closed. She pointed to an inch wide square aligned with the top of a hardback book. I walked over and felt its edges with my finger.

"No one could tell it was there," she said. "Jeff designed it that way. He said, if I was ever in trouble, to lock myself in and shoot anyone who came into the room."

I released my breath. "That was good thinking on his part," I said.

"I guess so," she whispered. Then her eyes locked on the bloody body of the African. He lay on his side, one arm twisted beneath his torso, the ankles touching each other. His eyes were wide and milky white around the dark pupils.

"You got anything to cover his face?" I asked, glancing around the room.

She shook her head. "He was here that night. I recognized his voice. He's the one who cut Jeff." A solitary tear ran down her face. "I suppose I got even, huh?"

"Yeah, and you saved my ass, too," I said. "Let's get out of here."

· · ·

In the front room, Cody sat leaning against the wall next to Serj Volkov. Cody had fastened a belt around Volkov's thigh and was holding it tight. Despite his injuries, Volkov's face was impassive, as if to convey he was unworried about his predicament. Cody, on the other hand, was grimacing in pain.

"Melanie, meet my partner, Cody Gibbons," I said. "Do you have a first aid kit?"

"Yes, and I know how to use it, too." She knelt and looked at the blood stained cloth I'd tied around Cody's wound.

"Can you come with me?" she asked Cody. "I'll shoot you with pain-killer and dress your wound."

"You sure?" Cody said.

"I trained for this," Melanie replied. "Part of being prepared."

Cody looked at me, then rose and followed her down the hallway.

"How about the tourniquet?" Serj Volkov said. He was bare chested and his shoulders and pecs were chiseled and no doubt the result of disciplined work outs. His waist was without fat, the abdominal muscles toned and prominent.

"No problem, Serj," I said, kneeling and cinching the belt tight above the wound in his thigh. "Let's also tend to your hand." I removed the sleeve still clinging to his arm and wrapped it around his damaged hand, gently covering the stub that remained of his thumb.

"The bitch said she had something for the pain, too," he said, cutting his eyes toward the hallway.

"I'm sure that can be arranged," I said. "I think you're gonna be okay, back to the gym in no time. As long as you answer a few questions first."

"No deal," he said, a forced smile on his face.

"You're the only one in your group left alive, my friend. I wouldn't take it for granted."

"Everybody dies sometime."

"I got to hand it to you Serj, you're pretty tough."

"You don't know a thing about it," he replied.

"Yeah, I do," I said, rising. I brought my foot down on his bleeding hand.

He gritted his jaw and tried to remain silent, but his lips were twisted into an unnatural scowl and beads of sweat broke out on his forehead.

"This can go on for a long time. It's your call."

"Eat shit and die," he hissed.

I shifted my weight, then kicked at the bullet hole in his thigh. He screamed and began panting, his breath ragged and his heart beating visibly beneath the skin.

"I'm not even out of first gear yet, Serj. Tell me about the black man."

I lifted my shoe from his hand. "Ready for round two? I asked. When he didn't respond I stomped his hand and pivoted. His eyes jerked wide, and he ineffectually punched at my leg as a cry escaped his lips. A moment later surrender flooded his face, his eyes pleading, spit bubbling from the corners of his lips. And then answers poured from his mouth as if he couldn't speak quickly enough.

• • •

When Cody and Melanie emerged from the hall a few minutes later, they were grinning, and if I didn't know better, I would have sworn they just had quick sex in the bathroom.

"What did you shoot him with?" I asked.

"A double dose of lidocaine. It numbs the tissue and reduces bleeding."

"She is one hell of a nurse, by god," Cody said.

"Cody told me you found Mia," Melanie said. "Is she, is she okay?"

"She looked fine, Melanie. I don't think they hurt her." I almost added, *not physically, anyway.*

Melanie smiled, but there were tears in her eyes. "Oh my god, thank you," she said, her voice cracking. "Thank you so much." She tried to continue, but then she dropped her head and put her hands to her face. Her shoulders shuddered, and she tried to mute a sob.

"I want to hear her voice," she said between sniffles. "Can I call her?"

"There, there," Cody said. "Sure you can, she's with the police in Vegas. I'll get you the number." He put his arm around her as he worked his phone, but he wasn't watching and his fingers bumped her breast.

"Hey!" she said, recovering in an instant. She spanked his butt with a quick swat.

"Sorry, my bad," Cody said. "How's he doing?" he added, nodding at Serj, who lay flat on his back, eyes closed. I'd tied the belt tight above the wound in his leg.

"I think he fainted," I said. "But first he told me what I needed to know."

"Everything?" Cody asked.

"Yup."

"Melanie," Cody said. "Go ahead and use my phone. But when you're done, I'd say celebration is called for. We all deserve a drink."

"You're already doped up," I said.

Cody ignored my remark. "You got any booze in the house?" he asked Melanie.

"Maybe a bottle of wine."

"That's it?" Cody said. "Just *wine*?"

"We never kept liquor in the house. Or beer."

Cody frowned, as if it was the worst news he'd heard all day. Given the circumstances, I couldn't help laughing. Melanie looked at me like I'd lost my mind, but before I could comment, Cody said, "Screw it, then. Bring on the vino."

•   •   •

While Melanie called Vegas PD, Cody and I walked out to the front yard. We stood in the cold light and he pulled a cigarette from his pack. He was searching his pockets for a light when my cell rang. It was Abbey, reporting she was on the way back with the Cedar City police. I handed my phone to Cody.

"Tell them the situation here is under control," Cody said. "That's right, Abbey, they're out of commission. What? No, it's all taken care of. Tell them to keep their guns in their holsters."

"Better enjoy the calm while it lasts," Cody said after he hung up. He gave me a smoke and we sat on the steps, looking out over the smoldering squad cars. The scene had a surreal quality, as if a war zone had been transplanted into the most unlikely of locales. Smoke still drifted upward from the blackened cruisers, and I dragged from my cigarette, hoping to mask the odor wafting from the yard. At least three patrolmen lay dead among the twisted wrecks, two of them burnt beyond recognition. To my left was the body of the gunman I'd shot when we first arrived, and inside the house, two more corpses were staining the floors. And I couldn't honestly say Serj Volkov wouldn't soon join them, for he'd lost a significant amount of blood and had fallen unconscious just as he'd answered my final question.

A holocaust survivor I met years ago had told me a story about his experience in the death camp. He'd found a secret cache of food, and to access it he needed to sneak through a room stacked with rotting corpses. The horror of the room never fazed him. The desire to survive deadened him to the fright or revulsion a person would normally experience. The survival instinct made all else trivial.

Sitting on the steps facing the yard, I wondered if I was experiencing the same phenomenon. For I felt nothing but numbness. Later, I knew I'd feel varying degrees of satisfaction, relief, triumph, and probably also guilt and regret, for death always brought that. But for the moment I was insensate.

Cody, on the other hand, was behaving as he always did after a shooting, which was not a great departure from how he behaved in most circumstances; he wanted a drink, and he hated drinking alone. When Melanie joined us a minute later, she held a serving tray with three glasses of red wine, and despite his proclaimed preference for hard booze, Cody didn't hesitate to grab a glass. He held it by the stem and sniffed the contents suspiciously. "I guess it will have to do," he said.

I took my own glass and Melanie sat between us. No one said anything at first, and I considered a toast, but I was out of words for the moment. But Melanie wasn't.

"Here's to you, Dan, for standing by me and rescuing Mia," she said. "And to you for your help, Cody." We clinked glasses, and I patted Melanie on the back, hoping to both console and thank her. And then I finally drank, ending my dry stint with a glass of merlot while sitting with my best friend and the woman who saved my life. I drank slowly, waiting for the cops in the brittle cold of the Utah desert, trying to ignore the grim carnage that lay before us.

12

WE SAT LISTENING AS the sirens grew louder, until we could see bursts of red and blue light flashing against the hillsides and the low clouds. When they finally roared into the clearing, Melanie jumped up, waving her arms over her head as if signaling a boat from a deserted island. The headlights poured over us, and her distorted shadow danced frenetically against the house. Then she seemed to realize the pointlessness of her gyrations and abruptly sat again.

And that's the way the Cedar City authorities found us, sitting on the porch, huddled in our coats, finishing the last of the red wine. There were three blue-and-whites, two Ford SUVs, a fire truck, and an ambulance. The firemen and paramedics ran to the charred patrol cars, while the policemen, followed by Abbey, converged on us.

"Dear, do you have another bottle?" Cody asked Melanie.

I spotted Taylor Humphries, the Cedar City plainclothes detective. He wore an oversize, puffy down jacket over the same pleated khaki pants and red rugby shirt he was wearing when I first met him. His light blue eyes were wide and jittery.

Next to him was a man about fifty with a square face and a five o'clock shadow. He started introducing himself as the Chief of Police, but stopped when I jerked my thumb toward the front door.

"Three bodies inside. Two dead, one might still be alive."

The chief gave rapid orders, and three uniformed cops went through the front door, guns drawn. Abbey walked around the remaining five policemen and sat next to her father. When she saw the empty wine glass, she rolled her eyes. "*Really?*" she said.

"We'll need to interview you separately," the chief said. He pointed at me. "You're in charge?"

"That's right."

I followed him to one of the unmarked cars and stood in the glare of its headlights.

"I understand you were hired by Melanie Jordan's parents, to investigate the murder of her husband."

"And her daughter's kidnapping."

"So how did it come down to this?" He spoke through clenched teeth and his words were clipped. He thrust his arm at where the paramedics were working to extract the two unfortunate officers from one of the burnt squad cars.

"The Volkovs, a Russian crime family from Vegas, had partnered with an African national who came to the U.S. to try to recover diamonds that were stolen from his clan. Turns out the diamonds ended up in Jeff Jordan's possession."

"How did that happen?"

"Jeff Jordan's father was a CIA operative in Africa. He stole the diamonds and smuggled them here through Los Angeles. For whatever reason, he gave them to Jeff."

"Wait a minute. You told Detective Humphries this was about gold, not diamonds."

"Jeff Jordan traded some of the diamonds for gold. It was through an unlicensed, black market trader. The Volkovs found out about it."

"But they dug up the gold when they killed Jeff, right?"

"Only a small part of it. They returned to get the rest."

"Tonight, you mean."

"Yes."

The chief shook his head, then turned to watch the paramedics pull one of the charred officers through a squad car window and lay the carbonized remains on a gurney.

"That officer was married with three young children," the chief said. His jaw was shiny and I could see black pits in his nose. "I've got to tell his family." He stared at the ground, and I watched him clench and unclench his hands. "Someone needs to pay for this," he said.

"They already have," I said, nodding toward the house. "With their lives."

His eyes flashed, and he stared at me. "You killed them?"

"In self-defense. They were all armed and firing. But maybe one survived—Serj Volkov. He's the one who blew up your cars."

"He's inside?"

I nodded, and when we looked at the house, two cops were carrying Volkov out the front door. They yelled for the paramedics.

"You want a live perp, there you go," I said.

Two paramedics rushed to tend to the bleeding mobster, leaving a hapless fireman behind to extract the second dead Cedar City policeman from the patrol car sitting thirty feet from us. The fireman had jammed a crowbar into the door frame, and it finally came open with a wretched screech. He reached in, fit his gloved hands around the rib cage of the corpse, and tried to lift it out the door, but it appeared affixed to what remained of the seat. He put his hands on his hips and looked around for help, then bent to the task again.

"What about the little Jordan girl?" the chief asked.

"My partner and I found her earlier today, locked up in a restaurant run by the Volkovs. She's safe with Vegas PD now."

The chief raised his eyes, and I saw a glimmer of hope, as if there was some small degree of redemption in my words. Then we both looked over at the fireman, who had his foot on the bottom of the door frame and was pulling hard on the body.

The chief took a quick step toward the car, but at that moment a loud crack sounded, and the fireman stumbled back, holding the blackened arm of the corpse, while the rest of the body remained upright in the seat.

"Ah, shit!" the fireman yelled. He tossed the arm aside and returned to the car.

"Good lord," the chief said. He bent over, his hands on his knees, and spit on the ground. "Good lord almighty."

"Are we done here?" I asked.

When he straightened, his eyes were red and watery and his mouth hung open. "God, I almost lost my cookies," he said. "No, we're not done. I need to call the state police and the FBI." He pointed at me. "Don't you or your friends leave town. You can stay at the hotel across from our station."

I looked around and didn't see Cody's hotrod, which meant that Abbey must have ridden here with the police. "Hey, Chief, we're gonna need a lift," I said.

He began marching back to the house. "Fine," he said. "We'll take you when we're done."

I knew better than to ask how long it would be. Instead, I walked away from the lights, over to the horse stables. It was dark, but then my eyes adjusted and a horse approached and whinnied softly. I patted his neck, checked the time on my cell, and found the number for Greg Stillman, my CIA contact. It was eight p.m. on a Wednesday night, and I knew Stillman had my number in his phone, so he'd know who was calling. Whether or not that would prompt him to take the call was a different matter. But he must have been in a curious mood because he answered after a single ring.

"Reno, I have to admit I never expected to hear from you again," he said.

"Evening, Greg."

"I take it this isn't a social call."

"No, I'm calling about one of your agents, Bur Jordan. Ring a bell?"

"What about him?"

"Have you been investigating his murder?"

He paused. "What do you know about it?"

"I know he was shot and killed in November. I also know who did it."

"How would you know that?"

"Because I was hired to investigate his son's murder. They were both shot and mutilated—arms hacked off. It was the same killer, an illegal from Africa. He's here now in Cedar City."

"You sure on your facts, Reno?"

"Damn sure."

"Is he being held by the police?"

"Not exactly."

"What, then?"

"His body will be on the way to the coroner shortly."

I heard Stillman tongue click in his mouth. "Let me guess—you shot him."

"Nope, not me. It was Melanie Jordan, wife of Jeff, Bur Jordan's son."

"What's the African's name?"

"I don't know. Why don't you hop on a plane, meet me at Cedar City PD tomorrow morning, and take possession of the body? You can probably still catch a flight to Las Vegas. It's only a two and a half hour drive."

"I'll alert our investigating agent."

"I'm sure he can sort it out with the FBI."

"The FBI?"

"The killer crossed state lines, along with some Russian mobsters. The Feds are probably already on their way."

Stillman cursed under his breath. The CIA and FBI have a long history of conflicting agendas. I knew Stillman would take a dim view of FBI involvement in Bur Jordan's murder case. I was hoping he'd react with a sense of urgency.

"Keep your cell on," he said. "You'll be contacted."

We hung up, and I stood in the darkness. I watched a van and a second ambulance drive into the clearing, their frames rocking on the uneven terrain. A fireman began sawing the crushed roof from the second destroyed police car. After a moment I turned away and saw that the porch was empty.

I walked to the house and went in, then followed the sound of Cody's voice to the dining room. He and Abbey were sitting at the table across from two plainclothesmen. When they saw me, the cops looked up with bewildered expressions.

"Yes?" one of them said.

"Sorry to interrupt," I said.

"That's all right," his partner said. "I guess we're about done." They closed their notebooks and slowly rose, as if uncertain what to do next.

I turned away and walked into the family room, where Melanie sat on the couch with Taylor Humphries and two uniformed officers. All three were silent, and none acknowledged me. I sat at the end of the couch and that seemed to snap the cops out of their stupor, but when they turned to me, I couldn't tell to what degree they were stunned, confused, angry, or suspicious.

"I'll take it from here," Humphries said. "You guys go and…" When he couldn't decide how to finish his sentence, he motioned with his hand, and the uniforms stood and walked out. As they left, Cody and Abbey walked in.

No one spoke for a minute, until Humphries rose from the couch. "Well," he said, "If you can all fit in my car, I'll drive you back to town."

· · ·

The small, family run hotel on Main Street was a minute's walk from the Cedar City PD building. A Mormon church sat next door, and its steeple loomed above, as if to remind all of the city's moral code.

"Hey, man, where's the nearest bar?" Cody asked the hotel clerk, a teenaged kid I assumed was the son of the patriarch. As if on cue, a bearded middle-aged man opened a door from behind the reception counter and peered at us over his spectacles.

"The tavern is two blocks up, on Hoover," he said.

"Right on, kemosabe."

The man hesitated and eyed Cody warily, trying to decide if a reply was advisable.

"They serve chow?" Cody asked.

"I believe they do," he said, and retreated to his office.

"Are you tired?" I asked Melanie.

"No, but I'm starving."

"Me too," Abbey said.

"Come on, then," Cody said, and he led us into the cold like the captain of a brigade on a life or death mission. We marched behind him for three minutes, past the dark shops on the main drag, until we came to a single-story, flat-roofed structure with neon beer lights in the windows.

We filed in dutifully, and inside it was warm and there was a long bar. Tables were set up in front of a stage, and the ceiling was covered with white acoustic tiles. The place looked like it could comfortably hold a hundred people, but there were only a dozen patrons scattered about; evidently nine p.m. on a Wednesday night was not prime time for partiers in Cedar City.

We took a table and ordered from the menu on the wall, which offered burgers, nachos, and wings. Cody began ordering a round of tequila from the waitress, then he paused.

"I'd like a vodka tonic," Abbey said.

"Could I get a glass of Chardonnay?" Melanie asked. I studied her face, looking for any hint that a mental breakdown might be looming. She had been kidnapped, her life threatened, and had shot a man dead. She'd also witnessed the violent death of innocent small town policemen simply trying to make a living. The stress of those events could cause even the most mentally stable person to fall apart. Given all that Melanie had been through, I was surprised she hadn't lost it yet. I prayed she wouldn't be beset by another migraine, or almost worse, an emergence of Sasha. I was still employed by the McDermotts and was responsible for Melanie's welfare as long as she was with me. The weight of that task had returned the moment after she killed the African.

"What about for you, Dan?" Abbey said.

"A Coke for now."

"What?" Cody said.

"Melanie, how are you feeling?" I asked.

"I'm happy to be alive. And I can't wait to see my daughter."

"Any headache, or light-headedness?"

"No, I feel pretty normal."

"You've been under a lot of strain."

"I guess I can handle it," she said, then reached over and patted my hand. "You shouldn't worry."

I crossed my arms. "I'll try not to," I said.

"That's the spirit," Cody said.

I sat looking at the bar, where the neon glow illuminated the rows of bottles with an almost magical radiance. I knew I had to call the McDermotts and give them an update. It was all good news, and they owed me their gratitude, but I doubted it would be forthcoming from Lillian McDermott. As long as I got paid I really didn't care, but the prospect of speaking to that woman made me feel as if nothing had been resolved and I had a lot of explaining to do. I knew that was illogical, but I simply wasn't in the mood to listen to her guff.

I rubbed my forehead with my fingertips, and thought, *What a bunch of crap. Call her and get it done with. Who cares what kind of bullshit she spews? It's her burden, not yours. Hang up on her if she cops an attitude.*

And then something clicked in my head, and I felt myself rise from my chair, the legs scraping loudly against the floor. I walked to the bar as if I were alone, hooked my boot on the rail, and motioned to the bartender.

"Double Canadian Club, straight up," I said.

Before the words left my mouth, Cody was beside me. "Feeling all right, old buddy?"

"It's time to blow off some fucking steam," I said.

"Easy, Dirt," Cody said, and I felt his giant paw massaging the muscles around my neck. "Have a drink or two, use it like medicine, but don't abuse it."

"That, from you?"

"I know how you are. You hold it all in, like nothing affects you. In the meantime it's grinding away in your gut. When you finally blow, you're out of control."

"Thanks for the analysis," I said, watching the bartender pour two measured one-ounce shots.

"Bring the booze back to the table and chill out. Eat some American food. Let the alcohol relax you. Don't start pounding and get obliterated."

"You got all the answers, don't you?"

"True enough," he replied, watching the bartender bring me two miserly shots. "Besides," he added, "This is Utah. It ain't easy getting ripped here."

"Just my luck," I said, but I was already feeling like a fool.

We went back to the table, and I sat with the shots before me and waited for the waitress to bring the rest of the drinks.

"Everything okay?" Abbey asked.

"Hey, we all been through a lot today," Cody said. "Some bad stuff, indeed. Let's not try to claim otherwise. But we should focus on the positive. We're the good guys, and the bad guys got what they had coming. Now Melanie's gonna get her daughter back, and Dan can get home to his fiancée. Abbey just had a valuable learning experience, and me, well, I…"

"Now you can be my dad, dum-dum," Abbey said.

"Yes, of course," Cody sputtered, his face startled. Then he smiled sheepishly as Abbey reached over to hug him. She tried to wrap her arms around him, but Cody's shoulders were too wide. "Thanks for being there when I needed you," she said.

"What did you expect? You're my daughter."

When Cody returned her hug, I saw him grimace, and I remembered he'd been wounded and should probably be at the hospital. But when I said as much, Cody waved me off. "Tomorrow," he said.

"And Candi's not my fiancée," I reminded him.

"I'm sure she will be soon enough," he replied, as the waitress delivered the drinks. I poured the two ounces of whiskey into my Coke and Cody raised a shot glass of silver tequila.

"To love and justice and wild times," he said, and if ever Cody had uttered words that better captured his outlook on life, I'd never heard them. I took a big swig from my highball and felt an amazed grin take hold on my face. Never in my life had a drink tasted so good.

●　●　●

After my second cocktail I felt decompressed enough to call Lillian McDermott. I informed her that Cody and I had rescued Melanie from her kidnappers, who would never bother anyone again.

"I'm appalled they were able to kidnap her in the first place," she said. "That never should have happened."

I ignored her comment and told her we'd be in Vegas in the morning. She started saying something else, and as soon as I heard her disparaging tone, I set my phone on table and jabbed the disconnect button. Then I called Candi. I let her know I'd be home soon, and the sound of her voice reminded me how much I'd missed her.

"It's been lonely around here without you," she said. "Smoky misses you, too."

"I'm sorry the case took longer than I hoped."

"It's only been a week."

"Huh. Sure feels like longer."

"Have you been burning the candles at both ends?"

"Yeah, pretty much."

"You'd best get your butt on home."

I suddenly became distracted by thoughts of taking Candi to bed, and I did not dwell upon Lillian McDermott for the rest of the night. But after another drink I did take Melanie aside to a quiet table.

"The diamonds were given to Jeff by his father," I told her. "Jeff traded a batch to a broker in Vegas for the gold coins."

"I never knew Jeff's father. Jeff never talked about him, either."

"They reconnected, somehow."

"But, why?"

"We can only guess, Melanie. My guess is Jeff's dad wanted to make up for being absent."

Melanie ran her thumb over a lipstick smear on her wine glass. "But look what happened. The diamonds got Jeff killed." Her eyebrows were raised, her lips parted.

"I'm sure Jeff's dad thought he was doing the right thing," I said.

She looked away, then her eyes narrowed. "I'm not buying it. Why wouldn't Jeff have told me?"

"Maybe he thought you would insist on managing the money, put it in the bank."

She frowned and rested her chin in her hand.

"Or maybe he was getting more paranoid and thought it would be best to not tell you until later."

When she raised her head, I saw a certain sadness in her eyes, as if she realized she would need to admit certain things to herself about her late husband if she wished to heal.

"He was getting more paranoid," she said, "and I couldn't stop it. But I never thought he didn't trust me."

When I didn't reply, she said, "I know he loved me. He was a good man, and I'll always remember him that way."

．　．　．

We left a little before midnight, after Cody's painkillers wore off and he conceded he'd better get stitched up. I left him at the emergency clinic, then returned to the hotel and fell into bed with a faded buzz. I knew there were interviews, or perhaps interrogations, in store for the morning, but I wasn't concerned. The mess that remained was one for the authorities to clean up. My part was done. Or so I thought.

13

It WAS 7:30 WHEN my cell rang the next morning, and I'd just woken. "Reno, Stillman here. Where are you?"

"In a hotel."

"Where?"

"Across the street from Cedar City PD."

"There's a coffee joint right there. You know where it is?"

"I'm sure I can find it."

"Meet me there at eight o'clock, please."

"All right."

I showered but didn't have time to shave. I put on yesterday's shirt and left the hotel at five before eight. It was a gray, cold morning, the skies heavy and colorless. Most of the shops on Main Street weren't open yet, and only a single flatbed truck rumbled down the road.

I crossed the intersection and found the restaurant. Once inside, I spotted Stillman right away. The CIA man wore a gray suit and a yellow necktie knotted perfectly against his white collar. He sat at a table at the rear of the small place, facing outward. His pitted face seemed gaunt, and when he spotted me his intense blue eyes looked mismatched to his complexion.

I sat across from him. I assumed he knew, at least in part, why I wanted him here.

"Good morning," he said, but he didn't offer his hand, nor did he bother with any further pleasantries. "Let's start with your investigation of Jeff Jordan."

"Are you recording this?"

"Yes."

I suspected he had a microphone hidden in his lapel. I began speaking, providing an outline of my investigation, leaving out any activities that stretched the boundaries of the law. I measured my words and condensed the details. He didn't question me until I got to the Volkovs.

"How did the African meet the Volkovs?"

"I think it was prearranged. Someone in Angola, maybe a clan leader, knew them."

"Which clan are we talking about?

"The only name Serj Volkov said was Savimbi."

Stillman leaned forward, his elbows on the table, his eyes probing and scrutinizing. "Jonas Savimbi was an Angolan kingpin. He died fifteen years ago."

"Did he ever do business with Russians?"

Stillman didn't answer, but nodded in the affirmative.

"Maybe this will help," I said, and took from my pocket the plastic baggie of Polaroid photos I'd found hidden in the African's mattress. I handed them to Stillman, and he looked at each picture, handling them carefully by the edges.

"I found these in the African's possession," I said. "Anybody look familiar?"

"Maybe." Stillman pocketed the photos.

"Did the U.S. government have any affiliation with Savimbi?" I asked.

"That's none of your concern."

"I imagine Savimbi had relatives, or associates, that stayed in the game."

"Like who?"

"Beats me. But I bet Bur Jordan knew them."

When he didn't respond, I added, "Seems the Volkovs knew them too."

Stillman leaned back and ran his hand over his salt and pepper hair. "Any idea why Bur Jordan would give diamonds to his estranged son?"

"Why do you assume they were estranged?"

Stillman tapped his fingers. "Because Jordan said so. At least that's what was in his file."

The waitress approached and poured me a cup of coffee. I took a sip, and said, "A couple possibilities. Maybe he had pangs of conscience over being an absent parent."

"Or?"

"Maybe he was using his son to launder the stones."

Stillman looked away, and I saw a twinge of sadness on his face. "I'd say that backfired," he said.

"You're betraying yourself."

"What?"

"You have kids, right? A son?"

He straightened in his chair, his body rigid. "My personal life is of no bearing. I think we've covered what we need to."

"Was Bur Jordan a good agent?"

Stillman reached into his jacket and fiddled with a hidden device. Then he straightened his coat and motioned for the check. When the waitress left it on the table he calculated the tip and left exact change on the table.

"Thanks for the coffee," I said.

He nodded and said, "Jordan served his country well. It's always a shame when a good agent goes off the tracks."

"Any theories why he did?"

Stillman eyed me for a long moment. "He spent two decades living in countries where the corrupt exploit the dirt poor on a daily basis. There's no fix for it. I suppose he felt it was time to take something for himself."

He stood, but before he walked away, I said, "Hey, Greg, I'd like to ask a favor. If the Feds or the state police try to hold me or Cody Gibbons, I could use your help."

I followed him out to the sidewalk, waiting for his reply. We were directly across from the police station, where a trio of dark Ford sedans were parked.

"You better get over there," he said. Then he held out his hand and we shook. His grip was firm and there was a tiny hint of amusement in his eyes.

"Don't worry, I'll be around," he said.

•   •   •

It didn't take long after entering the station lobby to see that the morning would be a three ring circus. First, the Cedar City Chief of Police tried to bring me to an interview room, but he was accosted by an overweight Utah State detective, and then two FBI agents in their trademark dark suits asserted their authority, and took me by the arm.

At that moment, Cody, Abbey, and Melanie walked in. The Cedar City chief tried to escort Cody away for an interview, but the state detective and the Feds intervened, and within short order voices were raised, and some ugly words were exchanged (the youngest of the FBI agents called the Utah State cop a fat son of a bitch). Cody and I stood next to each other, trying to repress our smiles. Then Cody raised his arms, as if he were a Grand Poohbah presiding over an unruly, drunken club meeting.

"Order in the court!" he shouted, and every cop in the room went silent and stared at him.

"We've got to be on the road in an hour, so you all need to get organized, if that's not too much to ask."

"Who are you?" one of the FBI men asked.

"Cody Gibbons, licensed private investigator, ex-San Jose PD." Cody walked forward, extending his hand, towering over the perplexed agent. "Let's assign each of us witnesses to a room and get started."

The older of the FBI agents nodded and said, "Make it happen, chief."

Within a few minutes I was seated in an office with the two Feds, who had chosen to take me first. It became clear from the onset of their questioning that their primary interest was in the Volkovs.

"What evidence do you have that the Volkovs kidnapped Mia Jordan?" the underling agent asked.

"I found her locked up in a secret room in the Café Leonov in Vegas. The Volkovs own the joint. Igor Volkov tried to stop Cody Gibbons and me from rescuing her, then he tried to get away. But Vegas PD took him into custody."

"I heard he was shot," the other agent said.

I shrugged. "He shot first."

The agents exchanged glances.

"Here's some more for you," I said. "The Volkovs rent a duplex in North Vegas where they keep women they've coerced into prostitution. And next, check out Towne Auto Salvage out near Nellis Air Force Base. The Volkovs muscled in and the legit owners fled. The Volkovs use the business to launder their crooked money. Go shut it down."

They interrogated me for another fifteen minutes, each question probing deeper into what I knew about the Volkovs. When they were satisfied I'd told them everything I could, I moved to the office of the Chief of Police, which was being used by the Utah State detective.

He was a fat, mustachioed man with eyes that looked small in his fleshy face. He wore suspenders and a .38 in a shoulder holster rested on his overflowing midsection. His girth was wedged into the chief's leather chair, and I could smell his garlic breath from six feet.

"I'm Detective Leonardo," he announced, his tone reminding me of cops I'd met who commanded respect but had not earned it.

"You know, I need a calculator to keep track of all the dead bodies you've racked up," he said. I looked for a hint of levity on his face, but all I got in return was a hard stare.

"I bet math was never your best subject," I said.

"Don't give me that smartass shit," he said, rising from the chair.

"Do you have any specific questions for me, detective?"

"I've got plenty," he said. He put his hands on the desk and leaned forward. "Let's talk about dead body number one, two bullet holes in the chest, out in front of the Jordan's house."

"He came at me with a pistol in his hand. I was quicker."

"What do think this is, the Wild West?"

"What would any cop do in that situation? Shoot, or wait to get shot?"

"Let's get one thing clear: you ain't a cop, not by a long shot. You're a pissant private dick scrounging to make a buck."

"Thanks for the glowing appraisal."

"Was there any witness to your murder of this man?"

"Murder? My partner Cody Gibbons was there. It was self-defense, and he'll testify to it. The gunman was also a member of the Volkov crime family, so maybe you can start drawing conclusions."

"I'm drawing conclusions, all right. Let's move on to victim two, the man in the kitchen who was shot to shit."

"That's Lexi Voronin. He's a Volkov hitman. He fired at me first. There's still a slug in the wall if you want to go dig it out."

"Any witnesses?" he asked, smirking, the corners of his mouth hidden by his jowls.

"Yup. Cody Gibbons."

"Oh, wonderful. I'm familiar with his background. I'm sure a jury will find him real credible."

"Cody Gibbons has put away more criminals than you ever will, *detective*, so you ought to check your attitude."

His beady eyes widened, and his mouth moved silently, as if he couldn't quite find the words to express what he was feeling. But I saw blood rise in his face, then he shouted, "Hands behind your back, you're under arrest!"

"On what charge?"

"Murder, to start, tough guy."

"It won't stick and you know it."

"You're coming with me to Salt Lake," he said. "I hope you have a good attorney."

"Neither the FBI nor the Cedar City PD will back your play."

He laughed, his teeth gray and small. "What makes you think I need anyone to back my play?"

"Because I solved a murder and kidnapping that the state police basically ignored. And the Feds and the Cedar City cops know it. And if you bring me in, I'll call the newspapers and make sure the whole damn country knows it."

"Jesus Christ, are you mentally retarded?"

"It's not only the Feds, the CIA's also involved. They're here now, taking possession of one of the bodies. Would you like me to call them?"

He yanked his cuffs from his belt loop and began coming around the desk. I pulled my cell and hit Stillman's number and moved away from the obese man, toward the opposite side of the desk. My phone rang, once, twice, and now I was behind the desk, and the cop was pointing at me and following. I let him get within a step, then I darted back to the front side.

"Reno? What's up?"

"Could use a little help. Got a Utah State detective trying to arrest me."

"Where are you?"

"The Chief of Police's office."

"Hang tight," he said.

The cop pulled his .38 and pointed it at my face. "Don't move a muscle or so help me god I'll blow you away."

I dropped my cell in my coat pocket and raised my hands. He came around the desk and said, "Hands behind your back."

I turned, conceding for the moment, but a second later the door opened.

"Good morning," Stillman said.

"Who the hell are you?" the cop said.

"Greg Stillman, Central Intelligence Agency. Holster your weapon now and don't make me ask again. Why are you harassing this man?"

"Harassing?"

"Provide your ID and step back, please," Stillman said, wrinkling his nose. "I need to contact your supervisor."

"What for?"

"To report misconduct. I'm aware of the details of this case, which has national implications. Do you understand what *national* means?"

"I do, but why should I care?"

"Dan Reno is innocent of any crime, you moron. Frankly, I'm amazed and disappointed that the great state of Utah has stooped so low to hire the likes of you. You are clearly unfit."

"You have no right to say that," the cop sputtered.

"Dan, take a picture of his ID card, please, and send it to me. I'll decide promptly whether a full investigation of this poor excuse for a policemen will be conducted. You better hope you're squeaky clean, detective. Because the CIA can find out things about your life that you don't even know exist."

The fat cop dropped his head, his feet splayed, and his frame looked like it could barely support the flab that hung below his beltline. I was sure his corpulence was paid for by dirty money. He knew it, Stillman knew it, and I knew it.

"Have a nice day," I said, and followed Stillman out.

"I don't think he'll cause you any problems," Stillman said, as we walked down the hallway.

"Appreciate it. You've got a way with words."

"Even the CIA gets to have fun sometimes," he replied, and for the first time I saw him smile. "Try to keep your nose clean, huh?"

"Do my best," I said.

·   ·   ·

It wasn't quite noon when we piled into the Hellfire Hooptie and set sail for Las Vegas. Melanie and Abbey sat in the back, where they chatted amiably, as if all we'd witnessed the previous day was impermanent and of little gravity. It may have just been a temporary respite, but I was glad to hear their light patter. I told myself that their spirits were resilient, and the intrusion of evil upon their lives would leave no permanent scars. I knew better, but sometimes you need to let optimism carry the day.

Cody, on the other hand, seemed in a dour mood.

"I guess I should see if Denise will take my call," he said.

"Did you ever send her the flowers?"

"When would I have had time?"

"Last night."

"Well," he said bitterly, "I guess I forgot."

"No worries, buddy. I'll do it from my phone. You got her home address?"

"She never gave it to me."

"Screw it then, let's send them to the station. Worst that can happen, she'll be a little embarrassed."

Cody smiled, then he laughed. "I'm sure she can handle that. Send the biggest freaking bouquet they got."

I spent a minute on my phone, and said, "It's done. I put a rush on it. Should be there by two o'clock."

"What do I owe you?"

"They're on me, old buddy."

"Why, that's very sweet of you, Dirt."

"Well, I probably owe you a few bucks for gas money."

"Step on it, would you, Dad?" Abbey said, leaning into Cody's ear. "Melanie wants to see Mia sometime this century."

Cody looked at me and I shrugged. "She asked for it," I said. Then he downshifted and we rocketed forward, blasting through the arid flats and eating miles like a starved hound, all the way into Las Vegas.

14

WHEN THE MCDERMOTTS MET us at the LVPD station lobby, we were standing in a quiet corner, away from a line of people on the opposite side of the room. We were waiting for an officer to bring Mia from a room where she was speaking with a trauma counselor.

As soon as they spotted us, Walter rushed forward. "Oh, Melanie," he said, embracing her in a hug. Lillian followed him at a measured pace. "Stop making a scene, Walter," she said. "This is a public place."

Walter ignored her and turned to me. "You came highly recommended, and by god, now I see why," he gushed. "Thank goodness we found you."

"You're making a fool of yourself, Walter," Lillian said, her syllables dripping with derision.

Walter squared his shoulders and his posture became rigid. When he turned to face Lillian, I could see a vein pulsing in his neck. He took two quick steps in her direction, and though he tried to hush his words, I heard everything he said.

"I've taken all I can take of your bitchiness, Lillian, and I won't hear it any more. You need help, and you better get it, because I'm done with this. Do you hear me?"

"How dare you address me in that manner."

"I'll address you as I see fit, so you better get used to it."

Lillian stepped back, and the stunned expression on her face was almost comical.

"Now," he continued, "I'm going to have a private word with Mr. Reno, while you wait here with your mouth shut."

Walter motioned to me, and I followed him out the front door. We walked toward the end of the building until we were looking out at Las Vegas Boulevard.

"I'm sorry you had to hear that," he said. "It's been a long time coming."

"She does have quite an attitude," I said.

"I don't mean to burden you with this, but I think you have a right to know. Lillian had a tough upbringing. She was raised in Kentucky, in the Appalachian Mountains. Her parents were part of a hillbilly clan, and for all intents and purposes, they were white trash. Lillian eventually rose above it, but one can never completely leave their past behind."

We watched a pair of squad cars bounce up the curb, then he continued. "Lillian was sexually abused as a child, and then her first husband abused Melanie."

"You're not Melanie's biological father?"

"No, I'm her stepfather. Lillian divorced her first husband shortly before he died of liver disease, when he was only forty years old. He was a horrible alcoholic, which explains Lillian's abhorrence to drinking. But I'm afraid her deepest scars are related to being molested by her father, and her guilt over Melanie suffering the attentions of Lillian's lecherous husband."

A jet took off from the nearby airport, and I waited until the roar of its motors subsided before I said, "That would explain Melanie's multiple personality issues."

"I suspect so," Walter replied. "I've been researching the subject since you brought it up. I have no doubt Melanie is harboring great pain from her past. But perhaps she doesn't consciously know it."

The wind blew a cloud of dust from an adjacent field, and it settled over the street traffic. "I hope Melanie can get the help she needs, Walter," I said. "I think she's a hell of a woman."

"Indeed. And thanks for saying so." He reached out and firmly shook my hand.

When we went back inside, Melanie was sitting with Mia on her lap, while Lillian sat apart, alone with her thoughts. Cody and Abbey stood near Melanie, watching over her. I started toward Lillian, but paused when a delivery man came into the lobby carrying a huge floral display overflowing with red roses. He looked at the line of people on the far side of the lobby, then he stopped a passing patrolman, who nodded and spoke on his radio.

I walked over to Cody and Abbey. "All good?" I asked.

"This should be interesting," Abbey said, as the deliveryman set the flowers on a chair.

A moment later a tall, attractive woman with strawberry-blond hair and an undeniably curvy figure came from a door behind the counter. When she saw the flowers, her jaw dropped. Then she saw Cody, and she put her hands on her hips and shook her head.

Cody walked toward her and she smiled shyly and met him in the middle of the lobby. He bent to kiss her, and someone started clapping, then a few more joined in, and a second later even the people waiting in line began applauding and whistling.

When Cody lifted his head, Denise Culligan's face was red with embarrassment, but also had a happy glow that suggested Cody might have an active evening.

I turned away and walked to where Lillian sat.

"You've done what you've been hired to do. You may go now," she said.

"I'll email you my bill," I said.

She looked away, apparently uninterested in further conversation. At least we were on the same page in that regard. Even though I understood the weight of her burden, I had no desire to speak with her for longer than necessary.

"What's her problem?" Abbey asked, when I went to where she stood away from the commotion.

"Negative energy."

"Sounds like a bummer."

"I tried to tell her, 'Don't worry, be happy,' but she didn't buy it."

Abbey elbowed me. "Is that a joke? Like, you're trying to be funny?"

"I get like that sometimes."

"Don't quit your day job," she said with a laugh.

Cody came over after Denise went back into the squad room.

"I need a lift to my truck," I said. "Over at the Plaza."

"Dan," Melanie said, standing, her arm around Mia. She motioned for me to come closer. "I need to talk to you before you go."

"All right. Out front?"

She followed me outside, bringing Mia by the hand. We stood near where I'd spoken with Walter.

"I want to give you something, as a way of thanks," she said.

"Not necessary," I replied.

"I know, but I want to." She reached into her purse and pulled out a rough diamond nearly three quarters of an inch round. She held it out on her palm, and said, "It's for your girlfriend."

The diamond sparkled in the cold sunlight. "Put it away, Melanie. That stone's probably worth a fortune."

"There's something I haven't told you yet. When I went to the safe last night, I was searching for the right ammo. I emptied all the zippered compartments and started pouring the bullets out, looking for the big ones. Guess what was in three of the ammo boxes?"

I looked at Melanie and saw Mia was staring up at me. Her little girl eyes were round, and definitely her mother's eyes.

"More diamonds," Melanie said. "Three more pouches, even more full than the first one you found."

I stared silently at her, then gazed out to where the boulevard led into the desert flats. My thoughts went to Bur Jordan. I wondered what the CIA agent was thinking when he decided to steal millions of dollars' worth of diamonds from African criminals who considered the most horrific atrocities trivial. I wondered what had motivated his greed, and how he so tragically miscalculated the risk, not only to himself, but also to his son and his son's family. I'd never know the answers, but I was satisfied with the knowledge that those who sought to harm Melanie and her daughter were either dead or facing long prison sentences.

I looked back at Melanie. "That's a lot of diamonds," I said. "No wonder the bad guys tried so hard to get them."

• • •

Cody dropped me off in front of the Plaza twenty minutes later, and when I steered my truck out of the parking lot, he and Abbey were standing in front of the hotel. I beeped my horn twice, stuck my fist out the window, and gave them the thumbs up. I watched in my mirror as they smiled and waved back.

Within fifteen minutes I was rolling northbound through the desert, heading toward a horizon dwarfed by columns of sunlight spilling from the white clouds. I did not ruminate as I drove, not on Cody and Abbey, nor on what the future held in store for Melanie and her daughter. Instead, once the last signs of Las Vegas faded behind me, I called Candi.

"I'm on my way home. Should be there in about seven hours," I said.

"Is your case done?"

"Yeah."

"And you're in one piece?"

"Of course. Listen, I've got a surprise for you." I felt the sharp edges of the diamond through my jeans pocket.

"What is it?" she asked.

I wedged my hand in my pocket and adjusted the diamond so it wouldn't jab my leg.

"If I told you, it wouldn't be a surprise," I said.

"Well, hurry, then. I hate being left in suspense."

My foot pushed down on the gas pedal as if I were wearing weighted boots, and my pickup launched forward, chasing the horizon and everything that waited beyond it.

Enjoy this Book? You Can Make a Difference

Reviews are extremely important to authors. Honest reviews are the best tool I have to get attention for my novels and attract readers.

If you enjoyed this book, I'd be grateful if you could spend a brief minute leaving a review (it can be as short or long as you like) on the book's Amazon page. To go there, see the appropriate links below.

Amazon US: http://bit.ly/DaveStanton
Amazon UK: http://bit.ly/DaveStantonUK

Thank you,
Dave Stanton

ABOUT THE AUTHOR

Born in Detroit, Michigan, in 1960, Dave Stanton moved to Northern California in 1961. He attended San Jose State University and received a BA in journalism in 1983. Over the years, he worked as a bartender, newspaper advertising salesman, furniture mover, debt collector, and technology salesman. He has two children, Austin and Haley. He and his wife, Heidi, live in San Jose, California.

Stanton is the author of six novels, all featuring private investigator Dan Reno and his ex-cop buddy, Cody Gibbons.

To learn more, visit the author's website at:

http://danrenonovels.com/

If you enjoyed **The Doomsday Girl**, please don't hesitate to leave a review at:

Amazon US: http://bit.ly/DaveStanton
Amazon UK: http://bit.ly/DaveStantonUK

To contact Dave Stanton or subscribe to his newsletter, go to:

http://danrenonovels.com/contact/

More Dan Reno Novels:

STATELINE

Cancel the wedding–the groom is dead.

When a tycoon's son is murdered the night before his wedding, the enraged and grief-stricken father offers investigator Dan Reno (that's *Reno, as in no problemo),* a life-changing bounty to find the killer. Reno, nearly broke, figures he's finally landed in the right place at the right time. It's a nice thought, but when a band of crooked cops get involved, Reno finds himself not only earning every penny of his paycheck, but also fighting for his life.

Who committed the murder, and why? And what of the dark sexual deviations that keep surfacing? Haunted by his murdered father and a violent, hard drinking past, Reno wants no more blood on his hands. But a man's got to make a living, and backing off is not in his DNA. Traversing the snowy alpine winter in the Sierras and the lonely deserts of Nevada, Reno must revert to his old ways to survive. Because the fat bounty won't do him much good if he's dead.

Dying for the Highlife

Jimmy Homestead's glory days as a high school stud were a distant memory. His adulthood had amounted to little more than temporary jobs, petty crime, and discount whiskey. But he always felt he was special, and winning the Lotto proved it.

Flush with millions, everything is great for Jimmy—until people from his past start coming out of the woodwork, seeking payback for transgressions Jimmy thought were long forgotten.

Caught in the middle are investigator Dan Reno and his good buddy Cody Gibbons, two guys just trying to make an honest paycheck. Reno, struggling to keep his home out of foreclosure, thinks that's his biggest problem. But his priorities change when he's drawn into a hard-boiled mess that leaves dead bodies scattered all over northern Nevada.

Speed Metal Blues

Bounty hunter Dan Reno never thought he'd be the prey.

It's a two-for-one deal when a pair of accused rapists from a New Jersey-based gang surface in South Lake Tahoe. The first is easy to catch, but the second, a Satanist suspected of a string of murders, is an adversary unlike any Reno has faced. After escaping Reno's clutches in the desert outside of Carson City, the target vanishes. That is, until he makes it clear he intends to settle the score.

To make matters worse, the criminal takes an interest in a teenage boy and his talented sister, both friends of Reno's. Wading through a drug-dealing turf war and a deadly feud between mobsters running a local casino, Reno can't figure out how his target fits in with the new outlaws in town. He only knows he's hunting for a ghost-like adversary calling all the shots.

The more Reno learns more about his target, the more he's convinced that mayhem is inevitable unless he can capture him quickly. He'd prefer to do it clean, without further bloodshed. But sometimes that ain't in the cards, especially when Reno's partner Cody Gibbons decides it's time for payback.

Dark Ice

Two murdered girls, and no motive…

While skiing deep in Lake Tahoe's backcountry, Private Eye Dan Reno finds the first naked body, buried under fresh snow. Reno's contacted by the grieving father, who wants to know who murdered his daughter, and why? And how could the body end up in such a remote, mountainous location? The questions become murkier when a second body is found. Is there a serial killer stalking promiscuous young women in South Lake Tahoe? Or are the murders linked to a different criminal agenda?

Searching for answers, Reno is accosted by a gang of racist bikers with a score to settle. He also must deal with his pal, Cody Gibbons, who the police consider a suspect. The clues lead to the owner of a strip club and a womanizing police captain, but is either the killer?

The bikers up the ante, but are unaware that Cody Gibbons has Reno's back at any cost. Meanwhile, the police won't tolerate Reno's continued involvement in the case. But Reno knows he's getting close. And the most critical clue comes from the last person he'd suspect…

Hard Prejudice

The DNA evidence should have made the rape a slam dunk case.

But after the evidence disappeared from a police locker, the black man accused of brutally raping a popular actor's daughter walked free. Hired by the actor, private detective Dan Reno's job seemed simple enough: discover who took the DNA, and why. Problem is, from the beginning of the investigation, neither Reno, the South Lake Tahoe police, nor anyone else have any idea what the motivation could be to see ghetto thug Duante Tucker get away with the crime. Not even Reno's best friend, fellow investigator Cody Gibbons, has a clue.

When Reno and Gibbons tail Tucker, they learn the rapist is linked to various criminals and even a deserter from the U.S. Marine Corps. But they still can't tell who would want him set free, and for what reason?

The clues continue to build until Reno and Cody find themselves targeted for death. That tells Reno he's getting close, so he and Gibbons put the pedal to the metal. The forces of evil are running out of time, and the action reaches a boiling point before an explosive conclusion that reveals a sinister plot and motivations that Reno never imagined.

Made in the USA
Las Vegas, NV
02 October 2022

56414553R00167